THE MINER'S CANARY

A NOVEL

BARBARA PRONIN

TouchPoint Press
Relax. Read. Repeat.

THE MINER'S CANARY
By Barbara Pronin
Published by TouchPoint Press
Brookland, AR 72417
www.touchpointpress.com

Softcover ISBN: 978-1-956851-41-0

TouchPoint Press books may be purchased in bulk or at special discounts for sales promotions, gifts, fundraising, or educational purposes. For details, contact the Sales and Distribution Staff: info@touchpointpress.com or via fax: 870-200-6702.

Editor: Kelly Esparza
Cover Design: David Ter-Avanesyan, @Ter33Design
Cover Image: ©Edmund Lowe Photography

Connect with Barbara Pronin online:
barbarapronin.com
Instagram @writerbobbi

First Edition

Printed in the United States of America.

To Jeffrey, Heather, Kendall, Mckenna and Sierra.
Fly, bubbelehs, and be the very best you can be!

Hats off to the National Park tour guides and local folk whose yarns and knowledge of the Black Hills region were the inspiration for this novel.

PROLOGUE

MAY 1994

He was relieved when Katy's body was discovered, face down in the shallow water of Spearfish Creek, not far from the highway.

She had been tall and solidly built, and heaving her dead weight down the embankment had taken an effort on his part. It had to be done, of course, no doubt about that. In the few minutes before he slipped the blade between her ribs, she had told him she was carrying his child, and that would never do, what with him already a married man.

As it turned out, according to the coroner, Katy was not pregnant after all. She had made a mistake—or maybe she'd lied to him. In either case, it was too late. He had done what he knew he had to do, though he would miss her. She had a gentle touch, and she knew how to make him feel special. It would have been sad to deny her a proper burial, laid to rest in the welcoming earth in the bosom of her friends and family.

In the packed church, filing past the closed casket, he thought for a moment that he caught a whiff of the lilac scent of her hair. But the moment passed, and when the choir sang and his wife slipped her hand into his, he sighed deeply and wept, as regretful as anyone that a young woman's life had been taken; that she had died such a cruel and tragic death only days before her twenty-first birthday.

ONE

If I hadn't been in such an all-fired hurry, I would have been home that morning when the phone rang. I could have said my goodbyes, moved on with my life, and none of the rest would have happened.

As it was, I had finagled Lulu into eating breakfast, getting dressed, and brushing her flyaway red hair into a ponytail in the back seat of my Chevy well before 7 a.m. It was a record in the bedlam of our daily routine, and I was halfway to her school on the edge of Newport Beach by the time my machine picked up the message.

Lulu's screech wrenched my attention from the traffic on Pacific Coast Highway. "My ice skates!" she wailed, and I rolled my eyes, a vision of the skates, tied together and looped over the bathroom doorknob, taking first position in my brain. I'd meant to remind Lulu to pack them in their case and sling them over her shoulder along with her backpack. But then, I meant to do a lot of things that somehow didn't get done.

Lulu had taken to the ice like a pig to mud, but detail was not her forte.

Not exactly a big surprise, the apple from the tree and all that. Still, at eleven, she shouldn't need to be reminded. What kind of a mother was I?

"No problem." I gritted my teeth. "Penny will pick you up from school, and you can stop by the apartment to pick up the skates on the way to the ice rink."

Penny was my lifesaver, the sometime nanny who looked after Lulu when I couldn't. A law school grad with a pretty smile and a short memory, Penny lived at home while she studied to take the California bar exam—for the third time. I felt bad for her lack of success so far, maybe worse than she did. But the good news for me was that a) she could really use the money I paid her, and b) she could generally manage to be available when I needed her, which was sometimes on pretty short notice.

I was the banquet manager for a little hotel near the beach in Dana Point, but you'd think I was an ER surgeon for the number of emergency calls I got outside of regular hours. Brides freaked out when the cake was late because the delivery truck broke down, and their mothers were even worse when there was no special meal ready for dear Aunt Fanny, who forgot to let them know in advance that she'd recently become a vegan.

But I am getting ahead of myself. My name is Julie Goldman. I'm thirty-five, tall and skinny. My husband, Marty, may he rest in peace, charitably called me willowy, with carrot-colored hair that has a will of its own and eyes that were either green or brown depending on my level of stress.

I didn't have too many skills or talents, but I seemed to have a knack for planning parties, which was how I wound up moving from waitress to supervisor to banquet manager for the chrome and glass Hotel Stevens Point. It's a boutique hotel—that meant small, eclectic, and expensive—not far from the beach, and if you paid attention to the rumors in the trades, it was almost always on the auction block.

Be that as it may, I hung on to my job because most of my clients—

remarkably—go away happy enough to refer their friends and neighbors, and also because I was not above clipping out the names of engaged couples from the local papers and making the first, all-important contacts.

My boss, Avery Bannerman, called me a scullery maid; it was his pathetic attempt at humor. But I knew, and he knew, how much my efforts contributed to the hotel's precarious bottom line, which was why he put up with the occasional clashes between my career and my motherly obligations.

Lulu, full name Louise Myra Goldman, named after my Marty's beloved grandma, Bubbe Lou, was truly the light of my life. Lulu was born on December 11, 2001, three months to the day after her father took a cab to the World Trade Center in New York to deliver some legal documents. . . .

I was still reeling when Bubbe Lou passed away in her sleep less than six weeks later, and suddenly there was nothing left for me in New York.

How and why we ended up in California is a story for another time. Suffice to say, I needed a fresh start in new surroundings after Marty was gone, and the fact that snow in the Golden State stayed in the mountains and out of the gutters might have had a little to do with it. Then, wouldn't you know it, my daughter took up ice skating! How's that for poetic justice?

But I digressed. Lulu bent forward to kiss my cheek as I pulled into the school parking lot. I reached back and squeezed her hand. "Penny will pick you up. Remind her to stop at home and pick up the skates and have a great practice at the rink."

The car door slammed. I called after her. "I expect to be home by six." She was long out of earshot. Just as well. With any luck, if all went well today, I might make it home by seven.

Traffic crawled along Pacific Coast highway, but the morning was surprisingly cloudless. The foggy June gloom had yet to settle in, and the ocean glinted in the bright May sunlight all the way to the horizon.

Someone once said if you're lucky enough to live by the ocean, you're lucky enough. I agreed. Okay, so I couldn't afford to live right by the ocean, but I made this drive at least five days a week. It was almost enough to make the traffic bearable, even when I was pressed for time.

Traffic thinned before I hit Golden Lantern, and I caught every stoplight green. I made it to the Stevens Point with time to spare, but before I ever got through the service entrance, I knew the feathers had hit the fan.

I could hear Juan, our head chef, bellowing in three languages. "Para amor de Dios, tú no comprendes. What am I to do with two hundred thawed lobster tails? Et le sabayon des peches–madre de Dios, non e possible arret–it must be eaten and eaten quickly! ¿Qué puedo hago ahora?"

I could hear Avery trying to get a word in edgewise around Juan's mix of languages, and I froze instantly in my tracks. Lobster tails were the entrée for the Frasee wedding, scheduled for Saturday afternoon. Juan's heavenly sabayon, one of the true stars of our catering menu, was to be served along with the wedding cake. What the heck was going on?

I stepped into the kitchen and locked eyes with Avery, who slouched on a stool like a lumpy dumpling, his pale complexion blanching to white under a thinning thatch of gray hair.

"Now, what?" I ventured.

Avery shook his head. "You will not . . ." He blinked. "I just, I do not believe it."

"Ok-aayy," I said, bracing myself. "I can take it . . . what's up with the lobster tails?"

"The Frasee wedding. It's off."

"It's off? It's all set for Saturday. What do you mean, it's off?"

Juan continued muttering, hands flailing, his gaze parked somewhere in the middle distance.

Avery heaved his bulk off the stool. "The wedding gown was sent over yesterday. It arrived about six in the evening. Harry, the only bellboy on duty last night, was busy moving in guests. So, Paco, who was leaving at the end of his shift, volunteered to take the gown up to the Frasee suite."

I squinted. Paco was the day janitor. Not the crispest cookie in the jar.

Avery sighed. "For some reason I will never understand, Paco hung the gown from a sprinkler hook."

How many ways can you spell disaster? Let me count the ways. . . .

"The sprinkler broke, the room flooded, and the dress is an unholy mess. The bride freaked, she hasn't stopped bawling, and Mrs. Frasee called off the wedding."

It was my turn to blink. "How is she planning to head off two hundred guests, plus the florist, the band, the entertainers, and who knows how many others?"

Avery sighed. "I have no idea, but that's what she said. She's planning to book another hotel and sue us for the damages incurred."

I took a beat. "When did she say that?"

"An hour ago," he said. "Mrs. Frasee and the bride checked in early, for hair appointments and whatever else. When they got upstairs, all hell broke loose, and it hasn't stopped flaming since."

My mind was racing. "Where are they now?"

"In the lobby—waiting for Mr. Frasee to collect them. He, as you may remember from the paperwork, is a powerhouse Newport Beach attorney."

Great. I looked around the huge kitchen, at the stainless-steel refrigerators full of thawing lobster tails and the ovens ready to cook them. I thought of Marisa Frasee, the flighty little bride, and her 200 disappointed guests, and lest you thought I was totally selfless, I thought about the hole this little debacle would punch in my commission check next month.

It was eight thirty. The kitchen staff began to straggle through the service entrance. I smiled at Juan, and at Avery, with as much confidence as I could muster. "Well, it ain't over till it's over," I said. "Let me see what I can do."

I flounced out, smoothing my skirt, aware of the stares directed at my back and glad I had worn my best blue linen suit for no reason I could fathom. I stopped in the office to check my Rolodex before I headed to the rococo lobby.

The would-be bride, face blotchy with tears, was perched on the edge of a damask sofa, blue eyes staring forlornly out the window. Her mother was seated on a high-backed chair, intent on the guest list propped up in her lap by her Louis Vuitton bag.

She was a large woman, dressed in a charcoal tweed suit too heavy for the spring weather. She had an unbending demeanor in the best of times, and her expression in her fleshy face hardened as she glanced up and saw me headed her way.

I flashed my most ingratiating smile. "Mrs. Frasee, Marisa, I just heard about the mishap!"

"Mishap?" Mrs. Frasee stood, grabbing her bag as though it were a lifeline as the guest list fluttered to the carpet. "I have never in my entire life seen such outright negligence. The dress is ruined! We are canceling the wedding, we will find another venue, and your hotel will pay for every cent the rescheduling costs."

I bent demurely to retrieve the guest list, aware that every eye in the little lobby was trained on our tête-à-tête. "I understand your feelings completely. But I think I know someone who can repair the damage, so the wedding can go on as planned."

Marisa turned, hope dawning like an early sunrise in her heart-shaped little face. But Mrs. Frasee sputtered, her complexion turning the color of eggplant. "Repair the damage?" Her voice cracked. "Repair—have you seen the dress?"

I had not, of course, but I seized the moment and crossed my fingers behind my back. "I'm certain it can be restored—clean, beautiful, and completely ready to make an entrance your guests will not soon forget."

Mrs. Frasee's eyes narrowed. "That would take nothing less than a miracle."

"I don't know about that, but I know how much this means to Marisa." The bride, bless her, whimpered pitifully. "Will you give me until four this afternoon?"

Mr. Frasee chose that moment to come barging through the heavy glass door, the wind at his back as he came to the rescue of his women. Mrs. Frasee glanced at him, then peered back at me. "Four this afternoon, you say . . ."

I nodded. "If we don't have the dress restored by four this afternoon, I will personally contact everyone on your guest list and cancel the wedding for you."

There was a moment of silence, punctuated by Marisa's quiet sobbing into her father's shoulder. Mrs. Frasee eyed me warily. She looked up at the clock over the desk. "Four o'clock. All right, you have it. But not one minute later. And I expect you to make good on your offer and to take full responsibility."

She turned on her heel and stalked off, Marisa and her bewildered father following in her wake, and left me standing there, with the guest list in my hand, wondering if I'd really lost it this time.

But I did have a chance, and her name was Flora Marquez, and her number was in my Rolodex. Flora owned a small bridal shop not far away in Costa Mesa, and we'd traded favors more than once, including the sizable professional discount I'd arranged for her at the Stevens Point for her daughter's wedding last summer.

I raced back to my office, grabbed up the Rolodex, and dialed Flora's number, aware that Avery was framed in my doorway looking like a deer in headlights.

I told Flora I would meet her at her shop in less than thirty minutes, and I very nearly tripped over Avery as I raced out the door and took the stairs up to the Frasee suite.

The gown hung from the broken sprinkler valve like a ghostly apparition, its stained, wet, bedraggled carcass twisting in the air-conditioned breeze. There was a moldy, damp smell I hoped was wet carpeting, but whatever it was, there was not a minute to waste. I snatched down the hanger, hung the sopping mess over one arm, and bolted for the stairs.

I found it reassuring that Flora did not blanch at her first glimpse of the disaster. She smiled sadly, clearly dismayed that something so lovely should be so bruised, but she bent over the stained areas with some sort of solvent, and I watched her nimble fingers work as the bruises began to fade.

Then she handed me a hair dryer, lifted the sequined tulle away, and as I moved the dryer over the fabric, she began to brush and fluff it. By noon, to my utter astonishment, the once-beautiful dress had begun to regain something of its former luster.

Breathing normally for the first time since morning, I asked if I could bring in lunch. "Go," she said, smiling, and when I returned with the sandwiches, she was working on the sequined tulle, drying, separating and fluffing the layers until they sparkled under the work lights.

By 3 p.m., I was hugging Flora's compact little body. "Boy, I owe you one," I said.

Flora smiled. "You owe me three. I have three more daughters at home."

Avery gaped as I sailed into the office, the iridescent wedding dress catching the light even under its plastic swaddling. I stopped in the kitchen long enough to assure Juan he could work his magic on the lobster tails. Then I took the dress upstairs, removed the plastic and hung it in the empty closet, fluffing it up to its glorious best before dialing the Frasee home.

They arrived in no time, and by the time they finished waxing poetic over the astonishing transformation, the wedding was back on, and I began to fantasize about being written into the family trust.

I called home. "I'll be there by six. What would you like for dinner?"

The consensus was pizza, and I stopped at Alfredo's to pick up an extra-large pepperoni.

When I got home, Lulu and Penny were curled up on the sofa watching *Sleepless in Seattle*. One of the things that made it bearable that Lulu was growing up was that now we could sit together and bawl shamelessly at all these schmaltzy chick flicks. So, I put the pizza box on the coffee table, got some paper plates, and curled up right alongside them.

By the time Sam and Annie and little Jonah headed down from the top of the Empire State Building hand in hand, it was time to dry our tears of relief and think about Lulu's bedtime.

After Penny left, Lulu dawdled through her bath and stalled her way to bedtime by begging to read the last two chapters of the latest in the *Twilight* series. How a healthy kid could get hooked on vampires was still a mystery to me, but in any case, it was after nine before I went into the kitchen and saw the answering machine blinking away.

The voice on the phone was not one I recognized. The message was coolly professional. "This is Charlie Banks, Chief of Police in Deadwood, South Dakota. I'm looking for a Julie Goldman who has an aunt named Sarah Lacey here in town. If you are that Julie Goldman, please give me a call." He rattled off the number.

I sat abruptly on a kitchen stool and replayed the message twice. I glanced around the little kitchen I had so carefully made my own. Then the world as I knew it fell away, and I was seventeen again, scared, angry, and alone.

TWO

The flight to Denver was uneventful, leaving me plenty of time to lean back, close my eyes, and dredge up memories of the teen years I had worked long and hard to forget. But the flight to Rapid City on a little prop plane was bone-jarring, and I gripped the arms of my narrow seat and prayed to get safely on the ground.

I had reached Police Chief Banks at just past eight in the morning. He told me, kindly and patiently, that my Aunt Sarah had suffered a heart attack and passed away in the night shortly before he'd left that message for me yesterday. In some paperwork held by her attorney, she had named me as her only living relative—believed, correctly as it turned out, to be living in Southern California.

I wrestled with a rush of conflicting feelings, not the least of which was relief that there was no way I could have gotten to South Dakota in time to say goodbye to Aunt Sarah, even if I'd received the message sooner. But in the end, I felt sadness and guilt at how many years had gone by with no attempt on my part to mend my broken fences. It was the guilt that made me tell the police chief I would be in Deadwood as soon as I could possibly manage it.

Reluctantly, I called the airline to make a reservation. I called Penny, who was fine with moving in and staying with Lulu for as long as I needed to be away. Finally, I called Avery who, as usual, was flush with meaningless busy work.

"Not to worry," he assured me, as though he loved a good crisis. "Everything's under control."

I threw a few things into a bag and stopped at school to give Lulu a quick hug and an even quicker explanation, and before I knew it, I was at the airport boarding the first of two flights to Rapid City. Now, as I tucked a road map I didn't really need into the side pocket of a rented Corolla, I drew a deep breath and headed out on the highway toward Deadwood.

If you had seen the TV series they called *Deadwood*, you would know the little city as the rough and tumble gambling mecca where Wild Bill Hickok met his Maker, a gun-slinging, honky-tonk Wild West town surrounded by the brooding Black Hills of the old Dakota Territory.

Way back in its gold mining days, it was probably pretty much the way the TV series depicted it. But when I saw it for the first time, at the age of ten when I went to live with Aunt Sarah and my cousin Katy, the mining was beginning to grind to a close, and the town's glory days of gold fever and gaming were pretty much a distant memory.

Deadwood when I got there was a dusty little town struggling to survive, and the only gambling going on was the weekly poker game in the parlor of Aunt Sarah's boarding house for the few miners who were too old to move on to the next possible stake.

Aunt Sarah used to say I brought a fresh breath into town, because the year I arrived was the year Deadwood picked itself up by its bootstraps and began to turn itself around, morphing back into an old-tyme gaming and gold-panning mecca in a bid to buck up the tourist trade.

I guess it worked, because it's still there, and I noticed the streets had been newly bricked and old-fashioned brass lampposts had replaced the rickety streetlights I remembered.

I recalled reading that Kevin Costner, who'd filmed *Dancing with Wolves* in the Lakota territory of the Black Hills, had opened a casino and restaurant in Deadwood called the Midnight Star, and sure enough, I caught sight of it as I cruised down the town's Main Street. But as I saw it now, ahead of the tourist season, the few blocks stretch of saloons and souvenir shops seemed lackluster in the sunlight, and the town itself looked almost as deserted as I remembered it on the day I waved goodbye to my aunt from the back of a Trailways bus.

The police station was just where it always had been, and I found it without any difficulty. A tall cowboy-type in a plaid shirt and jeans was preparing to get into a police car. He watched me lock my rental car and make my way across the gravel.

"I'm going to hazard a wild guess that you are Julie Goldman," he said.

I looked into clear and impossibly blue eyes. "I am. And you are?"

"Charlie Banks."

Deadwood's Chief of Police was broad shouldered and suntanned, somewhere in his early forties, I guessed, good-looking in a rough-hewn way. He smiled and held out a welcoming hand, and I wished I had checked my stubborn hair in the mirror before I got out of the car.

"Pleased to meet you, Ms. Goldman," he said. "Sorry to be the bearer of bad news."

"Thank you. I appreciate your making the effort to find me. How did— tell me about Aunt Sarah. . . ."

"Well, the good news, I guess, is it must have been quick. She put in a call to me early in the evening. I'm afraid I have no idea why. If she wasn't feeling well, she could have called 911. . . . In any case, by the time I got there—I was at a Kiwanis dinner when she left her message—and well, she was gone when I arrived."

The chief flashed a compassionate smile.

I nodded. "Where . . . where is she now?"

"At the funeral chapel up the road in Lead. We figured that's probably where you'd want her. Doc Rafferty—he's a deputy coroner here as well as a local doc—signed off on the death certificate."

I nodded again. "I see. So, I guess it's up to me to make arrangements?"

Chief Banks shrugged. "If there are other relatives, we haven't found them, so I guess it falls to you. You'll want to see Harrison Palmer. He was your aunt's attorney. We can call him if you like. I told him you were on your way here."

As it turned out, Harrison Palmer was in court in Rapid City, but he was expected back before the end of the day. I checked my watch. It was after three. I thanked the police chief again for his efforts and started back to my car.

"I was headed out for a late lunch when you drove in," Banks said. "You're welcome to come on along with me if you like. By then, Harrison may be back."

I'd been thinking I might drive by Aunt Sarah's house, but I was in no hurry to go there, for one thing, and anyway, I didn't have a key.

"Thanks," I smiled. "That's very nice. Those peanuts on that last flight didn't do much for my hunger."

We ended up in a little café with a bright red door and red checked cloths on the tables. Half a dozen diners nodded to the police chief and watched our progress toward a back booth by the window. Still standing, the chief nodded back, introducing me en masse as Julie Goldman, Sarah Lacey's niece. Half a dozen heads bobbed in my direction, murmuring hellos and condolences. Clearly, not much had changed in this town. Everyone knew everyone else's business.

Earlene, our waitress, was a scrappy little lady with a graying bun at the back of her head held in place with a couple of yellow pencils. She recommended the day's special, barbecued beef sandwiches.

Over sandwiches dripping with homemade sauce, I learned that Earlene was part owner of the café. I learned that Deadwood had grown to more than two thousand residents, that despite the gaming that mostly supported it, it considered itself a family town, and that Chief Charlie Banks, when he was off duty, raised horses on a thriving little ranch somewhere on the outskirts of town. He was also a widower, which gave us something in common, and I soon found myself prattling on about Lulu and the chaotic life of a single parent.

"I never was lucky enough to have kids," he told me. "It's one of the regrets of my life."

I nodded. "I understand. I don't know what I would have done without Lulu at the center of my life after my husband was killed."

An hour passed, and the chief took out his cell phone to call Harrison Palmer. As it turned out, his assistant said, the attorney would not be available today after all, but he would be in tomorrow morning, and he had instructed her to give me a key to Aunt Sarah's house if I wanted it.

I hesitated. In my head, I hadn't gotten as far as where I would spend the night, but it seemed foolish to spend money on a hotel if I didn't need to.

Chief Banks drove me to the attorney's office, where I picked up the key, and then back to my rental car at the police station. I thanked him again for his trouble.

"Not at all," he assured me. "You have a good night and be sure and call if you need anything."

So, just before dusk, as the hills slowly deepened to black and a chill settled on my shoulders, I turned into Bluebird Hill Lane and found myself gazing at the two-story Victorian where I had spent my adolescent years.

The vivid blue of the front door had faded, and there was paint peeling from the siding, but for a structure well over a century old, it seemed to be in fairly good shape. The rooster weathervane that had fascinated me as a child stood as proudly as it ever had atop the dome-shaped cupola.

I climbed the steps to the wraparound front porch and ran a hand over the old wood swing. It was worn smooth, and it bore my weight with the same raucous creaking sound I remembered, and I thought about the sad little girl I had been when I sat in it for the first time.

THREE

I was ten years old when my parents were killed in a fiery car accident that gave me nightmares still. I was tall and skinny even then, with hazel eyes and coppery hair that seemed to have a mind of its own. I had braided it into pigtails myself that morning before my grandma put me on a plane, but somewhere between Missouri and South Dakota, they had wiggled out of their restraints.

I'd been left in the care of a flight attendant; Grandma called her a stewardess. "Please take extra special care of this child," I heard my grandma whisper in her ear. "She was orphaned recently, and she is on her way to live with her aunt, who will be meeting her plane in Rapid City."

The stewardess bought me a comic book and an extra dessert, and she tried her best to make me smile. But my stomach was in knots, as it had been since my parents' accident, and all I could think of was what kind of person my aunt would turn out to be.

Aunt Sarah was my mother's older sister, though mother hadn't talked about her often, and the strange thing was, neither my mother nor my grandmother ever told me that Sarah had a daughter. Years later, I realized it was because they probably had never known. My indomitable Aunt Sarah, who had never married, had opted to keep her daughter a secret—a secret, as I was later to learn, that was only one of many.

So, I wondered, when Aunt Sarah claimed me from the stewardess, who the pretty girl was at her side. But I thought the moment Katy smiled and greeted me with a hug was the moment the knot in the pit of my stomach finally began to dissolve.

Katy was fifteen then, tall like me, but ever so much prettier, with kind blue eyes and silky blonde hair that, unlike mine, lay placidly around her shoulders.

Aunt Sarah did her best, in an awkward, stiff-backed way, to make me feel I was welcome in her home, but it was Katy who somehow, in her gentle way, managed to bring back my smile.

To make a long story short, I adored her from the get-go, and when she died five years later, it was as though, once again, the sun disappeared from my world. Whether I could have done something to prevent her death is a question that haunted me still. But then, if I had not left for New York when I did, I would never have met my husband, Marty, and Lulu would never have been born.

Beginning to shiver, I took a deep breath and turned the key in the lock of my aunt's old house. I heard the phone ring before I found the light switch, and I groped my way through the narrow entry and into the darkened kitchen. The phone still hung on the kitchen wall exactly where I remembered it.

"Julie?" a voice gushed over the phone line. "Julie, is it really you?"

"Yes . . . who is this?"

"Julie, it's Doreen. Tell me you remember. Doreen Hastings."

I stared at the receiver, calling into focus the chubby blonde girl who had appointed herself my first friend when I'd enrolled in school here in Deadwood.

"I heard from Nancy Jamison—she's Harrison's secretary—that you got here this afternoon. Julie, I'm so sorry about your Aunt Sarah. I saw her the afternoon before she died. . . . I want to tell you—well, I'll get to that, but I'm really glad you're here. How are you?"

I blinked. "I'm fine. Thanks, Doreen. How are you? Do you still live here in Deadwood?"

"Oh, yes. Some things never change. I'll probably be here till I die. But believe it or not, I'm a hospice nurse. I work out of Spearfish Regional Hospital. . . . My gosh, we have a lot to catch up on, Julie, and we really do need to talk."

I waited, but nothing more was forthcoming, except, "You haven't had dinner yet, have you?"

"Dinner? No. I'm afraid I had a late lunch."

"With Charlie Banks, I know."

I had to smile. Doreen was right. Some things never did change, and the café was clearly a conduit.

"That's right," I said. "I just got here."

"Well, get yourself settled. I'll be getting off shift soon. Then I'll swing by to pick you up—in an hour or so, if that's okay."

I wasn't sure I had the stamina to spend hours catching up with Doreen Hastings. But she had been a friend to me when I needed one years ago, and in truth, I was not looking forward to spending the evening by myself in Aunt Sarah's big old house.

"Okay," I managed. "I'll see you in an hour. Thanks."

I turned on lights in every room of the house, surprised to see that not much had been changed either in my old room or in Katy's. I changed out of my denim traveling suit into a pair of jeans and a sweatshirt. Then I went back downstairs, folded one leg under me in a wooden kitchen chair, and called Lulu and Penny.

"Hey, Mom! We're watching, *You've Got Mail*. It's cool. How was your trip?"

I spun the Meg Ryan and Tom Hanks film through my brain, and I didn't remember any steamy scenes I wouldn't want Lulu to see. "That's a good one, sweetie. My trip was fine. I hope I can get finished here in a few days. I miss you already . . . a lot!"

"Mom, you've only been gone a few hours. I would have been at school for most of that time—or at the skating rink."

There was no denying Lulu's cool-headed logic. "Right. Well, how was practice?"

"Fine. I started working on my double axel."

"Wow, Lu, that's great! I can hardly wait to see!"

"I know. Oops, the movie's back on. Call me tomorrow. Bye!"

I sat there a full minute with the phone in my hand and considered the ugly truth. Clearly, I ranked somewhere behind Lulu's love of chick flicks and her budding Olympics skating fantasies.

I wandered out to the back porch to have a look at the vista I remembered and was surprised to find the rickety porch had been remodeled into a sturdy wraparound deck. I stepped out to take a quick look at the starlit panorama behind it.

Doreen was right. Some things never changed, and others . . . well, they just did. I wandered back inside, checked to see what was in the kitchen cupboards, and stood in front of the chipped enamel sink where I'd washed or dried a thousand dishes during the years I'd lived in this house.

By the time I plopped down into the old, horsehair sofa, I felt tears prickling behind my eyes. I slapped myself soundly on the wrist. *Come on, get a grip*, I told myself, and then I burst into tears.

FOUR

It had been years since I'd allowed myself a good, all-purpose cry. Truth was, I wasn't even sure what I was crying about. But by the time I was through, I felt a strange sort of calm, and an even stranger kind of thankfulness for my life as I knew it now.

I washed my face in Aunt Sarah's downstairs bathroom, retouched my lipstick, and splashed on a little cologne. Then I picked up a magazine from the coffee table in the front room and settled in to wait for Doreen.

The next thing I knew, the sun was streaming in through the living room window, warming my face and making me blink as I struggled up from sleep. I glanced at my watch. Seven fifteen. I had slept the whole night through.

I sat up and thought a moment. *What had happened to Doreen? Surely, I would have heard if she had rang the doorbell, wouldn't I?* She must have been delayed, I told myself. Our catch-up session could wait another day.

Taking my overnight bag upstairs, I stripped off my clothes and laid them neatly on the bed in the room that used to be mine. I ran the water in the upstairs bath until it finally got warm, a process I remembered had always seemed to take forever. Then I stepped into the claw-footed tub and stood under the shower, scrubbing away old memories along with the tears and the travel grime.

Dressed again in jeans, with a red plaid shirt tied at my waist over a tee shirt, I hustled down the stairs to forage for some breakfast. The orange juice in the fridge was still fresh, and there was butter and homemade jam. I could picture Aunt Sarah gathering blueberries from behind the house and getting out her old jam pot.

I didn't see any bread, but I found some crackers and a jar of instant coffee, and soon I was sitting at the kitchen table scarfing it up while I mapped out my day.

First to the lawyer's office—Palmer, Harrison Palmer—to see about Aunt Sarah's last wishes. Then, I supposed, to the funeral home to make the necessary arrangements. Jewish families bury their dead within three days, Bubbe Lou had told me, and if that was okay for Bubbe Lou, it ought to be fine with Aunt Sarah. I finished the last of my instant coffee, thinking that with luck, I might catch a flight home within a few days at most.

I tidied up under the watchful eye of Aunt Sarah's cat-shaped clock, its plastic tail keeping spastic time to the thunk-thunk of the batteries. It was eerie to realize that just two days earlier, while I was busy thousands of miles away, my Aunt Sarah had breakfasted here on the last day of her life.

Shaking my head, I grabbed up my handbag and headed out for my rental car for the short drive into town. When I stepped into the storefront office of Harrison Palmer, Esq., the grandfather clock in his small reception area read eight twenty-two.

Nancy Jamison, the perky blonde clerk who had given me the key to Aunt Sarah's house a day earlier, looked up from her computer. "Good morning, Ms. Goldman, it's nice to see you again—"

"Please, call me Julie. Good morning to you. Is Mr. Palmer in yet?"

"Absolutely." She picked up the phone on her desk.

In a moment, a pleasant-looking guy with a receding hairline opened the door to an inner office. He ushered me in. "Julie Goldman, I presume. Nice to meet you. I'm Harrison Palmer."

When he smiled, I realized he was younger than I had realized—too young, in fact, to be losing his light brown hair. I focused in on his slightly crooked smile and found myself thinking that for a small town, Deadwood had some fine-looking men.

"I'm sorry for your loss," Palmer said, bringing me back to the reason I was here. "I know you hadn't been . . . close to your aunt for a while, but she always knew where you were. At least the last she was aware, you were living in Southern California."

"How did she know that?"

"I'm not sure exactly. But since you are her only heir, she wanted to be sure we could find you if and when we needed to."

I found myself frowning. "If she knew where I was, why didn't she ever contact me?"

He lifted his shoulders, the unspoken rejoinder floating in the air between us. Aunt Sarah had been in the same house for more than forty years. Why hadn't I contacted her?

Preferring not to think about it, I jumped into the breach. "Well, I'm glad Chief Banks was able to reach me."

Palmer smiled. "Me too, and this shouldn't take too long. As far as I know, you are Sarah's only living relative. Everything she had she left to you."

It was the first time I thought of my aunt's death in terms of what it might mean for me, except for taking on the minor responsibility of tying up her affairs.

"What exactly does that mean?" I asked. "Besides seeing to her final wishes?"

Palmer reached for a manila folder and handed me a thin sheaf of papers. "This is a copy of Sarah Lacey's last will and testament, updated and notarized at my office a little less than six months ago."

I glanced down at the papers in my hand but waited for the lawyer to continue.

"As of yesterday, Sarah had bank balances of a little over twelve hundred dollars in a checking account here in Deadwood, and just short of seventy thousand dollars in savings at First Dakota Bank in Rapid City. Those funds and the contents of a safety deposit box at First Dakota Bank are yours once you provide to them with proof of her death and a copy of this document."

I blinked. How in the world had Aunt Sarah managed to save this momentous sum? The idea that such a windfall would be coming to me nearly took my breath away.

Before I could respond, Palmer spoke again, his voice calm and reassuring. "But the largest part of Sarah's estate was, of course, her home. The house, which she owned outright, is worth somewhere in the neighborhood of four-hundred thousand dollars. You can check with any real estate agent in town to get a closer estimate, but that would be my guess based on today's market."

I looked at the lawyer, but my mouth was dry. I couldn't seem to find any words.

"You seem surprised."

I nodded. "Yes, I guess I am. . . . I had no idea first of all, that I would be inheriting at all and second, that there was anything much to inherit."

Palmer smiled again, more deeply this time, the skin crinkling around his eyes. "Well, then I'm glad to be the bearer of good news to help balance the sad."

I thought briefly of Chief Banks, who had used much the same phrase, and I shook my head, amazed yet again at the curveballs life expected us to field.

I could hardly wait to share the news with Lulu. Maybe, at last, we could afford to buy a little place of our own, not right at the beach, of course, but close.

But I was getting ahead of myself. "What happens now?" I asked. "What do I have to do before I go home?"

"If you look through the paperwork, you'll see that Sarah pre-paid her burial arrangements. Hank Fellows up at the funeral home in Lead can give you the details on that. He can also order copies of the death certificate for you, so you can present them to the banks when you're ready, and any real estate agent here in town can help you sell the house, if that's what you have in mind."

I blinked. *Of course that's what I had in mind. What else would I do with it?* But I didn't say that. I just got up from my chair on shaky legs and thrust out my hand. "Mr. Palmer, I can't thank you enough."

"Please, it's Harrison."

"Harrison, then. Thank you for helping me make sense of a situation I never expected to have to deal with."

He rose and took my hand in both of his, and I felt their warmth and strength. Why was it that everywhere I looked, people seemed to be getting younger?

"My pleasure," he said. "Please don't hesitate to call if you have any questions, or if there's anything else I can do for you."

I nodded gratefully, tucking the paperwork under my arm and gathering up my handbag.

"And please let me know when you make the funeral arrangements. Of course, I'd like to be there."

I nodded. "I will. Yes."

Nancy Jamison looked up as I closed the inner door behind me. "Ms. Goldman—Julie—can I ask you something? Did you meet up with Doreen last night?"

I shook my head. "No. She called and said she was going to pick me up, but I don't think she ever showed up. I'm ashamed to admit I fell asleep on the sofa, but I think I would have heard the doorbell if she'd rung."

Nancy frowned. "That's odd. She told me yesterday she was planning to have dinner with you. And she isn't at work today. I called the hospital a little bit ago, but they told me she hasn't shown up yet . . ."

I shrugged. "Maybe she isn't feeling well."

"I don't know. I tried her at home and on her cell."

"If she's sick, maybe she's just not answering."

"Maybe . . ." her voice trailed off. "Well, thanks, anyway. I just thought I'd ask. I guess I'll just try again later."

The hills around Deadwood were dense and green—a deep, dark green we rarely saw in water-starved Southern California—and the air was crisp despite the sunlight and heavy with the scent of pine. There was little traffic on the road to Lead, and no other cars in the parking lot at the mortuary except for one in the space marked, "Staff Only."

Like Harrison Palmer, Hank Fellows seemed very glad to see me, maybe because I was a welcome distraction in an otherwise boring day. He was tall and lanky, string bean thin, in fact, with a head full of carefully groomed gray hair. He uttered his condolences, then spread out the paperwork to show me what my aunt had decided she wanted for her burial.

"Mrs. Lacey was very thorough," he told me, pointing a long finger at a photo of the casket she had paid for and the site she had selected under a tree. "Father Ruggio, from St. Anne's Catholic Church, will do the service."

Startled, I realized that if my aunt was Catholic, this was the first I knew of it. She hadn't been raised Catholic, not in the family I knew. I thought of Katy, and I wondered how many other secrets my close-mouthed aunt had chosen not to share over the years.

In any case, as it turned out, there were no decisions I needed to make except for the time of services and interment. We agreed on Saturday—two days ahead—beginning at 11 a.m.

I thanked Fellows and walked out into the dappled sunshine. In the car, I hesitated. I could drive back to Deadwood and find a Realtor and make arrangements to sell Aunt Sarah's house. But maybe that would seem a little crass so soon after her death.

Or I could drive around to see how things had changed and maybe exorcise some of the ghosts I'd carried with me for so long. In the years I had lived with Aunt Sarah and Katy, they had taken me to see Mt. Rushmore, Crazy Horse Memorial, the Black Hills wildlife preserves, and all the sights tourists flocked to see. Maybe one day, now that I could afford it, I would take Lulu to see them, too. But now I found myself on the old Mickelson Trail, driving toward Sheridan Lake.

The sylvan lake, with the hills beyond, was just as I remembered it, lovely and serene, a balm to the senses, except in summer, when the area filled with campers. But now the marina was quiet and calm, a dozen little boats bobbing idly near the shore. On a spit of land facing the lake, a canopy was tethered to the ground, and facing the canopy were thirty or forty folding chairs festooned with white ribbon bows.

It reminded me of my wedding to Marty, of our sweet kiss under the wedding canopy—the *chupa,* they had called it—in Bubble Lou's garden. To my surprise, the memory now was as sweet as that long ago kiss; a remembered joy no longer tinged with sadness.

Likely a wedding would take place here on Saturday, the same day I buried my aunt. *Life goes on,* I reminded myself. I headed back to my car.

I made one more stop, in Spearfish Canyon, to the spot where my cousin's body had been found on that awful, unreal day. I tried not to dwell on what I had or had not done that might have contributed to her death. Instead, I thought about the sound of her laughter and released her soul from the depths of my memory to make its way to a better place.

It was half past four when I got back to Deadwood, and I realized I had not eaten since the crackers and jam at breakfast. I parked in front of the little café where I had eaten yesterday with Chief Banks.

I pushed open the cheery red door and started to wave to Earlene. It took less than a minute to wipe the smile off my face. Clearly, something was wrong.

FIVE

I spotted Nancy Jamison, Harrison Palmer's assistant, sobbing quietly in the back booth where I had lunched yesterday with Charlie Banks. Her straw-blonde hair obscured much of her face, but there was no mistaking her distress.

She was surrounded by a group of four or five women I did not know, who spoke to her in hushed tones. Earlene hovered protectively over all of them, absently shuffling a stack of menus. I stood in the doorway until she looked up and saw me.

"Oh, hello, Julie," she managed.

I peered at her, wondering what had become of the wide smile and hearty voice. "What happened? What's wrong?"

Earlene sighed, glancing at Nancy. "Well, Doreen was Nancy's best friend."

I hesitated, and Earlene stared at me as though I'd come from another planet. "Oh." Her hand fluttered to her mouth. "I guess maybe you haven't heard . . ."

She took my baffled silence for an answer, because she moved in a little closer and spoke in an exaggerated whisper. "Doreen Hastings. Her car went off the road last night. They found her body this morning."

I felt a chill snake its way down my spine. I swallowed hard and found myself stunned into silence. For a moment, I was nearly overcome by an old, familiar feeling—a ridiculous sense that where I was, death somehow followed. My parents . . . my cousin Katy . . . my husband . . . Aunt Sarah . . . and now someone I hadn't seen in years but had spoken to just last night. . . .

I had seen a therapist for months after Marty's death to try to work through these kinds of feelings, and the first time I gazed into Lulu's infant face I thought I had laid them to rest. Now I steadied myself with the nearest chair. I didn't know what to say.

Apparently, neither did Earlene. "Um," she murmured, fingering the pencil in her hair. "Sorry. Did you want something to eat?"

But my appetite was gone. I shook my head, murmured condolences, and backed out through the bright red door.

By the time I reached Aunt Sarah's house, my head had begun to clear, and I had pretty much assured myself that my coming back to Deadwood had nothing to do with Doreen's accident.

I barely remembered her, but I had just spoken to her, even planned to meet her for dinner. Now she was gone in the blink of an eye. An accident, Earlene had said. I wondered if her parents were still in town. If so, maybe I'd pay them a call.

For some reason, the thought made me realize I had not checked in with Avery. I punched his direct line into my cell phone, but it was after hours in California and all I got was voicemail.

But my hunger had come roaring back along with my equilibrium, so I rifled through Aunt Sarah's larder and settled on a box of linguini pasta and a jar of ready-made sauce. Putting a pot of water on the stove to boil, I dashed upstairs and washed my face, then traded in my jeans and sneakers for my comfy old terry robe.

I was halfway down the stairs, tying the robe around my waist, when I heard a knock at the door. To my surprise, Police Chief Charlie Banks was standing on the other side of it.

I pulled the robe a little tighter. "Oh, hi. Sorry. I wasn't expecting company."

He smiled. "No problem. I'm afraid I'm not company. I'm here on official business."

"Official—" I opened the door wider. "Something to do with my aunt?"

"No, not at all," he said, stepping over the threshold. "I'm sad to say there's been another death."

I nodded. "I heard. Doreen Hastings." I motioned him to the sofa and took a seat across from him.

He sat, a huge presence in Aunt Sarah's little front room, and nodded soberly. "You've heard."

"Just a little bit ago, at the café. What happened?"

He grimaced. "What a tragedy. Hard to imagine how it happened. Doreen's driven these mountain roads all her life. But apparently, she lost control of her car last night on her way back from an assignment."

"An assignment?"

"Doreen was a hospice nurse out of the regional hospital. She drove these mountains all the time, to patients in a lot of remote areas." The chief rubbed a hand over his face. "Sorry, I thought you might know that."

I shook my head. "She mentioned she was a hospice nurse, but to tell the truth, I don't know much about Doreen. I hadn't seen or heard from her in years until last night. I guess she heard I was in town. She called to offer condolences, and she asked me to join her for dinner. But she never showed up. . . . Now I know why. . . . What a horrible thing to happen."

The chief nodded. "The weather was good, the roads were clear, and she loved that little Miata she drove. Of course, the investigation is still ongoing. But I heard she might have been on her way to see you last night. I wondered if maybe you'd actually connected, if she seemed despondent or anything . . ."

Again, I shook my head. "We only spoke on the phone, but she sounded fine. In fact, she said she was looking forward to seeing me. There was something she wanted to tell me. But we never got the chance. Now we never will. Poor Doreen. Is her family still in town?"

"Her dad's in a rest home in Rapid City. Not doing too well, from what I hear. Her mom died a couple years back. Not sure yet about other relatives. Well." He stood. "Sorry I bothered you. If you think of anything else . . ."

I got up to let him out. I heard the pasta water boiling away. "Chief Banks—"

"Charlie."

"Charlie, then. I was just wondering . . . have you stopped long enough to have some dinner?"

A rueful chuckle. "No, not yet. I'm afraid it's been a rough day."

"Well, it isn't much, but I have some water boiling for pasta. If you're done for the day, you're welcome to stay and join me."

Charlie checked his watch and shifted his weight. "I wouldn't want to impose . . ."

"No imposition. To tell you the truth, I'm not terribly comfortable yet, alone here in this big old house. I'd enjoy the company if you'd like to stay."

He nodded. "Well, I don't know how much more I can do tonight . . ."

I led the way into the kitchen and poured spaghetti into the boiling water. "It's not fancy, but pasta always works when you're hungry. I spent most of the day today doing errands, the funeral arrangements for Saturday, and meeting with Aunt Sarah's attorney. . . . The day kind of slipped through my fingers. I stopped in to get a bite at the café, but then I heard about Doreen . . ."

"I can imagine. Welcome back to Deadwood. Forget the radio, the phone or the Internet. If you want to know what's going on in town, just stop in at the café."

I poured a jar of sauce into a pan to heat and rummaged around for a colander, which I found right in front of me on the kitchen counter, full of lemons and ripening tomatoes.

"Hey, I don't cook too often anymore," Charlie said, "but I can make a pretty decent salad."

"Check the fridge, then. See what you can find to go with these tomatoes."

He turned up a head of wilting romaine lettuce, which he stripped down to the heart, chopping and tossing it with tomatoes, red onion, and splashes of olive oil and lemon juice.

In the end, it was a humble but satisfying meal, which we ate at the kitchen table, chatting about Lulu, and the old days in Deadwood, and how you never knew what the fates were going to hand you. When his cell phone buzzed, I glanced at my watch, amazed to realize it was after nine.

"Sorry," he said, pushing back from the table. "Duty calls after all."

"No problem. Do whatever you have to. I need to call Lulu, anyway."

"If you're sure . . ."

"I'm sure."

"Well, then," he smiled. "Thanks for dinner . . . and the company. I enjoyed it. How long will you be in town?"

"The funeral is set for Saturday at eleven, and I have some other things to take care of. But I can't afford to take too much time off work. I hope to go home by early next week."

Charlie nodded. "I can understand that."

At the door, he turned. "There's a nice little steak house up the road apiece. If we can work out the timing, I'd be happy to buy you dinner before you head back to California."

I smiled. "Anywhere except the café. Too many prying eyes."

"You got it." He grinned. "Well, you take good care."

"You, too."

I walked him to the door, closed and locked it, and headed back to the kitchen. I tried to remember how long it had been since I'd said good night to someone at the door.

Oh, bosh . . . that's what Aunt Sarah would have said. I picked up the phone to call Lulu.

SIX

I slept that night in my old bed, the narrow bed under a dormer window where I had spent my teenage years. But I tossed and turned, plagued by dreams about the night Katy died.

I was fifteen then, shy and quiet, and taller than most of the boys my age. But height had never seemed to hinder Katy, who, at going on twenty-one, was turning heads wherever she went.

I think I guessed she was seeing someone special. Her room was next to mine, and though I couldn't make out the words through the thick old walls, I knew there were late night calls on the hall telephone, which she smuggled into her room.

I felt betrayed—hurt, really, because we had been so close, and now she didn't seem to trust me with whatever secrets she was hiding. She didn't invite me into her room much anymore either or laugh with me about the goofy boys in town.

Then one night, a little after midnight, I heard her stirring around in her room. I heard her door close softly. I heard her moving down the stairs, slowly to mask the creaking. I heard the heavy *thu-thunk* of the front door as she pulled it firmly shut.

Everything in me wanted to run downstairs after her, to find out where she was going. I wanted to stop her from running out into the night. But I lay there, immobile, afraid she would brush me aside—or, worse yet, be angry with me for butting into her business.

Eventually, I padded quietly down the hall, fearful of waking Aunt Sarah. I opened Katy's door ever so slowly and crept inside, hoping maybe I could find something—anything—that might give me a clue about where she was going, or whom she might be planning to meet.

In the pale moonlight, I scanned the shelf above her bed, a mishmash of stuffed animals, little framed photos, and kewpie dolls that had been won for her by various dates over years at the county fair. But the photos were all familiar to me and nothing suggested who her new boyfriend might be.

I looked through the stuff on her dresser top, a tangle of brushes, colognes and hair goodies, some coins, and a couple of mismatched earrings.

Stuffed into the mirror were a picture of the Backstreet Boys we'd ripped from a *Tiger Beat* magazine, a photo of the two of us in raffia hula skirts at a Kiwanis Halloween dance, and a photo of our once beloved Scallion, a spunky little kitten who probably met her end sparring with a mountain lion, but who we preferred to think had simply run away.

Nothing I saw offered any clues. Finally, I rummaged in the dark through the drawer of Katy's nightstand, my hand fumbling with a small flashlight and a few strands of beads and something that felt like a bulky little ring.

As I closed my hand around it, I heard the toilet flush and Aunt Sarah coughing in the hallway, and I panicked. I heard a door close and open again, and I ran back to my room, skidding on a rug and bumping my head on the corner of my own nightstand.

"Julie, is that you?" Aunt Sarah called. "Are you all right?"

"F-fine, Aunt Sarah." I plopped onto my bed, praying she would not come down the hall to check.

I lay there quietly, figuring I'd look under my bed later to find the little ring-thing that had slipped from my grasp when I fell. But the next thing I knew, it was morning, and Aunt Sarah was calling us to breakfast, and Katy didn't appear, and Aunt Sarah went upstairs to shake her out of bed and found the bed had not been slept in.

Then all hell broke loose, and for some ungodly reason, I did not tell Aunt Sarah that I had heard Katy slip out during the night.

The police came, and a flurry of neighbors, and air seemed to rush though my ears, and time stopped until two days later, when Katy's body was found in a shallow grave in the waters of Spearfish Creek.

Now I heard myself moaning in my sleep, but it was a shrill ringing, a piercing sound that brought me finally awake. I sat up, groggy, trying to remember where I was. Forgetting for a moment about the hall phone, I stumbled down the stairs to pick up the phone in the kitchen.

"Julie, is that you? It's Annie."

I fell into a chair. It was Annie Lewis, Avery's fresh-faced assistant at the Stevens Point Hotel in Dana Point. The hotel, the beach, my life as I knew it seemed oddly far away. But I blinked and ran a hand over my eyes. "Annie, yes, it's me."

"How are things going in South Dakota?"

"Um okay, I guess. How are things going there?"

"Smooth as silk, at the moment, anyway. Everyone seems to be happy."

I nodded. "Well, that's good for a change. I guess it's safe to breathe."

"Anyway, I was listening to Avery's voicemail, and I heard your message, so I wanted to let you know he won't be in today. He's out with the hotel brass in Los Angeles. Some hush-hush meeting, last minute. I'll probably hear from him later today, but I'd guess he won't be back till Monday."

"Oh. Well, fine, then. Thanks, Annie. I really only wanted to let him know I expect to be back very soon. As soon as I know when, for sure, I'll call in again and let you know."

"No problem. You take care. Talk to you soon. Bye."

I leaned back in my chair, thinking hard just to remember what day it was. Friday, I realized, and I would not be home to light the Shabbos candles with Lulu.

I'm not Jewish by birth, and neither is Lulu, according to most traditional Jewish thinking. But Friday nights when I was married to Marty meant dinner at Bubbe Lou's, and I was always transfixed when she covered her head to light the Shabbos candles before we ate. It was as though, for a moment, she retreated into a place of private peace, and the ritual seemed to fill me with a sense of well-being; it was a far cry from the vague uneasiness that plagued me much of the time.

So, after Marty and Bubbe Lou were gone and Lulu came into the world, I bought myself a pair of silver candlesticks, found an old Hebrew prayer book in a used bookstore, and studied the Friday night Sabbath prayer. I'm not even certain I pronounce it right, but I say it phonetically, the way I remember hearing Bubbe Lou say it, and when Lulu and I recite it together, I am filled with a sense of peace. It's a fragile connection to the happiest time in my life and to the daddy and grandma Lulu never knew.

Now I sighed and drummed my fingers on the table. I missed Lulu terribly. I'd never been away from her this long before. But today was also the day before my Aunt Sarah's funeral, and it occurred to me the one thing she had not planned for in advance was flowers. Making those arrangements seemed as good a way as any for me to pass some time away today.

It was already mid-morning, and I decided to stop by the café and treat myself to a late breakfast and while I was there, to find out from the well-oiled community pipeline if there was any more news about Doreen.

There wasn't, as it turned out, except the investigation was still ongoing, and word had not yet begun to circulate about when Doreen's funeral service might be held. But Earlene did point me to the nearest florist, also up the road in Lead, so after demolishing a stack of pancakes, I hit the road again.

The flower shop was bright and fragrant, filled with bowers of healthy greenery and the bubbling of an indoor fountain. A no-nonsense woman with lively brown eyes and a ready smile helped me to choose a simple spray of gardenias, which had been Aunt Sarah's favorite, and a couple of pots of blooming jasmine. My aunt had requested only a graveside service, so there would be no need for chapel flowers.

"If you want," the florist told me, tucking a few strands of gray-blonde hair behind her ear, "we can pick up the pots of jasmine after the service and deliver them to the regional hospital. They're always happy to have fresh plants. They seem to cheer up the patients."

That seemed like a good idea to me. I rummaged in my purse and pulled out my plastic to pay. "It seems pretty quiet around here," I said. "How do you manage to keep busy?"

"Oh, you'd be surprised," she told me. "Delivery orders from out of town help, and we draw from a pretty big area. Fortunately or unfortunately, the mortuary keeps us busy, too. In fact, there'll probably be another funeral next week."

I looked up. "Doreen Hastings?"

"Yes. Did you know Doreen?"

"A little," I said. "My cousin and I went to school with her. It was a long time ago . . ."

"Your cousin?"

"Yes, my Aunt Sarah's daughter, Katy Lacey."

"Oh, my goodness, you're Sarah Lacey's niece! My very deepest condolences. Goodness, Katy's funeral seems so long ago. We did her flowers, too."

I signed the charge slip. "Did you know her? Katy?"

"Not well, although she went to school with my daughter, Faye, and I knew she was Sarah's daughter. It was just so horrible—the way Katy died, so young . . ."

I looked up. "They never found her killer . . ."

"No," she said. "I don't think they ever did. . . . Do you still live around here?"

I shook my head. "No. I left for New York right after I finished high school. This is my first time back."

The woman nodded. "I'll bet you see a lot of changes."

"Yes. And I wish the circumstances were different. First Aunt Sarah, and now Doreen."

The woman nodded. "Another life too young to be taken. Doreen, of all people. The way she tore around these hills in that little red car of hers. You have to wonder, how could it happen?"

"That's what Chief Banks said, too."

The florist handed me a colorful business card. "Well, don't you worry about a thing, Ms. Goldman. We'll do a really nice job for Sarah."

"It's Julie." I tucked the card away in my wallet. "Thanks so much for your help." I smiled. "You made a sad job a little easier."

At a roadside stand, I bought some locally grown plums and a basket of red, ripe strawberries. At a lookout point, I stopped again and picnicked on the fruit in the afternoon sun until darkness began to settle into the canyons. As I watched, the sun began to sink, a brilliant ball of yellow amid the shadows. When the afternoon breeze picked up and ruffled my thin shirt, I headed back to my car.

At home, I found two messages on Aunt Sarah's machine. The first was from a Mrs. Kovich, president of the Ladies' Guild at the church, letting me know that the ladies would set out a luncheon repast in the rectory hall following my aunt's funeral. Everyone in town was invited, and I was not to do a thing except show up to greet Aunt Sarah's friends.

The second call was from Charlie Banks, who wondered, if I was free this evening, if he could pick me up at seven o'clock and pay me back for last night's dinner.

If this were a date, I would probably be flustered. How uncool, Lulu would say. But I looked at it as a neighborly gesture, like the church ladies setting out lunch. I could live with that. And I loved a good steak. And I happened to have packed a basic black dress, which I planned to wear to the funeral.

I checked Aunt Sarah's ticking cat clock. It was just past five. I started to call Lulu and realized, as the phone began to ring, that it was still school hours in California. Just as well. I'd have time for a soak and enough time to condition my hair and try to coax it into submission.

SEVEN

I was dressed and ready when I called Lulu after school hours in California. She was doing her homework because Penny had promised her a shopping trip on Saturday if all her homework was done. "We're going to check out some skinny jeans—just looking," she assured me.

Oh, boy. No matter how I wanted to slow it down, my little girl was growing up. "Listen," I told her. "If you find a pair you like, tell Penny it's okay. You can use some of the money I left. I should be home soon, anyway."

"Really?" I could sense the joy in her face, and I missed her more than ever.

"Really," I said. "And if you find a top you like, you can go ahead and get that, too."

"Cool. Thanks . . . and Mom?"

"Yes?"

"It's Friday, and I'm planning to light the Shabbos candles tonight, even if you're not here."

I swallowed hard, surprised and touched that my daughter remembered. "That's great. That's wonderful, Lulu. I love you very much."

I had washed my face and was applying fresh mascara when the doorbell rang promptly at seven. Charlie Banks, in a navy sport coat and khaki slacks, was not at all hard to look at.

"Hey," I said. "You clean up pretty good. You know you didn't have to do this."

"No, but I like to repay my debts. And I thought you could use a little cheering up before the funeral tomorrow."

Right, of course. Ah, well.

"That was thoughtful," I said. "Would you like to come in? As I recall, Aunt Sarah always kept some sherry hidden on the lower left shelf of the china cabinet."

He laughed. "I have to say, I'm starved. Thanks, anyway. But why don't we just get going?"

I followed him out. "Do I need to lock the door?"

"Probably not. But do it anyway."

I turned the key in the ancient lock. "So, how was your day?"

He opened the door of a silvery Camry with the convertible top down. "Spent a good part of it crawling up and down the hills around the bend in the road where Doreen's car went down. Lots of skid marks, but nothing unexplainable. The car's been towed into town."

I slipped into his Camry, and he closed the door. "Will the wind be too much for your hair?"

I shrugged. "Doesn't matter. My hair has a mind of its own anyway. This'll be fine. Thanks for asking."

We ended up at a steak house in Hill City, just north of Custer. I remembered the area from a childhood outing with Aunt Sarah and Katy. "Isn't there an old-fashioned train that runs through these hills?"

"Yep. An old steam train. It winds through the hills to Keystone, puffing steam all the way."

"I remember. We sat in the first car, me leaning out the window every time we went around a bend. I thought it was pretty exciting."

We were seated in a red leather booth, a little the worse for wear. There was sawdust on the floor, antlers mounted on the wall, and Tammy Wynette was standing by her man from somewhere in the depths of the room. I felt like I had been teleported in one fell swoop into the Deadwood of yore.

Charlie studied the wine list as I studied him. "I'm not much on this stuff," he mumbled after a minute. "Do you prefer red or white?"

We settled on a Merlot the waiter recommended and sipped it as we waited for our steaks. Charlie settled back in his seat. "So, what else do you remember about your wayward youth in Deadwood?"

I smiled. "I remember the gold mine, of course."

"Yep. Still there but long since closed. The tourists like to explore the Open Cut."

"Oddly enough, I never did that."

Charlie raised his brows. "Well, we'll have to take care of that. Part of my job as chief of police is to be sure it stays safe for tourists."

I nodded. "I do remember seeing Mt. Rushmore for the first time. I remember thinking it was really awesome, especially the huge, craggy face of Abe Lincoln, because we'd studied him so much at school."

"How old were you?"

"Ten. That's when I got here, to live with Aunt Sarah and her daughter, Katy, after my parents died. My aunt did her best to make me feel at home, but Katy was the one I adored."

I felt the prickle of tears, but I blinked them back. "I was fifteen when Katy died."

Charlie regarded me, his blue eyes soft. "Yes. I sort of remember when it happened."

I looked at him. "Were you on the police force then?"

The waiter brought our steaks, cooked perfectly, and mammoth baked potatoes on a separate plate, topped with a mountain of sour cream.

Charlie picked up his fork. "I was a rookie that year. I remember being more than a little ticked. First murder we'd had in Deadwood in years, and they told me I was still too wet behind the ears to be an active part of the investigation."

I stared at my plate. "Maybe they should have let you try. As it turned out, they never found her killer."

"Well," he said, slicing into his steak, "as I recall, they didn't have much to go on. It likely wasn't a random killing, since Katy had no reason to be out on her own sometime in the middle of the night. But if she had a boyfriend, or someone she planned to meet, nobody seemed to know who he was."

I nodded. "I had thought for some time that she might have been dating someone, but I had no idea who, either. I remember being questioned after her . . . after she was found. All I knew for sure—all I could tell them—was that I heard her leave the house sometime in the night . . ."

I looked at Charlie, but I was seeing the face of the officer who had questioned me that awful morning. "I could have stopped her," I told him. "I should have stopped her. I should have told Aunt Sarah. . . . But I didn't . . ."

I looked down at my plate. "And then, for some reason, I couldn't tell her. Not when we spent so many silent nights, when we let Katy's birthday pass without a word, as though it wasn't her birthday at all . . ."

I felt the prickle of tears, but I blinked them back. "I didn't tell Aunt Sarah for a very long time. She was—well, she was pretty closed up for so long after Katy died."

I had told all this to Marty years ago, baring my soul, trying desperately to exorcise my ghosts, and he had held me, listened with infinite patience, and wiped the tears from my face. But being back in Deadwood brought it all back, and this time, the tears sprang freely. The wound was fresh again. I realized how much I missed Katy to this day, and the memory of our time together cut through my being like a knife.

"Julie—" Charlie prompted, and I looked up, surprised to hear my name.

"So, I lived with the guilt for nearly a year," I went on, "and then one day, it just spilled out. I told Aunt Sarah what I'd heard that night and that I'd been too scared, or too stupid, to stop Katy from leaving . . ."

Mechanically, I cut into my steak. "And it was never the same—my life with Aunt Sarah after that. She couldn't find it in her heart to forgive me for not alerting her the night it happened. Why would she, when I couldn't forgive myself? Try as we might, neither one of us could ever manage to reach across the chasm."

"So, you left town."

"As soon as I could, when I was eighteen, right after high school. And I never looked back. Not until now, anyway."

Once again, I blinked back tears. "And the worst of it is, it's too late now. I'll never know if she forgave me."

Charlie paused, his fork in midair. "Sounds to me like she did."

I looked at him. "What makes you say that?"

"The way I hear it around town," he said, "your aunt left you everything she had. . . . Why would she have done that unless she finally forgave you?"

I was stunned into silence, a rarity for me. Then I stared at Charlie and nodded. I managed a smile. "I guess there's some truth in that. Thank you."

Suddenly, the steak tasted wonderful. "So," I said, digging in. "How did you get into police work?"

"Well." Charlie poured more wine. "Believe it or not, I was an aimless kid, putting in hours at my dad's liquor store in Lead. Fell in love with the mayor's daughter. I wanted to marry her, but I had no money, and when they posted the opening for a cop in Deadwood, it seemed like the perfect opportunity."

I grinned. "Did you marry the mayor's daughter?"

"Yes, I surely did."

"Wow. So, you started out as a lowly cop and worked your way up to Chief."

"Don't have to work as hard," he chuckled. "I don't often have to get my hands dirty, except when I'm crawling around safety-checking the mine, or inspecting every inch of a mountain pass, like today, looking for evidence in the accident."

The waiter appeared with a dessert menu. Charlie didn't bother to look at it. He ordered blackberry cobbler with two spoons. "And put some ice cream on it."

I had to admit, it felt good to have someone else make decisions for a change. I was feeling relaxed, and my natural curiosity bubbled up.

"Tell me if it's none of my business . . . but what happened to your wife?"

Charlie's face sobered. "I don't mind. Lot of water's gone over that bridge . . ." He took a deep breath. "Laura had a series of miscarriages . . . three, actually, one year after another. Then we finally had a child—a beautiful little girl. We named her Merry. . . . But she died before she was eight weeks old. Crib death, they called it."

He pressed his lips together, cleared his throat. "Laura just—well, she never got over it. Doctor said she died of a congenital heart murmur. I think she died of grief."

I looked at him. I remembered the other day, when he told me that not having children was the deepest regret of his life.

"I'm so sorry," I whispered.

"Don't be," he said. "It was a long time ago . . . but I do know a little something about loss."

He smiled crookedly, and we both watched as the ice cream melted into the cobbler. We talked some more, but I felt self-conscious, as though I'd somehow popped a big balloon, and the air around us felt different.

It was half past nine when he pulled into Aunt Sarah's driveway and walked me up the porch stairs.

"Would you like me to come in and have a look around?" he asked. "You said you felt a little skittish."

"Thanks, not necessary. I'll be all right. I left all the lights on downstairs. And thanks, Charlie, for everything, really. I feel like I've made a friend."

"Me, too. No thanks needed. I'll see you tomorrow at the funeral service."

I nodded, and something I wasn't ready to process hung between us for a moment. Then he nodded and turned away. I watched him get into his car.

I was bolting the door from the inside before I realized I'd been holding my breath.

EIGHT

I was truly surprised at the number of people who turned out for the graveside service. There must have been forty or fifty, most of whom I had never seen before. Charlie Banks was there, and Harrison Palmer, the attorney, who had insisted on picking me up and driving me out to the cemetery.

I recognized Harrison's secretary, Nancy Jamison, looking paler than I remembered and totally devoid of makeup, and Earlene from the café, dressed soberly in a dark gray dress, a far cry from her cheerful red and white waitress' uniform. And I recognized the florist, Hannah Wilkerson, whom I'd met at her shop the other morning.

It was a day Aunt Sarah would have called "fit for beating the blankets," warm and sunny with a mountain breeze whistling through the Ponderosa pines.

Father Ruggio, a slight, white-haired slip of a man, officiated at the service. He described my aunt as a warm, loving, compassionate soul and a pillar of the mountain community. I wondered for a brief minute if he had known the same woman I had.

Then I gave myself a proverbial slap because who was I to be an ungrateful brat after all she had done for me? Not for the first time, I felt truly ashamed that my own selfish, unresolved feelings had kept me from being there for her in the last years of her life.

By the time the service was over, I was blubbering, and Aunt Sarah's friends gathered around me like mama hens guarding the nest. Nobody asked me where I'd been all these years, and that made me feel even worse.

Finally, as the mourners began to break away and head for their cars, Harrison appeared at my side to offer a steadying arm as we made our way over the hilly terrain to his dark green Explorer.

I leaned back into the leather seat. "I never expected such a crowd."

Harrison smiled. "It's a small town. Sarah was one of our own."

I blinked. "Yes, I suppose she was. . . . Father Ruggio called her a pillar of the community. What did he mean by that?"

Harrison pulled into the stream of cars leaving for the repast at the rectory hall. "Well, for one thing, after she lost Katy, she set up a charitable foundation here in town. It's pretty low key, but my father handled the legal work for her, and since he's been gone, I kind of oversee it. It's called Katy's Legacy, and it provides assistance to grieving families and children in South Dakota—counseling, scholarships, financial help for burial, whatever it takes to put people back on their feet after they've lost a loved one."

I was floored. "Oh, my gosh. I never knew!"

"There's a board of directors and a part-time administrator, and in addition to the assets your aunt willed to you, she funded the foundation in perpetuity."

I sat in shocked silence for the rest of the ride, wondering what else about my Aunt Sarah I'd been totally clueless about.

But I couldn't dwell on it because the crowd at the rectory hall was even larger than it had been at the cemetery, and the newcomers quickly gathered around me, eager to share stories and memories.

The serving tables were loaded with platters of chicken and cold cuts and a vast array of breads, salads, and desserts, and it wasn't long before a robust woman with a plate in her hand bustled her way through the crowd.

"Give this poor young woman some space," she said, leading me to a cloth-covered table. "I'm Genevieve Kovich from the Ladies Auxiliary." She backed me into a chair and set the plate in front of me. "I spoke to you yesterday, you may remember. You probably don't remember me from when you were here years ago as a girl."

I shook my head, the woman's snow-white hair and double chins doing nothing to jog my memory. "I'm so sorry. There seems to be so much I don't remember."

"Well, no matter. You were only a child. Sarah would have been glad to know you got back here for her when it counted."

I blinked.

"You know she was thinking of calling you . . ."

I shook my head. "I didn't know . . ."

"Oh, yes. She told me so herself, not more than a day or two before she died."

Once again, I was stunned. "Why?"

"Well, I don't rightly know. She only said she was going to try to reach you."

I tried to compose myself, sorting through questions I probably should have asked sooner. "Had Aunt Sarah been ill?"

"I don't think so, no. No more than the rest of us old biddies. The usual aches and pains." Mrs. Kovich raised a plump finger. "Getting older is no walk in the park. But these things happen, you know."

Mrs. Kovich dropped into her chair. "A heart attack can just come and find you in your sleep. It happened last fall to Mary Cavendish."

I nodded.

"When you think about it, it's not a bad way to go. But of course, you do leave some things unfinished."

"I suppose," I murmured, humbled to know that my aunt had wanted to find me and feeling guiltier still that I'd made no effort over the years to close the breach between us.

Mrs. Kovich pushed at the plate in front of me. "Eat, my dear. It will make you feel better. You'll see."

But one by one or two by two, people appeared at my side, a blur of eyes and faces and beards, shaking my hand, sharing stories, leaning in to offer a hug. For a person like me, basically a loner, it was almost overwhelming. I smiled until my face actually hurt, and I felt a headache brewing behind my eyes.

Finally, Harrison Palmer appeared and asked if I was ready to go. I could have kissed him, I was so ready, but propriety trumped relief, so I jumped up, mumbled my thanks, and managed some feeble goodbyes. I looked for Charlie, but he was nowhere in sight. Duty had called, I assumed.

Mrs. Kovich assured me the leftover food would be delivered to Aunt Sarah's house. I tried to tell her I didn't expect to be there long enough to enjoy it, but she waved me off, put on an apron, and busied herself with a roll of aluminum foil big enough to wrap the whole table.

As she'd promised, two burly old guys arrived at Aunt Sarah's house not long after Harrison left, piling bowls and platters into the fridge and pies and cakes on the kitchen counter.

I started to protest, but the mild headache was by now beginning to grow claws, and I realized there was nothing much but this morning's cup of coffee standing between me and starvation.

So, I made myself a ham sandwich and piled potato salad on the plate. I ate slowly, processing the food, which tasted better than anything I'd had in a while, and thought about all the flabbergasting things I had seen and heard that day.

My aunt was a philanthropist. A foundation in Katy's name, funded in perpetuity with funds I never knew she had. Perfect strangers at the repast had stood wringing their hands, looking deep into my eyes, wanting me to know what Aunt Sarah had done for them in their time of grief and need.

Bubbe Lou once told me that no matter how well you thought you knew a person, you could never really live inside their heads. She had a Yiddish expression for it, which I can't remember, but it struck me not for the first time how true a thought that was.

I sighed, tidying the kitchen as best I could and missing Lulu so much it hurt. I ached to get back to my real life and even to my job at the Stevens Point.

There were loose ends still to be tied up here—putting the house up for sale, for one, and making whatever arrangements needed to be made with Aunt Sarah's banks. But I couldn't do much until I had copies of Aunt Sarah's death certificates, and that would take a couple of weeks at least.

It would be several days yet before Doreen was laid to rest, and while it might have been courteous for me attend, I could not think of a single reason why I really needed to.

I called the airline in Rapid City and found there was a flight to Los Angeles by way of Denver leaving at 6 p.m. With luck, I would be home by midnight, and what a nice surprise it would be for Lulu when she woke up tomorrow morning.

I made the reservation and set about cramming whatever leftovers I could into Aunt Sarah's freezer. Then I left a message on Harrison's cell phone.

"It's Julie, Harrison. Thanks for everything. I wanted to let you know I've decided to go home tonight. I'll be back as soon as I can to get things finalized here, and you can reach me at home if you need to. Oh, and please see that Nancy or Mrs. Kovich or somebody gets a key to the house, because the leftover food I can't fit in the freezer needs to find people to eat it . . ."

I thought a few seconds, but I seemed to have said it all. "Thanks again. For everything. Bye."

I ran upstairs to pack my few things and took a last look around my old room. I didn't want to deal with the conflicting feelings that were rattling through my brain. But then something occurred to me, and I put down my bag and got down on my hands and knees.

I felt around, deep under the bed, clear up into the dusty corners, and sure enough, my fingers closed around something small and hard and vaguely rounded. The bulky little ring-thing I'd found in Katy's dresser drawer so many years ago had remained right here all these years, under the bed where I had dropped it in haste when I heard Aunt Sarah that fateful night.

On my belly, I eased back out, brushed off the dust bunnies, and brought the object into view. It was a ring of some sort, some kind of silver or pewter ring with an insignia I did not recognize. Stumped, I dropped it into a side pocket of my suitcase and headed for the stairs.

If I left for the airport now, I'd have plenty of time to return my car before it was time to board. I thought about calling Charlie Banks, but for some reason, I felt a little shy, and I was fairly certain he would hear my story from Harrison.

So, I locked the front door, threw my things in the back, eased out of Bluebird Hill Lane, and tried not to look back.

NINE

Waking in my own bed on Sunday morning was better than an unexpected gift. It was early—my brain was still on South Dakota time—and Lulu and Penny were sound asleep on the upper and lower bunks of Lulu's trundle bed.

I padded down the hall to the kitchen, put on a pot of coffee, and peeled an orange. I had barely brought in the Sunday papers and settled into the sofa when Lulu came screeching down the hall.

"Mom? Mom! I smelled the coffee!" She landed right on top of me. "Why didn't you tell me you were coming home?"

I hugged her. "Because that would have spoiled the surprise! Oh, Lulu, I love you."

"Yeah, I know. I love you, too." She began righting sections of the strewn newspaper. "You wanna see my skinny jeans?"

"Of course. But don't wake Penny if she's still asleep."

"Yeah, I'll be quiet. I'll be right back. Don't move. Okay?"

I did not move except to turn a page of the Arts section, my favorite part of the Sunday paper, including the back page Crossword. But Lulu was back in a few minutes, Penny trailing sleepily in her wake.

I had to admit, my heart did a flip-flop seeing Lu in her new outfit. She looked long and lean in her skinny jeans, longer and leaner than I remembered. Her hair was taking on a burnished copper cast, and in the coral sweater top with the matching cap and scarf, she could have posed for the cover of *Seventeen*, if, in fact, *Seventeen* was still being published and hadn't morphed into an online app.

"Wow," I managed. "You look truly cool. You look a kid out of *iCarly*." It was her favorite show on TV at the moment, full of teens running cheerfully amok.

"I know," she said, striking a model's pose before apprehension bloomed on her face. "I wasn't sure you'd be okay with it . . ."

I took a breath. "I'm okay with it."

"Yay! Penny saved the receipts in case you had a cow."

I laughed. "I am not completely out of it, you know . . ."

"I know, but you're pretty bossy!"

"Bossy?"

"Bossy, Mom. If *you* don't like it, *I* don't get to wear it."

I made a face at her. "That's what mothers are for. Right, Penny?"

Penny giggled. "It's good to have you back, Julie."

Penny was in her mid-twenties, but standing there in her shortie pajamas, face scrubbed, long brown hair framing a pixie face, she looked like a little more than a teenager herself. For the umpteenth time, I realized how lucky we were to have her in our chaotic lives.

"Thanks, Pen. It's good to be home. I missed you, too. I missed both of you."

"How did it go?" Penny asked, plucking out a section of the peeled orange. She was not a coffee drinker, but I knew it wouldn't be long before she got up to brew herself some tea.

"Okay, I guess. I have lots of stuff to process, but I'm not ready to do that yet. Today is for fun. Lulu can decide what she wants us to do. And

Penny, you can come with us, if you want. We'll have a Girl's Day—wherever you guys want."

Lulu was hopping up and down, once again my little girl. "The mall! They're having a *Back to the Beach* fashion show. We saw it advertised yesterday."

The mall? I tried to mentally review what was left in my checking account. Of course, I could always fall back on the plastic, and with luck, I might have something of Aunt Sarah's bequest before the credit card bill came in.

Penny shook her head. "Thanks. But I've got plenty to catch up on. Another Bar Review class, for one thing. There's another exam coming up."

"Bummer. But I have a really good feeling you're going to pass it this time."

I spread my hands and gestured toward Lulu. "Okay, then. The mall. Done deal. But it won't be open for a couple of hours, so let me try to do my crossword."

Lulu clapped her hands and plopped down in front of the TV while Penny went back to get her things together. I happily settled in with the papers, trying to tune out the latest shenanigans on the Nickelodeon channel. I stopped only long enough to give Penny a hug and stuff some bills into her hand.

"Thanks, Pen," I hugged her again. "I don't know what I'd do without you."

"Pleasure," she murmured. "Lulu's the best."

I knew that, but it was good to hear it anyway.

By eleven, Lulu and I had taken front row seats in the center court of the mall, and we did our share of oohing and aahing as the newest take on teen couture pranced across the runway. I even took some notes, so we could find the styles Lulu was crazy about when the time came to shop.

At nearly two, having spent every dollar I could talk myself into, we were sliding into a booth at Scooters, where the milkshakes were thick, and the wait staff tooled around on roller skates.

"Hey," I said. "So, what's new on the ice?"

"I'm practicing my axel," Lulu told me. "I'm getting pretty good, but I wish I could get to the rink to practice more than once or twice a week."

I did, too, since it meant so much to her, but one private lesson and one practice session a week was just about all I could afford. I thought briefly about the commission check I would get for the on-again Frasee wedding. *And then, of course. . . .* But I didn't want to think about that. The inheritance still didn't seem real.

"Well," I said. "We'll just have to see. I promise to get over to the rink this week to see your lesson and your practice."

A pretty young waitress with a bouncy ponytail rolled to a stop at our table. We ordered double burgers and vanilla shakes, our long-time tradition at Scooters.

"So, tell me about your trip." Lulu busied herself lining up the bottled condiments. "Tell me about Deadwood. Were you sad?"

I had told her when I left that I was going back to South Dakota to say goodbye to my aunt, who had passed away in her sleep. "Yes," I said now, "it's always sad when someone dies."

Over the years, I had told Lulu snips and snatches about my childhood. She knew that my parents, like her daddy, had died when they were very young. But she didn't know much about where I had grown up, except that I had lived with an aunt.

"Deadwood's an interesting little town," I told her. "Once upon a time, it was a gold mining town, and it's still a little cowboy-ish in some ways. But the Black Hills are beautiful, and it's very cold in winter. People can ice skate on the frozen lakes; they don't even need a skating rink."

Her eyes lit up. "Really? Can I go?"

It seemed as good a time as any to tell her that she might be seeing Deadwood sooner than she thought.

"Well, as it turns out, I'm going to have to go back to tie up some business," I said. "Maybe we can go back together right after school is out."

"Cool!" Lulu was so excited she nearly knocked over her milk shake.

"You won't be able to skate," I cautioned her. "It'll be summer, after all. But you can see the lakes and the old gold mine and the house where I grew up, and we can even take a ride on the old steam train."

I did not tell her that we were coming into some money, and that at long last, once we got back, we might be able to buy a house of our own somewhere not far from the beach. It seemed too much to hope for, too fragile to grasp, for someone like me, whose dreams had been shattered too many times in one lifetime.

But a tiny bubble of anticipation was beginning deep inside me. Bubbe Lou would have warned me, *"Don't give it a 'kinnehora."* I knew it meant something like, "Don't think about it, or you might just jinx it."

"Hey," I said. "Now that we've shopped till we nearly dropped, how about we go see a movie?"

TEN

It was nearly seven by the time we got home, laden with shopping bags and way too full of popcorn. We cut the tags off Lulu's new clothes.

"Thanks, Mom."

I looked at her. "Bossy, eh? Is that what you really think?"

She grinned, and then, because I thought we ought to, we heated some vegetable soup for dinner.

We ate on trays and watched the end of an Angels game. They gave it away in the ninth. Lulu snuggled against me the way she had when she was little. Eventually, her head sagged against my shoulder. It felt so good, I hated to disturb her, but I walked her to her bed without fully waking her, tucked her in, and kissed her good night.

I cleaned up the dishes, threw my traveling clothes in the laundry, and worked a little more on the Sunday puzzle. By nine, I was nodding off myself. *Jet lag*, I told myself. But in truth, I was ready to get a good night's sleep and get back on schedule in the morning.

I woke on Monday morning with a rare sense of buoyancy, showered, and put on a yellow sundress that seemed to match my mood. To my amazement, Lulu was bathed and dressed and had poured cereal for both of us. I dropped her off at school before eight and dodged enough traffic to make it to the hotel parking lot on the dot of eight thirty.

It was quiet in the kitchen, but the door to Avery's office was open, and I could see him sitting at his computer, the stray hairs on his balding crown standing at attention.

"Hey," I said, peering around the door. "I'm back a little sooner than I expected."

Avery looked flummoxed in the best of times, but this morning he appeared totally bewildered. "Oh," he said. "Welcome back. I wish I had better news."

I dropped into a chair. *Nothing like the promise of disaster to get your juices flowing.* "What's the matter?" I asked.

"The hotel has been sold."

Bam. Just like that.

"Are you sure?"

He blinked. "Of course I'm sure. They called me to a meeting Friday. Trotted out a beautiful Monte Cristo sandwich and then they dropped it on me."

"The sandwich?"

"The news. It's a done deal."

"Ah. . . . So, what happens now?"

The hotel had been up for sale so long that the specter of sudden unemployment had long since ceased to pester us, but it settled now in Avery's doughy face like a fly in rice pudding.

He hitched up his shoulders. "Don't know. Apparently, we've been sold to some big conglomerate, and the new management has yet to decide which, if any, of our present staff will be retained."

My eyebrows shot up. "Wow. Great. Nothing like living on the edge."

Avery shrugged again. "Not much we can do. Dust off our resumes, I guess, and carry on until somebody shows up and shows us out the door."

That was easy for him to say, I thought. Avery didn't have a child at home, and he was close to retirement anyway. But I supposed he was right—on both counts. There was nothing much else we could do. So, I nodded sagely. "Well . . . so, let's have a look at our calendar."

With summer coming, there were three weddings scheduled, plus a bar mitzvah and a service club convention, which would be plenty to keep me busy. In between, I would dust off my resume and bring it up to date and maybe even make a few discreet inquiries. Come fall, if I was still employed, I would start combing the engagement announcements for wedding prospects down the line.

For now, I would, as Avery suggested, simply carry on, and that meant phone calls and linen selections, menu consultations with Juan in the kitchen, and endless meetings with brides-to-be and a succession of overbearing mothers.

Bossy, I heard Lulu say. She didn't know the half of it.

In my cubbyhole of an office, I found a voicemail message from Nancy Jamison, Harrison Palmer's assistant in Deadwood. Doreen's funeral was set for Friday. Nancy thought I would want to know.

Apparently, to Nancy's way of thinking, Doreen and I had been best friends in the old days. In fact, despite what Doreen might have told her, the enthusiasm had been pretty one-sided. But I thought I owed Nancy a return phone call to thank her for her courtesy.

She answered on the first ring. "Attorney's office. Can I help you?"

"Nancy? It's Julie Goldman. I got your message, and thanks for thinking of me. But I'm afraid I won't be able to get back to Deadwood for the funeral."

"I figured as much, since you only just left. But I was pretty sure you would want to know, you being such good friends and all . . ."

I hesitated, thinking silence was the better part of valor, but Nancy broke into the silence.

"She really wanted to see you, you know, that first night you were in town. I don't know what it was, but she said there was something important."

I remembered Doreen saying as much on the phone, but I couldn't imagine what it might have been.

"Well, I guess we'll never know," I said now.

"She wouldn't tell me . . . even though I'm—well, I *was* her best friend. But it must have been important because she was hell-bent to get finished with work and back into town to see you."

"Nancy, I'm so sorry . . ."

"They're telling me it was an accident—a simple accident. She lost control of the car. But I don't know . . ."

I waited.

"Nothing to indicate foul play. That's what they say in the police report. But I'm not so sure. Doreen was an awfully good driver." A quaver crept into Nancy's voice.

I remembered the florist, Hannah Wilkerson, saying much the same thing—and Charlie Banks, too. But brakes gave out all the time, and accidents did happen.

"Well," I said, as kindly as I could, "if that's what the investigators believe . . ."

Nancy sniffled. "That's what they said. It's just so hard to believe she's gone . . ."

I stifled a sigh. Nancy was upset, but there wasn't much I could say to make her feel better, and I had problems of my own.

"I'm really sorry," I managed finally, "and thanks for letting me know about the funeral. Please say hello for me to Doreen's father, if he remembers me. And of course, I'll send some flowers."

When we ended the call, I fished in my purse for Hannah Wilkerson's card and dialed the florist shop.

"Hi, Mrs. Wilkerson. This is Julie Goldman. I'm back in California, but I'd like to place an order for some flowers for Doreen Hastings' funeral."

"Hello, Julie. You can call me Hannah. Yes, it's set for Friday."

"I heard. Well, you knew Doreen better than I did, so whatever you suggest is fine with me."

"Such a shame," Hannah said. "Doreen was such a dedicated young woman. How they can suspect her of some kind of shenanigans is really beyond me."

I shook my head. "Shenanigans?"

"Something about drug tampering. I don't know the whole story, but they're saying some drugs were missing from the hospital where she worked. They think Doreen may have taken them."

I blinked. This was more than I wanted to know, but it would have been rude to cut her off.

"My sister told me," Hannah said. "She works in intake at the hospital. But why now, when Doreen is gone? She isn't even here to defend herself . . ."

"Well, I'm sure they'll get it all cleared up." I didn't know what else to say. "Um, about the flowers for Friday? Do you still have my credit card on file?"

"Oh, yes, of course, I do. I'll fix up something pretty."

"Great. Well, thank you, Hannah."

"No problem. Thanks for calling, Julie. Take care."

I hung up the phone and spread the new season's linen catalogues all over my desk, as much to make a pretense of working as to put Doreen, Deadwood, and the prospect of unemployment as far out of my head as possible.

ELEVEN

As it turned out, the strategy worked. By the end of the day, I had updated the sample books, made half a dozen phone calls, and booked preliminary food and wine tastings with the three scheduled wedding couples.

I was feeling pretty good overall, and I had just arrived home at ten minutes to five when the phone rang. It was Charlie Banks.

"You kind of skipped out on us," the police chief chided. "I never got to say goodbye."

I felt my face flush. "I looked for you before we left the rectory hall, but I guess you had already left."

"Duty called."

"I figured as much. But once I got back to Aunt Sarah's house, there didn't seem to be much point in staying longer. There isn't much I can do until I have death certificates. I missed my daughter, I was feeling a little blue, and I found out I could book a quick flight out of Rapid City."

"Yep, I get it. But it was nice to meet you. Are you planning a trip back here anytime soon?"

I didn't know where Lulu was, but I lowered my voice anyway. "I've got some business to finish there. I want to put the house on the market and settle the rest of my aunt's estate—whatever that means. I expect to be back there sometime this summer, when Lulu's out of school."

"Good. I'm looking forward to meeting her."

"I'll let you know when we get back, if the café hotline doesn't beat me to it, and thanks, Charlie, for checking in. It was very sweet."

Lulu, as it turned out, had been lounging over the kitchen counter and hanging on my every word. I tried to sound nonchalant.

"Well, that was nice. That was the police chief in Deadwood, the man who called me when my Aunt Sarah passed away. He was just calling to be sure I got home all right and that everything was okay."

Lulu started to say something but apparently thought better of it. She watched me stow my bag and my briefcase.

Penny opened the oven and sniffed. "We made macaroni and cheese for dinner."

"Great. Can you stay?"

"Sure, I guess so. I'll have all evening to study."

It was a good week. My brides were almost reasonable, the menus came together, my deliveries showed up on time. I even got to watch Lulu glide across the ice late on Tuesday afternoon.

Her axel wasn't perfect, but she was getting more confident, and once again I was forced to realize she was not my baby anymore. She was mastering her sport and loving it, and in a fit of extravagance I couldn't yet afford, I agreed she could have an extra lesson on Thursday.

All in all, the hard little knot of impending doom that had lived in my gut for years seemed to loosen just the tiniest little bit. The world was manageable. We were going to make it. I could be the master of my fate.

The axe fell on Friday. Avery called a meeting, and the staff shuffled into a conference room.

* * *

The axe fell on Friday. Avery called a meeting, and the staff shuffled into a conference room.

"I know it's been tough." Avery rocked on his feet as we held our collective breath. "New management called this morning, and it's not good, but it isn't a wholesale slaughter, either."

Avery was being retained as hotel manager, at least for a while as the new management took over. The housekeeping and reception staffs would stay, and Juan and his kitchen staff would have a "performance trial" of sixty to ninety days. The accounting staff was out, the bell captain would be replaced by a "qualified concierge," and the grounds crew by an outside vendor.

As for me, I had thirty days "to get my files in order" and to make way for an event staff of three who would handle marketing, banquet management, and consumer advocacy, whatever the heck that was. Maybe it was convincing a skeptical bride that a ruined wedding dress could be saved.

On the one hand, I was gratified to know it would take three people to do the job I was doing by myself. On the other hand, it was little consolation to take with me into an anemic job market. Of course, I had not even looked at my resume, but if you asked me, I would assure you that the new "event staff" could figure out my files on their own. I would be using my thirty days to do some heavy-duty networking.

I did a little commiserating with the other employees who were about to join me on the trash heap, and I tried to lighten up by focusing on the view on my drive up Pacific Coast Highway. The sunshine was brilliant, the sea was like glass, and an onshore breeze ruffled the palms that lined the Dana Point Marina.

But I could tell you I was pretty bummed by the time I made it home. It was only the safety net of Aunt Sarah's bequest that kept me from plunging into depression.

As though to underline the reality of a lifeline, there was a thick manila envelope in my mailbox. In it were copies of Aunt Sarah's death certificates. How was that for timing?

I flopped down on the sofa, home for a change long before Lulu and Penny, and allowed myself the luxury of yet another good cry. Then I blew my nose, walked into the kitchen, and ate a half pint of Ben and Jerry's chocolate chip while standing over the sink.

I felt better. The die was cast. I had survived worse in my lifetime. Lulu would be out of school next week, and I had promised a trip to Deadwood.

By the time she and Penny got home, I had called the airline and pretty much maxed out my credit card. I would put Aunt Sarah's house on the market, transfer my inherited funds from her banks to mine, and put off my job-hunting until after we were back in California.

At sundown that night, I stood beside Lulu, white shawls draped over our heads. Together, we said the Hebrew prayer and lighted the Shabbos candles. With my eyes closed behind upraised hands, I felt the comforting presence of Bubbe Lou.

And why not? Her indomitable spirit was here in my daughter. How bad could things be?

TWELVE

We arrived in Deadwood on a Sunday, the weekend after Lulu was out of school. Flights were cheapest early on Sunday morning, and I was very aware that we were still in penny-pinching mode.

Lulu had flown only once before, a short flight to San Francisco, so she was jazzed by the whole experience, changing planes and all. She fell asleep briefly on the drive from Rapid City in our rented car, but by the time we drove onto Deadwood's Main Street, she was wide-eyed and raring to go.

The summer tourists had begun to stream into town, and I had to admit, the casino lights looked brighter, and the vibe was more exciting than they'd seemed to be just a few weeks earlier. Lulu's red head swiveled from one side of the street to the other like a little bird watching a tennis match. "Wow, Mom. Cool," she muttered. "Did you see that huge wooden Indian? Was he here when you were a kid?"

It was nearing three, and except for a bag of trail mix I'd stuffed into my purse, we hadn't eaten since a quick bite at the Denver airport. I had not called anyone to let them know we were coming, and I figured the quickest way to spread the word would be to show up at the café.

"Are you hungry?" I asked Lulu.

"Starving."

"I figured." I drove into the corner parking lot.

The café was half full of customers, though I didn't recognize anyone. But Earlene greeted us at the door, her round face creasing into a smile. "Julie Goldman! What a surprise! Welcome back to town!"

Her glance slid down to Lulu.

"This is my amazing daughter, Louise. Everyone calls her Lulu. Lu, this is Miss Earlene. She's one of the café owners."

"Hey, Lulu," Earlene said and led us to a table, every eye in the place watching. "Welcome to Deadwood. If you like burgers, we've got the best in town. Even buffalo burgers, if you like 'em."

Lulu's eyes widened. "Buffalo burgers?"

"You bet. They're our specialty. Butchered right here in town."

"Wow." Lulu thought about it, scrunching up her face. "Well, thanks, but I think I'll have a regular burger. Mom, can I have a Coke?"

What the heck? It was a vacation—sort of. "Sure. And the same for me."

We were just biting into our burgers when Nancy Jamison walked in. She scanned the room, fastened on me, and rushed up to our booth. "Julie! What a nice surprise. I left work early. I need to get home to fix a leaky pipe under my bathroom sink. But I never had lunch, and now I'm starving."

"You know how to fix a leaky pipe?"

"When you live alone, you learn to do a lot of things." She looked pointedly at Lulu. "Can I join you?"

I scooted over to make room. "Nancy, this is my daughter, Lulu. Lu, this is Miss Jamison."

"Nancy's fine. Nice to meet you, Lulu. So, Julie, are you back for good?"

"No, no. Just some loose ends to tie up and I want to show Lulu the sights. We'll be here for a week, and then it's back to California."

Earlene hovered over us, pencil poised. Nancy ordered the daily special without bothering to look at a menu. "Well." She looked at me. "I can understand . . . what with your job and all."

I toyed with the tray of condiments. "I wish. My job, unfortunately, has gone bye-bye." I glanced over at Lulu, to whom I'd given the news just as we were packing for the trip. "It seems the hotel where I work has been sold. I'm joining the ranks of the unemployed."

Lulu ate, glancing around her, no doubt cataloguing every nuance of the café and its inhabitants.

"Well, that's a bummer." Nancy dug into some kind of pasta dish. "What is it you do, anyway?".

"Hotel event planner. Weddings and stuff. I coordinate the menus and all."

"Really? I don't think we have event planners here. Maybe you could use your aunt's old house. Turn it into a banquet hall or something."

It was the first time the idea was broached, though it wasn't to be the last.

"Nancy." I sipped my Coke. "I'm sorry I haven't stayed in touch. What was the result of the investigation after Doreen's—" I stopped.

"Are you talking about the so-called accident? Or the drug the hospital seems so sure she pilfered?"

I hesitated. "Hannah Wilkerson mentioned the drug thing so both, I guess, really."

Nancy made a sour face. "Her death was ruled accidental. So, what if she knew these mountain roads better than the back of her hand? Tooled up, down and around those mountain curves every day since she was sixteen years old? The roads were dry and anyway, she would have kept her cool if the car had started to skid."

"I'm sorry. I know you miss her . . ."

"And the drug thing? They're still saying she did it. Took a vial of some kind of drug. Some powerful paralyzing stuff. It's stupid. There was no reason Doreen would have done that."

I nodded.

"Although it seems now like the whole criminal thing might just fade away, with Doreen not here to give any answers."

I didn't know what to say.

"It makes me sick. There's a connection somewhere, and I'm not the only one with questions. If only she had made it back to Deadwood that night. I know she was onto *something*. In my heart of hearts, I think that's why she never made it back that night."

The thought was unsettling, and in truth, I wished I knew what Doreen had had on her mind. But I would never know, and Lulu was clearly through with her meal, fidgeting and wanting to move on. I was ready to leave, but Earlene served Nancy a slab of pie, and it would have been rude to ask her to move so we could get out and get going.

"So, Lulu." Nancy seemed to sense her boredom. "What grade are you in?"

"Sophomore."

"Do you like school?"

"It's okay. What I like to do is skate. Ice skating."

"You should be here in the winter, when the lake freezes."

"My mom told me. It sounds like fun. Maybe we can come back then."

"That would be great. I'd love to take you. I like to skate, too."

Nancy scooped up the last of her pie, and Earlene set our checks on the table. "Come back soon." She winked at Lulu. "Everyone in town will want to meet you."

I smiled, scooting out of the booth. By the time we got to Aunt Sarah's house, our arrival would be the talk of the town.

While I brought our bags in from the car, Lulu went from room to room, perusing every inch of the nooks and crannies in the unfamiliar old house. I was closing the door behind me when the phone rang.

"Hey, welcome back!" Charlie Banks sounded happily surprised. "I thought you were going to call me."

"Yes, sorry." I ran a hand through my hair. "Things have been a little hectic."

"So I hear. You lost your job?"

I grinned. The café struck again. "Yes, I really did. But it's okay. I needed to come back here for a week or so to tie up all the loose ends."

"I get it. Anything I can do, just ask. I'm anxious to meet your daughter, too. Can I take you both to dinner?"

"We just ate at the café."

"So I heard. But you'll get hungry again. Why don't I let you get settled in, and come by to get you about six thirty?"

I looked at my watch. It was after four. "Okay," I said. "See you soon."

"No problem. Oh, and I just saw Harrison. He said to tell you he has more paperwork for you. You can stop by his office anytime."

I put Lulu in Katy's old room and threw my stuff into mine. For some reason, I wasn't ready to take over Aunt Sarah's bedroom.

"Mom! How cool—the view from the back porch!"

"Isn't it?" I joined her to watch the afternoon clouds move in over the hills, soft and billowy, like a down quilt settling onto the bed. "This porch wasn't safe to stand on when I lived here as a girl," I told her. "Aunt Sarah must have had it rebuilt sometime after I left for New York."

The phone rang again. It was the florist, Hannah Wilkerson. "Hello, Julie. Glad to have you back."

"Thanks. It's nice to be back. But it's only for a week or so."

"I know. You have some business to take care of. That's the reason I called. I'd be happy to show your daughter around while you do what you need to do. It'll be a lot easier if you're on your own. I'll introduce Lulu to my granddaughter, Morgan. She's fourteen-going-on-twenty."

I smiled again. We were in town for an hour, and even the florist already knew Lulu by name. "Well, if you're sure . . ."

"No problem. I take Mondays off, anyway. My daughter, Faye, runs the shop. I can swing by for Lulu about ten tomorrow morning, if that's all right with you. And don't make plans for dinner, either. I'll throw something in the crockpot before I leave."

I didn't know what to say. "Hannah, are you sure?"

"Of course I'm sure. See you tomorrow morning at ten o'clock."

I stood there for a moment with my hand on the phone, then dug Harrison Palmer's business card out of my purse.

"Attorney's office." It was Harrison on the line.

"Hey, it's Julie Goldman. Is that you, Harrison?"

"Yep. Nancy went home early."

"To fix a leaky pipe. I know."

"How'd you know that?"

"We ran into her at the café."

"Ah. Figures. Welcome back. How are you doing?"

"Fine, thanks. Charlie tells me you have some paperwork for me."

"Just some forms to sign to give you power of attorney over business at your aunt's foundation. Remember, I mentioned that."

I remembered a foundation in Katy's name for families who needed assistance. But I couldn't see where I fit in. "Why? I don't expect to be involved."

"Well, you never know. As your aunt's heir, you have the tie-breaking vote over any foundation business."

I considered that. "I don't know, Harrison. I don't know anything about the foundation's business."

"You will. It's a short course. You might have met the director, Rennie Malcolm, at your aunt's funeral, though I'm sure the names and faces are a blur. Oh, and I did call Sarah's banks, both here and in Rapid City, to let them know you'd be stopping by. You have copies of the death certificate, don't you?"

"Yes."

"Good. That's all you'll need. I have extra copies of the will here for you."

I blinked, stunned. For the first time in a long time, I was out of decision-making mode. Dinner . . . arranged. Child care . . . done. Bank transfers . . . ready to roll. Everything was being done for me. Either I was being treated like visiting royalty or hoodwinked into giving up control.

THIRTEEN

True to his word, Charlie Banks rang the doorbell at precisely six thirty. He looked rugged and fit in a well-tailored blue plaid shirt, and I had to admit the sight of him filling the doorway brought a smile to my face.

We had unpacked and rested for a while in front of the TV before we showered and dressed, Lulu in her new skinny jeans and me in my trusty denim pantsuit.

Lulu seemed unusually shy, hanging back behind me.

"Lu, this is Chief Charlie Banks, the police chief here in Deadwood. Charlie, meet my beautiful daughter, Louise. She likes to be called Lulu."

Charlie folded his six-foot frame down to Lulu's height. "Delighted to meet you, Lulu." He smiled. "I've heard a lot about you."

Lulu looked at me, no doubt wondering what I had told this hulking stranger. But she gamely stuck out her hand to shake. "Thanks. I heard about you, too."

In fact, I had said little or nothing to Lulu about Police Chief Charlie Banks. But he looked pleased as he straightened up. "I hope you've had a chance to work up an appetite. I'm taking you to one of my favorite places."

It was a steak and soda shop in Hill City—mama, papa, and baby bear-sized steaks and big, thick ice cream sodas, served with a fat dollop of whipped cream in tall, shapely glasses.

"Cool!" Lulu devoured her steak and took deep draws of her soda.

"Has your mom told you about the steam train here?"

Lulu shook her head as she sipped.

"She rode on it when she was a kid. Now it seems like it's your turn." He looked at me. "I know you've got things to do, Julie, but I hope you built in some fun time. You name the day, and I'll slack off the job and take you girls out and about. You have about a week here, is that right?"

I nodded. "I appreciate the offer, Charlie. But you really don't need to do that."

"No, but I want to. It's no trouble. You just name the day."

On the way home, we stopped at a market, so I could pick up some breakfast things and basics. By the time we got back to Bluebird Hill, Lulu's eyes were at half-mast. She didn't argue when I told her to go upstairs and get ready for bed. "I'll be up in a bit to tuck you in."

Charlie made a cursory circuit through the house. "Everything looks fine," he announced.

I was getting accustomed to being back in the old house, and I didn't feel quite as jittery as I had on that first night. But it was nice, feeling that Charlie cared about our safety. I smiled. "Would you like a cup of coffee?"

He looked at his watch. "Only if you're not too tired. You've had a long day, too."

"No problem, have a seat while I put on the coffee. Then I'll run upstairs to say good night, and I'll be ready to kick off my shoes."

Lulu roused herself long enough for a goodnight kiss, then snuggled contentedly into the folds of Katy's old feather quilt.

Downstairs, I poured the coffee, took it into the parlor, and sat next to Charlie on the sofa, happy to kick off my shoes.

"You look exhausted," Charlie said. "Maybe I should go."

"Just a little jet-lagged, maybe, but I'm okay. In fact, I've got a couple questions."

"Shoot."

I took a beat. "It's about Doreen. I was talking today to Nancy Jamison. For some reason, she seems to have more questions than answers about what happened to her best friend. She's convinced that Doreen had something on her mind, something she wanted to tell me. And when I spoke to Doreen, I had the same impression. But then, as you know, the accident happened before she got back here into town."

Charlie offered a sympathetic smile. "I don't have a clue what she might have had in mind. But it *was* an accident, I can tell you that, a sad and unusual accident, maybe, given that Doreen had a rep for being a pretty good driver. But the investigation was thorough and pretty conclusive. For some reason, her brakes failed, and she lost control. It's just as simple as that. There was no reason then, and no reason now, to believe anything more sinister."

I processed that. "But there was something about a stolen drug. As I understand it, Doreen was suspected of taking some drug from the hospital . . ."

"If you're thinking she ran her car off the road because she was looking at a drug charge, you should know it was only a single dose that went missing—one vial of some drug with an unpronounceable name. That's all the hospital reported missing, and they weren't likely to file charges over that."

It did seem to be much ado about little.

"Besides, even if Doreen did commandeer that vial," Charlie said, "it surely wasn't worth her life. Nor is it likely that anyone else would have staged an accident to cover up a missing dose of a drug."

He shook his head. "It doesn't add up, and I think once the hospital board reviews the situation, no charges will be filed. What's the point of prosecuting someone who's not here to answer to charges anyway, especially when the amount of the missing drug was so miniscule in the first place?"

I had to agree. "Sad that no one will ever know what was going through the poor woman's head. But I don't blame Nancy for being upset. She lost her best friend, after all."

Charlie drained his cup. "You and I both know a lot about losing someone you care for. It can make you crazy if you let it."

My gaze met his for a long moment. There was a tantalizing moment before his lips drew close to mine. A gentle kiss, over in an instant.

I could feel my heart beat as we broke apart, unsure what to feel. But then, I had let it happen.

And then he rose and so did I.

We nearly collided as we stood up.

"Sorry," he said. "I think maybe it's time to call it a night."

"Don't be sorry. I'm not. But you're right. It's time for you to go."

I walked him to the door, turned on the porch light, and he turned to face me from the doorway. "You've got plans tomorrow?"

"Yes. Lots to do in town and dinner afterwards with Hannah Wilkerson."

"The florist."

"Yes. She's coming by to pick up Lulu in the morning, so I can get on with my errands."

"Good," he said. "Get a lot done and save Wednesday or Thursday for me. I'm mapping out a route. We can do the Black Hills tourist circuit to show Lulu the highlights."

It sounded like fun, and I told him so.

He leaned in and trailed a finger down my cheek. "Good night, then."

There was a lump in my throat as I closed the door. I took the coffee cups to the kitchen. I turned out the lights, climbed the stairs, and looked in on Lulu.

I tried not to think about it, but I had to admit I felt that touch on my cheek even as I crawled into bed.

FOURTEEN

Downtown Deadwood on that sunny June morning looked like a picture postcard—casinos restored to their old glamour, quirky little shops and outdoor bistros, and the brooding Black Hills under rolling clouds a vast, surprising backdrop.

Hannah had brought her granddaughter, Morgan, when she came to collect Lulu. Morgan was half a head taller than Lu, with a mischievous grin and her grandmother's big, expressive eyes. There was no hesitation on Lulu's part at meeting the two strangers. She sized up the pair of them, dropped her cereal bowl in the sink, and hopped into Hannah's Jeep without so much as a "Bye, Mom."

Hannah told me to "just give a jingle" when my errands for the day were concluded, and I had to admit there was a spring in my step when I opened the door to Harrison's law office at just after ten in the morning.

Nancy was on the phone, dressed in her version of country professional, jeans, turquoise Indian jewelry, and a neatly pressed yellow linen shirt. She waggled her fingers and motioned me to a seat in the small reception area. I was rifling through a stack of magazines on the table when the door to Harrison's office opened, and a nattily dressed man, short and slender, brushed by me so quickly that I actually felt a rush of air.

The door was swinging closed behind him when the inner door opened again, and Harrison peered out and looked around.

"Where'd he go?" Harrison glanced at Nancy, as though she might have stashed the guy behind a chair.

"A man in a hurry," I said.

Harrison reached for my hand. "Hey, Julie, good to see you. That was Rennie Malcolm, the director of your family foundation. If I'd realized you were out here, I would have been sure to introduce you."

"I think I might have seen him at the funeral," I said, following him into his office. "But it's no big deal. As I said, I don't expect to be involved much, anyway. For one thing, I'll be a couple thousand miles away."

"Still." Harrison indicated a chair and took a seat behind his desk. "The ongoing work of Katy's Legacy will, to some extent, rest with you, unless you choose to abdicate the role your aunt intended you to have."

It made me uncomfortable, but I let it go. Harrison didn't wait for a response. He reached into a stack of files and set one in front of him. "So, how are you coping, Julie?"

"Fine, I guess. I have a fair idea what I have to do. My daughter, Lulu, is anxious to see the sights. I just want to get this all behind me."

"I understand." He sorted through the file and took out a sheaf of papers. "These are extra copies of your aunt's directive naming you her heir and a couple extra copies of her death certificate, too, in case anybody asks for one. As I told you, I've called ahead to her banks to let them know you'd be stopping by, and here are the bankers' names, by the way. There shouldn't be any problem in transferring your inherited assets to whatever accounts you wish in California."

I nodded. "Thanks, Harrison. You've been a really great help."

He paused briefly. "Can I ask you a question?"

"Sure."

"Are you planning to sell the house?"

I didn't hesitate. "Yes, I think so."

"Well, before you put it on the market, here's a little something to consider. There's a guy here in town, who's been here all his life, a nice guy, an Iraq war veteran. I believe he has some interest in buying it. His name is Nate Miller. He's the guy your aunt hired to rebuild and expand the back porch."

"Really? Wow, he did a great job. When I lived in the house, that porch was a mess. We weren't allowed to go out there."

Harrison nodded. "Well, now he's talking about renovating the rest of the house. Maybe turning it into a hotel or a bed and breakfast. The problem is, I don't think he has the cash to buy the property outright."

I listened.

"Your aunt knew he was interested. She had talked to me about it more than once, and I think Nate believed she might even leave the old house to him. But her guess, I think, was that by the time she was ready to sell, he might be able to raise the cash he needed."

"I see." I drew a deep breath. I certainly had as much empathy as anyone, maybe even more, for Iraq war vets and the survivors of nine-eleven and its aftermath. But I also had a child to support, and the proceeds from the sale of the house would go a long way to securing her future.

"It's just a thought," Harrison said, sliding the papers I needed into a manila envelope. "I understand you may prefer a quick sale, and you're certainly entitled to do that. I mention it only as something to consider as you're making all your decisions."

He plucked another file out of the stack and slid it toward me. "Meanwhile, these are the other forms I'd like you to review and sign while you're here, a signature card granting you authority to sign foundation checks and a form acknowledging to the governing board that you retain the tie-breaking vote."

I looked at him.

"One of the issues Sarah's death left unanswered was the future of Katy's Legacy. It was pretty much assumed Malcolm would take over the reins if you opted not to, so until you decide, this gives you the right to sit in on foundation board meetings whenever you like. No duties, no obligations, but the right to weigh in if you wish to."

"I guess I'm surprised the foundation is big enough or formal enough to need a governing board."

"But it is." Harrison smiled. "I think I mentioned that Sarah funded Katy's Legacy in perpetuity. At the moment, there are accumulating assets of over half a million dollars in the foundation budget, and nearly a third of that amount is disbursed to recipients every year."

I blinked. "Should I ask who serves on the board?"

"You probably met them all at the memorial service, along with Rennie Malcolm, who is employed on a half-time basis. Would you like to see a copy of the foundation charter and a current list of directors?"

That was way beyond what I needed to know. "No thanks, I don't think that's necessary." But I couldn't see the harm in signing the forms, so I did. I looked up. "Is that it?"

"That's it."

I stood up, and Harrison followed. "You know where the bank is here in Deadwood," he said. "The one in Rapid City is right on Main. You won't be able to miss it."

I gathered up my things and headed out, thanking Harrison again as he held the door for me, and stopping at the front desk to say hello.

"Hey, Nancy. How are you? Were you able to get that leaky pipe fixed?"

"Good as new. No problem." She shrugged. "Now I'll have to fiddle with the old water heater. There's something wrong with that."

"I envy you. I'm afraid that screwing in a light bulb is the extent of my mechanical know-how."

"It's a gift." Her smile seemed a little forced. "And it keeps me occupied. I need to do something to keep my mind off Doreen's accident."

All I could do was nod.

"I keep thinking it's *something* to do with that missing vial of drugs. But I think there was more than that. I said so again, just the other day, to Chief Charlie."

"And?"

A ragged sigh. "He told me again the investigation's been closed. Nothing to indicate foul play. But he did agree to revisit the hospital part. Nose around a little to see if maybe someone had a grudge against Doreen or knew something about why she might have taken that vial of drugs . . . if she did take it . . ."

Nancy's frustration showed on her face. "I don't know. Maybe it's just me . . ."

Not for the first time, I felt a twinge of regret that my dinner with Doreen had never happened. *She had said she wanted to tell me something but what? And would it have made any difference?*

I shook my head. "I'm so sorry. I know how hard it is to lose someone you care about."

Nancy shrugged. "And how about you, Julie? How are you doing these days?"

"Lots to do, but I'm fine, I guess. Just a lot of running around." I thought about asking Nancy out to lunch, but I really wanted to get going. I tried my best for an encouraging smile. "Thanks for asking. See you later."

It took only minutes, once I'd presented the documentation, to withdraw the funds from my aunt's local account and have them transferred to my bank in California. In the half hour it took to drive to Rapid City, I entertained visions of a long string of dollar bills passing through miles of invisible wire and swan diving, one by one, into my anemic checking account thousands of miles away.

The transfer process was just as quick in Rapid City, where I was also accompanied by a bank employee to a bank of safety deposit boxes.

In Aunt Sarah's box, I found a little case containing a pearl and diamond pendant and matching earrings. It occurred to me Aunt Sarah might have planned to give them to Katy on her twenty-first birthday and put them here for safekeeping after Katy was taken from us.

I put the case in the bottom of my big handbag. Maybe one day Lulu would wear them. I couldn't think of a nicer tribute to her great-aunt and cousin.

There was a packet old silver dollars in the box—souvenirs of Deadwood's heyday—and a tarnished little silver piggy bank I guessed might once have belonged to Katy. There were insurance papers I would go through later—mostly liability insurance for the house—and an envelope containing some black-and-white photos of people I did not recognize.

I scrutinized the photos closely, hoping to find likenesses of my parents. There was one creased photo of a laughing young couple swinging a baby at a park. It wasn't me, and it wasn't my parents. I would have recognized the faces. Was it Katy? Was it a young Aunt Sarah and the man who had been Katy's father?

Try as I might, I could put no names to any of the faces I was looking at, and there was nothing written on the back of the photos to help identify them.

I chalked it up to what seemed like a history of strange family secrets, including Katy's very existence, and stuffed the pile of photos and papers into my big handbag. All in all, I left the bank in Rapid City torn between regret that I had no way to thank my Aunt Sarah for all she had done for me and the giddy, unfamiliar feeling that I was now a rich woman.

Of course, I wasn't really rich—not by most sane people's standards, anyway—although I might be considered so in earnest once I collected the proceeds from selling the old Victorian.

That gave me pause. By all rights, I should go right back to Deadwood, head for the nearest realty office, and list the house for sale. But what Harrison had told me about the tacit understanding between my aunt and Nate Miller hovered over me like a bee at a picnic. I wondered what Aunt Sarah would want me to do.

I was also hungry, and I decided to ponder it over a yummy lunch with no regard for calories or cost. I spotted a little French bistro across the street and headed for an outdoor table. In short order, I was munching happily on curried chicken crepes, which I washed down with mango iced tea and finished with a silky crème brûlée.

I felt totally stuffed, absolutely decadent, and more than just a little guilty over my urge to splurge.

But I was no closer to making a decision about listing the house for sale.

FIFTEEN

On impulse, I stopped at a funky little boutique down the street and bought a sparkly *Twilight* T-shirt and another pair of skinny jeans for Lulu. I picked up a knotted thread bracelet for Sarah's granddaughter, Morgan—just to say thanks for keeping Lulu company—and a sky-blue silk scarf for Hannah.

By four, I was on the road back to Deadwood. I called Hannah to let her know I was on the way, and I rang the doorbell of her neat little house just before four o'clock. Lulu met me at the door, bouncing up and down in Morgan's wake, eager to show me her newly painted purple fingernails.

"Dinner's in the crockpot," Hannah said. "The girls have been having such a good time. We're glad you can join us—that is, if you're done for the day."

I was, and whatever was in the crockpot smelled great. Lulu shot me a beseeching look, but I could have saved her the trouble. "If you're sure," I said, and the girls cheered, and Lulu reached for the boutique bags I'd brought in.

Morgan, tall and rangy like her grandmother, loved her little bracelet, and the girls ran happily up the stairs so Lulu could try on her new clothes. I followed Hannah into the kitchen. "Thanks," I said. "I really appreciate the babysitting."

"No trouble." Hannah set a pitcher of lemonade on the table. "And no need for the scarf, although it's lovely. Faye's at a Scout meeting tonight with Morgan's brother, Petey, and the girls have been having a great time. The whole idea was to let you get your errands done with as few interruptions as possible."

"And I did," I said, sitting at the breakfast bar. "It was a lot easier than I expected. The only thing I didn't do, and I have to admit I've been dragging my feet on it, was put my aunt's house up for sale."

Hannah rummaged around in the fridge and brought out an armful of salad fixings. "The old house should be worth a pretty penny." She began tearing lettuce into a bowl.

"So I understand, but there's a little wrinkle. Hannah, do you know a Nate Miller?"

"Sure. Everyone in town knows Nate. He's a long, tall drink of water, looks a little like a young Abe Lincoln, with the same kind of neat, little black beard. He's an Iraq war vet, never smiles much, earns his living as a handyman. Why?"

I watched Hannah. "Harrison Palmer tells me Nate has long-standing designs on the house. He wants to turn it into some kind of hotel or a bed and breakfast. Apparently, he didn't have the money to buy it outright while Aunt Sarah was alive, but they had some sort of informal arrangement that he might get first crack at the house whenever she was ready to sell."

Hannah shrugged. "I don't know anything about that. But it sounds like something your aunt would do. She always was a champion of the underdog."

I waited.

"Nate grew up here in town. Married really young, right out of high school, actually. But his wife—well, she partied a lot while he was off in Iraq. Eventually, she ran off with somebody else without so much as a Dear John to Nate."

She began to slice cucumbers. "In any case, I don't think it needs to concern you now that Sarah is gone. I'm sure Harrison told you the house is yours to do with as you wish."

I asked if I could help with dinner, and Hannah handed over a grater, a bowl, and a wedge of cheddar.

"Well . . ." I began grating the cheese. "As it turns out, there was quite a lot I never knew about my aunt. It's too late to do anything about most of it now, but in light of what she's done for me and Lulu, I wish I knew what she would have wanted me to do."

"I'll say one thing," Hannah mused, beginning to slice tomatoes. "I don't know about a hotel per se, but this town could use a good bed and breakfast. We have a couple of half-hearted efforts, but believe it or not, there hasn't been a dedicated B and B here since the Quincys packed it in a couple of years ago and left for a family farm in Iowa."

"Really?" My overactive imagination kicked in, and I spent a fanciful couple of minutes grating cheese and picturing a montage of homey little scenes: oak four posters with hand-quilted coverlets, lacey placemats on a long, pine table; Tiffany lamps, a busy little herb garden, big pitchers of hot, spiced cider; and a skinny redhead in a frilly apron pulling hot biscuits out of the oven.

Then I laughed as a dose of reality pulled me back from the edge. It was a long way from hotel banquet manager to bed-and-breakfast proprietor, and anyway, what would Lulu and I live on until, if ever, such a venture took off?

"What's funny?"

"Me. For a minute there, that actually seemed like an option. But I need to get back to California, where there are plenty of hotels, and find myself another job." I put the bowl of cheese on the table. "Is there anything else I can do?"

"Call the girls to dinner." Hannah put down the salad. "And maybe have a chat with Nate Miller before you make up your mind."

The chili bubbling in Hannah's crockpot tasted as wonderful as it smelled, and we shared stories and laughed a lot at the girls' silly antics. Dessert was an amazing peach cobbler, made with fresh peaches the girls had plucked from the tree in Hannah's backyard.

I felt as though we were making good friends, and it occurred to me that, apart from Penny, friends were something I'd been short of for a very long time. I wasn't sure that Penny counted since I more or less paid for her time. It was a sobering thought. Job track . . . mommy track . . . there hadn't been a lot of me left over to give.

I had hoped to find a minute to ask Hannah if she'd heard anything more about the issue of the stolen drugs or to ask what she thought about Nancy's feeling that they had something to do with Doreen's accident. But the evening was so pleasant, and the girls so full of chatter, that the time just never seemed right.

In any case, it was after eight before Lulu and I got home. She never stopped talking on the drive back to Bluebird Hill Lane.

"Morgan likes to ice skate. She said she'd show me the best spots if we're still here in the winter. Morgan loves vampire stories, same as me. She has a puppy. His name is Nuisance. And she has her own phone."

She was nosing around a couple of sore subjects. Dogs were not allowed in our apartment building, a rule Lulu had been grousing about for years, and I had thus far nixed the phone. I was tempted to suggest that when we bought our own house, we might get a puppy. But for reasons I wasn't ready to address, I kept my big mouth firmly shut and listened to her prattle on.

The phone was ringing as I opened the front door. "Go run a bath," I told Lulu. I sprinted for the kitchen and grabbed the phone.

"Hi . . . Julie? It's Charlie Banks. I was just about to leave a message."

"We just got in. We just got back from Hannah's."

"Great. Listen, I have no idea what's on your agenda, but if you can make it tomorrow, I'll take the day off to take you and Lulu for that tour."

In fact, there was nothing I needed to do, except maybe, look up Nate Miller before I listed the house for sale and Charlie, who surely knew everyone in town, might have some ideas about that.

"Are you sure? I mean, about taking time off?"

"Not a problem, I assure you. I'd like to think I'm indispensable, but they can get along without me for a day. Anyway, I'm always reachable by cell . . . sometimes more than I'd like to be. How about I pick you both up at ten tomorrow morning? I'll even bring donuts if you have the coffee on."

"Deal." I was surprised to find myself grinning. "See you in the morning. Good night."

SIXTEEN

"So, how long will you two ladies be gracing our fair city?" Charlie asked over a second cup of coffee.

He looked relaxed and at home in jeans and a crisp blue denim shirt. "Not that we're anxious to let you go, you understand. Personally, I'd like nothing better than to add two to the population sign out there on the edge of town."

It was nice to hear, and in a dim corner of my feeble brain lurked a vivid recall of the kiss we'd shared, though sometimes I wondered if I'd really only dreamt it. But reality prevailed and I blinked myself back into the kitchen.

Lulu was polishing off a maple bar doughnut, a treat I didn't often allow. I asked her to run upstairs and get her things together for our outing.

Once she was gone, I turned to Charlie. "To answer your question, we're here until Saturday. Then I'm afraid I have to get home. Looking for a job is serious business."

"Understood."

"Funny you should hint at something permanent, though. Hannah suggested I open a bed and breakfast right here in my aunt's old Victorian."

"Really?" Charlie's eyes were wide. "Wow. Would you consider it?"

I shrugged. "Probably not. The idea is appealing, but I don't think I can afford it. It makes more sense for me to sell the house, put some money in the bank, and head back to California to find another job."

Charlie drained the last of his coffee. "Maybe. There's probably more work out there, for one thing, and you're right. The proceeds from the old house would give you a nice sense of security."

I could hear Lulu stomping around upstairs, probably looking for the mock suede boots she'd kicked off in the parlor when we came in last night.

"Charlie," I said slowly. What was the harm in asking? "What do you think of Nate Miller?"

"Nate? An okay guy, as far as I know. Quiet. Keeps to himself. He's great with carpentry. In fact, I think he remodeled your aunt's back porch a while back."

"He did. And I understand he's interested in remodeling the rest of the house—turning it into a hotel or a B and B."

Charlie scratched his chin. "To tell you the truth, I don't really know if this town could support another hotel or even a full-time bed and breakfast, now that you mention it. Last one or two packed it in for lack of a steady trade. But if anyone could do a bang-up job of remodeling the place, I guess it would be Nate."

If I'd expected encouragement from Charlie, his response was a rude awakening. But I forged ahead. "Do you happen to know where I can reach him?"

"I think he's been working on the Ridley place, adding a room or something. I ran into him at the lumber yard the other day. He's probably in the phone book."

Lulu barreled down the stairs. "Mom, where are my boots?"

"In the parlor, Lu, right where you left them." I began carrying dishes to the sink, and Charlie got up to help.

Lulu sat on a kitchen chair to pull on the well-worn boots.

"Glad you've got those," Charlie told her. "You'll need them to get up on horseback."

Her eyes got wide. "Horseback?"

"Not today, maybe, but I've got a couple of quarter horses on my ranch outside of town. I thought maybe you'd like to get acquainted with them—that is, if it's okay with your mom."

Lulu turned her big eyes to me. "Can I, Mom? Please?"

It was nice of him to make the offer. "Maybe. If Chief Charlie can find the time."

He winked at Lulu. "We'll find the time, don't you worry, missy. Right now, what say we get going?"

For a kid who'd never even heard of Wyatt Earp, the lore and history of the Black Hills had every right to be a bore. But Charlie brought it alive for her as we drove, with colorful stories about larger than life, shoot-'em-up characters like Calamity Jane and Wild Bill Hickok and the crusty prospectors who panned the mines for the first precious grams of gold.

"Back when General Custer roamed these hills," he told her, "those old miners were fighting each other hard to stake their claims and get rich. That led to a gold rush right here in South Dakota that would make the California gold rush seem puny."

"Really?" Lulu was wide-eyed. "We just finished a study session about the California gold rush!"

"Well, the truth is the old Homestake Mine right here in the Black Hills was the oldest and the deepest mine in the country, somewhere around eight thousand feet deep. That's something like a mile and half down into the earth."

"Wow." There was awe in Lulu's voice. "Can we see it?"

"Well, it's closed now, except for tourist visits, but sure. We'll get you over to see it."

We started our tour at Mt. Rushmore, where Lulu's mouth opened wide at the sight of the sixty-foot-tall presidential faces hewn from the great granite mountains, not because the carvings were a soul-stirring shrine to the power of American ingenuity, but because she actually recognized the faces.

We ate lunch at Crazy Horse Monument, where the Lakota warrior and his trusty steed were slowly being coaxed to life out of the grey rock of Thunder Mountain. "On target," Charlie told Lu as we watched, "to become the world's largest sculpture once it's finished."

Driving slowly through the national park, he pointed out herds of buffalo and bison, haughty, majestic big horn sheep, and dozens of playful little prairie dogs, and he asked Lulu to keep a sharp eye out for the lightning-fast jackrabbits who at any moment might decide to cross our path on the road.

Once, we stopped at a splintered piling sitting in a patch of wild iris and watched a lone bluebird, only inches from our faces, trill a melancholy song.

Lulu was captivated, and who could blame her? We couldn't have asked for a better guide. It occurred to me that Charlie was meant to be a dad, and the thought both saddened and intrigued me.

The sun was fading as we drove out of the park, and by the time we left the roadside café where we stopped for a barbecue dinner, the night had cooled, and the Black Hills had faded into the starless night sky. In minutes, Lulu was asleep in the back seat of Charlie's car.

"I don't know how to thank you," I told him. "I could have shown Lulu all those sights myself, but your stories and your incredible knowledge of the area made it a day she'll never forget."

"No thanks necessary, I enjoyed it," he assured me, focused on the winding road ahead. "And I meant it when I offered to get her out to the ranch. If it's okay with you, just work me into your schedule one day before you leave."

Not exactly a hardship, I thought ruefully as he pulled into the driveway of the old Victorian, and the thought of leaving Deadwood behind forever held distinctly less appeal than it once had.

"No sense waking her," Charlie whispered, leaning into the back seat. "I'll just carry her into the house and take a look around the premises to be sure everything is secured."

He hefted Lu as if she were weightless, and I smiled, moving ahead of him to open the door and turn on a light. "Just put her on the sofa. She'll be fine, and there's really no need for you to do a look-around. For what it's worth, the old house is beginning to feel more like home."

"If you're sure you're okay." He deposited Lulu on the old sofa and turned to look at me. He didn't move to kiss me, but his fingers grazed my cheek for a moment before he straightened up to go.

"Thanks again, Charlie."

"No problem. Be sure to call if there's anything you need." He was out the door before I knew it.

Well, there's a mixed message. I ran upstairs to get a blanket for Lulu. Did he want me to stay or go? Or was there nothing more between us than friendship and a soft spot for kids? Had I imagined the warmth of that one impromptu kiss that now seemed so long ago?

Still pondering the question, I gently pulled off Lulu's boots and covered her with a hand-knit afghan. I was turning off lights when I heard scuffling sounds, and I froze, rooted to the spot.

It sounded like something, or maybe someone, moving around on the back porch—slow, heavy, deliberate footfalls, too heavy for a roving coyote.

I wondered if Charlie had decided to look around after all. But why, when I'd said there was no need? I groped in my handbag, on a chair near the sofa, for my cell phone.

I heard them again. They were definitely footfalls, and I felt my heart beat faster and faster still as I followed the sound of them in the deep stillness, moving toward the front of the house.

I was pretty sure I had bolted the front door after Charlie left. Cell phone in hand, I crept toward it to be certain, the beating of my own pulse loud and rhythmic in my ears. I drew myself up to my full height to peer through the peephole, and I made out a shadow moving down the front steps toward the driveway.

I will never know if what happened next was misplaced bravery or sheer idiocy, but I threw back the bolt, turned on the porch light, pulled the door open and yelled, "Who are you and what are you doing here?"

The man turned toward me, a tall, thin figure in a plaid mackinaw, hands jammed into his pockets. He stared at me for a few seconds, looking more surprised than guilty. "Sorry," he said. "I didn't see any lights. I didn't think anyone was home . . ."

In the circle of light, I saw a thatch of dark hair, a long face with a neatly trimmed short beard. Hannah's description of Nate Miller came into my head. He did look a little like a young Abe Lincoln.

He cleared his throat, and I stared.

"My name is Nate Miller," he said finally, as I was about to voice the question. "I'm sorry if I scared you. I guess I should have rung the bell."

"Yes, you should have." My heartbeat slowed as fear became indignation. "What on earth are you doing here at this hour? I thought I heard someone prowling around out back."

He rubbed a big hand over his face. "Yes. Again, I apologize. I built that porch for Mrs. Lacey a while ago. I was in the neighborhood, and I began to wonder how the cantilevering was holding up."

"The cantilevering."

"Yes, ma'am. It's my own design, to accommodate the grading of the lot.

We're just over a serious rainy season. I just . . . I thought I'd better check it out . . ."

It was my turn to stare. "I'm Julie Goldman," I said finally. "I'm Sarah Lacey's niece. My aunt has passed on, as you may know. The house belongs to me now."

"Yes, I do know that. I heard it from Harrison Palmer. . . . Actually," he said and stuffed his hands deeper into his pockets. "Actually, I was planning to call you."

"Mmm," I muttered. "That might have been smarter. As it is, you nearly scared me to death."

Nate Miller's face was inscrutable. "I do apologize. It was stupid."

"Mmm," I said again. "Well, listen, it's late and I've got a kid asleep in here. Why don't you come by in the morning, when I can see you in the light of day?"

"Yes, ma'am, I'll be glad to do that, and again, I'm sorry if I frightened you."

"My aunt was ma'am." I started to close the door. "Julie is fine. Good night."

SEVENTEEN

Nate Miller had struck me as earnest, literal, and single-minded of purpose, if not well schooled in the social graces, so I was not surprised when the doorbell rang at nine thirty sharp the next morning, and there he stood, in the same plaid mackinaw, with a worn leather briefcase at his side.

"Good morning," he murmured, his gaze resting somewhere between his shoes and the worn porch floorboards. "I hope it's not too early and again, my apologies for poking around here last night."

I nodded. "Forgiven. Although I have to admit, you may have scared a year off my life. In any case, come in. You saved me the trouble of looking you up, and by the way, you did a fabulous job on the back porch. It was one of the first things I noticed when I got here."

"Thank you." His face held no expression.

Lulu had followed me to the front door, a slice of buttered toast in her hand. "Lulu, this is Mr. Miller. He's the man who rebuilt the back porch. Remember, I told you what it used to be like when I was a kid."

She nodded, scrutinizing the visitor.

I showed Nate to the sofa, recently cleared of my daughter and the colorful afghan, and sat across from him, Lulu following.

"So," I began, "Harrison told me about your interest in buying this property."

His Adam's apple bobbed. "First off, I'm sorry for your loss. Your aunt was a fine lady. I never knew she had any family, but that's another issue. I'd make an offer on the property today, if I thought I had enough for a down payment—that is, if you plan to put it up for sale."

It was disconcerting that he hadn't met my gaze, but I put it down to social uneasiness. "To tell the truth," I said, "I haven't decided whether or not to sell, but I'd like to know what you have in mind."

He reached for his briefcase. As he rifled through it, Lulu leaned over my shoulder to whisper in my ear. "Mom, I swear he looks like Abe Lincoln!"

I had to smile. "Finish your breakfast, Lu, and run upstairs to shower and change. When I'm done here, I thought we'd drive over to Hill City and take a ride on the old steam train."

I didn't need to tell her again. She took the stairs two at a time.

Nate rolled out a sheaf of papers on the coffee table. Clearly, he was well prepared.

"These are the plans I showed Mrs. Lacey. She loved the idea of the renovation, but she thought she was too old to deal with it. So, I shelved the idea for a while, hoping maybe I could make it happen once—well, sometime in the future."

And here I come along, putting another layer of distance between his expectations and his plans. I wondered if Nate had known of my existence, much less of Aunt Sarah's plan to leave the house to me. But I decided not to pursue it just then and bent instead to look at his diagrams.

Hand-drawn in crisp architectural detail, the plans were easy to visualize. The remodel would tear down walls to create more open space between the kitchen, dining and living rooms, expand the guest bathroom, and add a reception area adjacent to the stairwell. In effect, he would open the entire living space into a spacious and functional common area.

"Upstairs," he told me, laying a second sheet of plans over the first, "I'd redesign the bedrooms, steal a few square feet from each of them to add two more bedrooms and another bath, for a total of five and two. It would make the place perfect for a little boutique hotel or maybe a bed and breakfast."

It was the most animated I had seen Nate Miller. "Do you think the tourist trade in Deadwood can support a B and B?"

He didn't hesitate. "Absolutely. Tourist numbers here go up every year, and we lost our one dedicated B and B over a year ago."

I nodded. That was just the opposite of what Charlie had said. But Hannah had thought it could work, and the possibilities were intriguing.

Lulu came bouncing down the stairs, dressed in jeans and a purple Taylor Swift T-shirt, her hair pulled back in a ponytail.

"Ready!" she announced, and I knew instinctively that serious discussion was over.

"Look," I said, straightening up. "The plans look great, but I have some thinking to do. I live in California. It may be more practical for me to sell."

Nate began to roll up the plans. "I've been thinking, too. I'm hoping maybe we could forge some kind of partnership. I'd put up the cash I have saved and all the labor in exchange for a stake in the finished property. We could even—"

I stopped him. "Nate, I need to think it through, maybe get Harrison involved. I might agree it bears some discussion, but no promises, for certain."

Nate stuffed the plans back in his briefcase and stood, towering over me. "I understand. Thanks for listening." He handed me a card. "Here's my number. Call when you want to talk some more."

I walked him to the door, Lulu following, and he bent down to meet her eye to eye. "Abe Lincoln, eh?" He winked broadly without cracking a smile. "What if I told you I was the model for that likeness over at Mt. Rushmore?"

Lulu turned to me after he left. "Weak joke, right?"

That Miller had any sense of humor at all was a revelation to me. I laughed. "Yep. Let me get my bag and we're out of here."

The narrow gauge railroad was just as I remembered it, an old-fashioned.

* * *

The narrow gauge railroad was just as I remembered it, an old-fashioned chug-chug, steam-powered train that twisted through the wooded hills and rolling, green open spaces. Horses and sheep grazed in the meadows, and once, I spotted a small herd of buffalo. Lulu's head was stuck so far out the window that I felt compelled to keep a firm grasp on the back of her purple shirt.

We stopped for lunch in the same soda shop where Charlie had taken us for dinner. Lulu was pensive. "I like it here, Mom. There's so much to do and see."

"That's because you've never been here before. Trust me, it isn't nearly as exciting when you live here."

"But it's horse country, and it's great for climbing and skating on a frozen lake . . ."

I sipped my diet root beer. "Sounds great, I know. But there's also clearing snow out of the driveway and being miles from the nearest mall."

I decided it was as good a time as any to let Lulu in on plans I hadn't shared.

"I've been thinking, Lu. My aunt left some money. Maybe we can buy our own place back home, someplace nearer to the coast, with a yard so you can finally have a dog."

She shrugged her shoulders. "I could get a dog here. And you don't need to pay to skate on the lake, so you wouldn't need to pay for my sessions."

My cell phone chimed. It was Charlie.

"Hey," he began. "Glad I caught you. Hope this is a good time."

"As good as any. We just got off the steam train. We're having lunch at the soda shop you brought us to."

"Perfect. I'm just about to leave the mine. We did an inspection here this morning. I can drag my feet a bit if you like, give Lulu a personal tour."

I hesitated for the blink of an eye. "Okay. I'm sure she'd like that. We can be there in half an hour."

Charlie was waiting near the entrance to the visitor's center, where a knot of tourists had gathered for a tour of what was left of the old Homestake Gold Mine.

"We'll give these folks a five-minute head start," he told Lulu. "Then we'll take our own little tour."

We bypassed much of the museum display, an illustrated history of the mine's glory days, but Charlie once again brought the era alive with tales of greed and gold fever.

"In its time, some say this was the wickedest gold mine in the whole Western hemisphere," he told her. "In its heyday, they hauled out some 40 million ounces of pure gold—so much gold they had to look out for robbers every time they had to transport a load."

We peered down into the Open Cut, a bottomless black abyss surrounded by what seemed to me to be a dubious steel railing. Lulu listened to the echoing sound of her voice as she yelled down into the pit.

"Wow." She looked up at Charlie. "You can't even see to the bottom."

Charlie kneeled to point out the tiered ridges along the cratered sides of the pit, the rails where rickety, wooden mining cars had spiraled for a hundred years, hauling out the precious metal.

"Matter of fact," he told Lu, "the mine is so deep that the air at the bottom could kill you."

"How?"

"It's carbon monoxide. It's poisonous."

"That'd be enough to scare me out."

"But those old prospectors wanted the gold so bad, they figured out a way to beat the odds. A smart miner would take a healthy canary down with him into the mine. If the bird keeled over, the miner would go no further, because he knew the air below him was poisoned."

Lulu frowned. "What about the poor canaries?"

Charlie shrugged. "I guess maybe a few survived. But better to lose a canary or two than kill off the miner, don't you think?"

From the look on her face, Lulu wasn't convinced. She peered down into the mine. "I don't think I like this place."

Before I could answer, she grabbed my arm. "Mom, let's get out of here."

EIGHTEEN

The canaries were forgotten over pizza for dinner, and we made it an early night. It was a good thing, because the phone began ringing early the next morning. The first call was from Hannah, wanting to set up a date on Friday for her granddaughter, Morgan, and Lulu.

"There is no way," she told me, "that this kid is going to let your daughter go home without saying a proper goodbye."

She offered to take the girls for a picnic by the lake, while Faye, Morgan's mom, manned the florist shop. Lulu's. "Yeesss!" pierced the air when I told her.

The second call was from Nate Miller.

"I don't mean to rush the situation," he said, "but I don't know how much longer you'll be in Deadwood. Would it be okay if we met with Harrison Palmer one day, to kick around whether some kind of partnership might be feasible . . . that is, of course, if you're still willing to consider it . . ."

I hesitated. We had only two more days in Deadwood before our flight home on Saturday, and though the options were never far from my train of thought, I had made no decision about the house. I wasn't eager to examine the reasons why not, but in the end, I decided there was nothing to be lost by talking it out in front of an attorney.

"All right," I said, finally. "I can't do it today. Tomorrow, though, sometime mid-morning. If you can schedule something, just leave me a message about the time."

On the way home from the mine the day before, Lulu reminded Charlie, without so much as a pretext of tact, that we would be going back home on Saturday.

"That doesn't leave too much time for horse riding," she'd said pointedly, "if you meant what you said the other day."

I thought she was pushing it, but Charlie laughed. "Glad you reminded me, Lu." He winked at me. "If it's okay with your mom, how does tomorrow sound?"

In a matter of minutes, and over any objection I might have been tempted to formulate, the issue had been decided. We were to meet Charlie at the police station at noon and follow him out to his ranch.

He was in a staff meeting when we arrived, and Lulu busied herself in

* * *

He was in a staff meeting when we arrived, and Lulu busied herself in the waiting room, examining the neat rows of notices and "Wanted" posters lining the drab green walls.

"Looks like something out of an old Western movie," she whispered. "There must be a jail in here."

"I'm sure there is," I said, reasonably certain. "Why, do you want to check it out?"

"No, not really, but I wouldn't be surprised to see John Wayne coming around the corner."

She was doing her bow-legged John Wayne imitation when Charlie appeared around the corner, in uniform, to say he'd be right with us. Lulu looked like she'd been caught with her pants down, and we all had a good laugh.

When Charlie appeared again a few minutes later, he wore well-worn jeans and a blue flannel shirt over a navy T-shirt. Why don't the two of you ride with me?" he suggested. "I can run you back later this afternoon. I need to be back here, anyway."

I decided I'd rather have my own car, though I really couldn't say why.

"Why?" Lulu begged the question.

I gave her "the look."

"Bossy . . ."

"I am not bossy. I'm just being practical. What if Charlie gets called away?"

She knew enough not to argue any further as she climbed into the front seat of my car.

We followed Charlie a few miles out of town to a narrow, unmarked road I figured was halfway between Deadwood and Lead. Then we turned into an even narrower road and finally into a long, graveled driveway.

Two big German Shepherds came roaring out of nowhere to greet their returning master, who calmed them down, held them by their collars, and instructed them to say hello to his guests. Lulu hung back for a few seconds, then cautiously made her way forward to scratch one of the dogs behind an ear.

"That's Peaches," Charlie told her. "And this big guy here is Woody."

We stood still long enough to let the dogs sniff us all over and decide we were welcome to stay. Then, with Lulu looking over her shoulder at what was clearly the barn, Charlie led us into the house, a neatly kept ranch-style farmhouse with white wood siding and a wide front porch.

"Okay, who's hungry?" he asked, heading for the fridge.

The kitchen table was set for three, but Lulu's behind hardly touched the chair. She was so anxious to get to the horses. I gave her "the look" again and made a face, and she held still long enough to swallow a few bites of a tuna sandwich and some fruit salad.

Finally, Charlie pushed his chair back. "Ready to meet Sparkle and Henry?"

Lulu bounced out of her chair like a balloon cut from its moorings. She was out the door so fast in Charlie's wake that the screen door nearly hit me in the face as I followed. By the time I made my way out to the barn, Charlie and Lulu were already inside, standing in front of the stalls.

"This is Sparkle," he told her, patting the rump of a chestnut-colored mare. "And this big guy here is Henry."

As if in acknowledgment, the larger horse—a roan, I thought—whinnied and took a step forward.

"Wow." Lulu, the city kid, reared back. "They're a lot bigger than I thought."

"They won't hurt you," Charlie said. "They've been with me for a long time. They're almost like part of the family."

Opening the door to one of the stalls, he led the little mare toward the rear of the barn. Lulu kept a step or two behind him as we headed out to a small riding ring enclosed within a split rail fence.

"Sparkle here is pretty gentle," Charlie said, "but let's give her a chance to get to know you." He reached into his shirt pocket and drew out something small, which he put into Lulu's hand. "Now, hold your hand out slowly, and let her take the sugar cube out of it."

Lulu did as she was told, standing nearly nose to nose with the mare, a nice-looking animal with a spray of white facial markings that probably explained her name. The mare snorted and opened her mouth, revealing a row of enormous teeth, and Lulu jumped a foot back, losing her balance and tumbling, butt-first, to the ground.

I started forward, but Charlie signaled me back, squatting down to support Lulu as the horse nosed all around her body in search of the sugar cube.

"It's okay," he said, helping Lulu up. "She's just looking for her treat. Slowly, now, open your hand and let her have it."

Still sitting on the ground, Lulu stretched out her open hand and watched, fascinated, as the sugar cube disappeared into the horse's gaping mouth.

"Wow, she took it," she whispered, clambering to her feet.

"Of course she did." Charlie rubbed behind the horse's ear. "Sparkle likes her treats. Now she knows you're a friend. Here, talk to her a minute. Maybe rub her nose a little, while I go get some tack."

Lulu turned to me. "What's tack?"

"A saddle and stuff . . . the equipment you need to ride."

She nodded, turning back and reaching gingerly toward the spray of white markings on Sparkle's muzzle. It was a long reach, but the mare seemed to get the idea and relaxed her long neck downward.

"Hey, Sparkle," Lulu crooned, as if the mare were a puppy. The horse seemed to nod, and Lulu grinned. "Look, Mom, she likes me! Hey, Sparkle, do you want to go for a ride?"

Charlie came back to tack up the mare, Lulu watching every move, and soon he was hoisting her up in the air and buckling her into the saddle.

Nervous, I forced myself to lean back against the split log railing as Charlie gave Lu a quick course in using the reins and the heels of her fake leather boots to give directions to the mare. I held my breath as he finally began to lead the horse forward.

It takes a mom to fully appreciate the joy in her kid's face. I hadn't seen Lulu so excited and happy since the first time her skating instructor let go of her hand to set her sailing over the ice on her own. I blinked away a tear and watched my plucky daughter guide the horse around the ring.

"Do you ride?" Charlie asked, joining me at the railing.

"Used to, a little. But it's been a while."

"Well, look at her go. She's a natural, don't you think? Next time, we'll get her out of the ring and out on an easy trail."

When, if ever, there would be another ride, especially here at Charlie's ranch, was a question I didn't want to think about. There was no point in denying the pull of what felt like a growing connection with Charlie, with the allure of a country life, even with the stultifying little town I was glad to leave behind so many years ago.

But I had trusted to fate a time or two before and had only disappointment to show for it, and at this age and stage of my life, I wasn't sure I had what it takes to trust that way again.

Wordlessly, we watched Lulu lead Sparkle around the ring, digging her heels in to bring her to a halt each time Charlie asked her to.

"See?" he grinned. "She's a natural."

I was afraid it might take a stick of dynamite to separate Lulu from the mare, but after an hour, she reluctantly admitted her bottom was getting a little sore.

"Saddle-weary," Charlie told her. "It takes a while to get used to it. But you did great, Lulu." He hoisted her off the mare. "Next time you're here, we'll head out on a trail, and then you can learn how to cool her down and groom her after the ride."

Lulu looked at me, as if for confirmation that this was a real possibility. I flashed her an enigmatic smile and rushed over to give her a hug.

"Good job! I'm proud of you, Lu. Charlie says you're a natural!"

Charlie bent to buss the top of her head, a gesture that took me by surprise, and while Lulu squirmed at the unaccustomed male attention, he leaned over to kiss me lightly on the forehead.

Lulu looked up in time to see him do it. I didn't know which of us was more flustered.

NINETEEN

Hannah came by with Morgan at nine o'clock on Friday, promising to get Lulu back by four in time to clean up, eat some dinner, and get a decent night's sleep before we had to leave for the airport early the following morning.

Nate had left a message for me indicating Harrison could see us today at eleven, which left me an hour to get a head start on packing before I headed into town. I was chasing down the missing mate to one of my slippers when the phone rang.

"Hi, Julie, it's Nancy," Harrison's assistant said. "I know you're coming in at eleven, but I wanted to say a personal goodbye in case I'm busy or something when you get here and tell you I hope you and Lulu will be coming back here very soon."

"That's sweet of you, Nancy. I appreciate that. I'll miss all of you a lot."

"Also," her voice became a stage whisper, "I thought you would want to know I'm working on the State Highway Patrol to reopen the investigation into Doreen's so-called accident."

I hesitated, first because I knew from Charlie that the case had been officially closed, and second because of Nancy's curious assumption that I was somehow in league with her suspicions.

"Well, good, Nancy, if that's what you want." It was the best that I could manage. "It's always better to know the truth than to go on whistling in the wind."

"Oops," Nancy said, "the other phone is ringing. I'll try to give you a hug when you're in here."

I hung up and went back to my packing.

Nate was waiting when I arrived at Harrison's office at a few minutes before eleven. He rose when he saw me, clutching his battered briefcase in one hand and thrusting the other in my direction. He was wearing a tie and a worn navy sport jacket that barely contained his rangy frame, and he looked distinctly ill at ease.

I smiled as I shook his outstretched hand, though in truth I think I was as unsure as he was about what we might accomplish at this meeting.

Nancy was on the phone, but at precisely eleven, Harrison peered around his open door and motioned us into his office. He was dressed, as if for court, in a crisp dove gray shirt and charcoal tie, making Nate's attempt at dress-up seem even shabbier, but he shook hands with each of us and did his best to put Nate at ease.

He offered coffee, but we both declined, and there was silence for a long moment as we settled into our seats.

"So," Harrison started, "if I understand this right, there's a chance you two are considering a partnership to remodel Julie's old Victorian and turn it into a bed and breakfast."

It sounded odd to hear it called Julie's old Victorian, but I had, in fact, spent a good part of a sleepless night mulling the pros and cons of such an arrangement.

If I sold the house outright, Lu and I could live anywhere we wanted, and thanks to Aunt Sarah's generosity, I would never have to worry again about Lulu's future or my own. I could put the ghosts of Deadwood to rest, as I thought I had done years earlier, and go on with the life I had somehow managed to build.

If I didn't sell, there might still be enough money to secure a reasonable future, but there was no point holding on to the old house unless I planned to live here, and that's the point at which I kept getting stuck, like a needle in an old record.

"Considering is the right word," I jumped into the silence. "I haven't fully decided whether I would rather just sell it outright . . ."

Nate shifted in his seat.

"If I do decide to sell, however . . ." I glanced over at him. "I would like, if possible, to honor my aunt's willingness to give Nate priority as the buyer, maybe even at a below-market price, assuming he has the assets to make some sort of down payment and take on the responsibility of a mortgage."

Nate shot up out of his chair. "Wait a minute," he said, his craggy face taking on a mottled hue. I had a fleeting image of him prowling around at the back of the house and how frightened I had been at the time. But to his credit, his voice was level when he spoke.

"I'm proposing to put up a little cash," he said, "but I'll be putting up a lot of time, probably several months, and all my considerable work skills. In return, I would expect a reasonable stake in the value of the improved property especially if it becomes an income-producing venture. I thought that's what we were talking about."

Harrison and I remained silent, and Nate's frustration showed in his eyes.

"Your property and my remodel." He looked directly at me as if I hadn't understood. "Then we share in the value of the upgrade, maybe even sell it at that point and split the profit."

Unless I decide to stay and live in it. How would the partnership work then? I sighed, feeling out of my depth and no closer to a decision.

Finally, Harrison stepped into the breach. "Okay," he said in a measured voice. "At least I know now what each of you is thinking, and I would have to advise you, based on what I hear, to make no decisions at this point."

He looked at me. "Julie, this whole situation is new to you, and I understand it's hard to take in. Take some time. Figure out your next steps and get a financial advisor to help you sort out the money issues. In other words, don't make any decisions until you have a better handle on your options."

He gestured to Nate, who sat down, his brooding face unreadable. "Nate, you and I need to get together and come up with a viable plan—an actual plan of action with financial ramifications, so Julie has something concrete to consider. We'll need to list your assets, get a market price on the house as it sits today, and try to place a dollar value on the time and skills you would contribute going forward."

It seemed reasonable, and I was grateful to Harrison for getting me off the hook—at least for now. I glanced sideways at Nate, whose Adam's apple was working furiously as he considered what Harrison was proposing.

At last, he stood, half a foot taller than Harrison and towering over me.

"Right," he mumbled. "Give me some time to get some numbers together. Then I'll call you again, Harrison, and hopefully we can come up with something Ms. Goldman finds acceptable."

He glared at me. "I can only hope that she is as reasonable."

I was still flustered when I got back to the house. I thought about our life in California and how much easier everything would be if I sold the house and banked the proceeds. But I wasn't ready to call a real estate agent here in Deadwood, and I wasn't even sure why not.

I checked my to-do list. I had said some goodbyes, assured Harrison I would stay in touch, and made arrangements for Nancy to come by after work and take home any perishable food that remained in the old refrigerator.

In the kitchen, I found a phone message from Charlie wishing us a good flight home. He asked me to call if I could. But I felt stymied, totally incapable of making decisions about anything, even, maybe especially, about him.

I still wasn't myself when Lulu and Morgan came bounding into the house, Hannah close behind them. But Hannah came to my rescue again, this time with a pizza balanced on one hip. "So, you don't need to think about dinner," she said.

There was a pair of silver candlesticks in Aunt Sarah's sideboard. It was Friday, after all, and Morgan and Hannah watched, rapt, as Lulu and I covered our heads, said our prayers, and lighted the Shabbos candles. It was a lovely moment, as it always was, and it helped somehow to restore a little calm.

"We'll miss you," I told Hannah. We ate in the kitchen while the girls ate in front of the TV. "I feel like we've made some really good friends."

She smiled. "Well, don't talk as though you'll never be back. This will all be continued, you know."

I smiled back, not yet ready to share my misgivings even with my new friend. Time flew, and then it was bedtime, and I checked our airline tickets for the umpteenth time before crawling into my girlhood bed.

I closed my eyes and let myself be lulled by the ticking of the old wind-up alarm clock. I found myself thinking of my cousin Katy, ripped so rudely from my life, and of Marty, my husband, whose reassuring presence had been just as ruthlessly torn away, and even of my aunt, whose unexpected gift from the grave had led me to yet another crossroads.

I pulled the covers close around me. *What would they want me to do?*

Finally, I thought of Police Chief Charlie Banks and the message he'd left earlier and whom I hadn't called because I wasn't sure what I wanted to say or hear.

I hoped I was tired enough to sleep soundly, and I guess I actually was, because the next thing I knew, the alarm went off, telling me it was 5 a.m.

We had returned the rental car and were waiting in the lounge for our flight to be called when I realized Lulu had hardly said a word since we'd pulled out of the driveway. I put it down to the early hour, but I turned in my seat and turned her face toward me just in time to see a big, fat tear rolling down her cheek.

I was startled. "Lu? What's the matter?"

Her voice was the plaintive little-girl voice I hadn't heard for a while. "I don't want to go home. I like it here. Why can't we live in South Dakota?"

I took a deep breath, already regretting that I hadn't returned Charlie's call, and I asked myself, maybe for the first time, what there really was to keep me in California. I had no job, no home of my own, and no one I could really call a BFF, never mind a prospect for romance.

Why, indeed? I asked myself, just as they called our flight.

But it wasn't until we were buckled into our seats that I felt the first stirrings of commitment.

TWENTY

The only one who was not surprised was Penny.

"I knew it," she told me, stuffing pillows and blankets into a big carton and sealing it with brown packing tape. "Who would choose a stuffy apartment on the outer edge of Surfer's Paradise when you have this great big old Victorian house just waiting for you in some idyllic little town in South Dakota?"

I stacked the carton on top another in a corner of the little living room that was rapidly filling up with packed boxes.

"I'm not sure idyllic is the word I'd use to describe Deadwood," I said. "It's a little hick town with big ideas and a few buffalo and slot machines."

"Oh, yeah?" Penny threw a sofa pillow at me. "What about all those good-looking cowboys?"

"It has its share of those," I admitted. "Some men tend to look pretty good in tight jeans and riding boots." I threw the pillow back at her and made a silly face. "And they don't look bad in uniform, either" I said.

I'd made the mistake, in a weak moment, of telling Penny about Charlie, who'd greeted the news that we were moving back with a mix of awe and something I couldn't quite fathom.

"I never really thought you'd decide to pull up roots," he said when I'd finally called to tell him. "But I'll be waiting when you get here."

On Harrison's advice, I met with a financial planner, who helped me squirrel away enough of my inherited cash to ensure Lulu's education. It didn't leave much, but with the house in Deadwood free and clear of a mortgage, and Nate providing all the necessary labor, the renovation of the old house in Deadwood seemed to be a worthwhile investment.

In fact, I told myself, it was relatively risk-free since it could always be sold if the idealistic plan for a B and B turned out to be a bust.

As for everyone else I knew—and there weren't that many with whom I shared the news of our departure—they'd reacted with little more than mild interest to my cross-country relocation.

Avery Bannerman, my boss at the hotel, turned only a slight shade greyer when I informed him I wouldn't be finishing out my thirty days.

"I suppose we'll manage without you," he'd sniffed, as though my untimely exit was but one more weight on his overburdened shoulders. "Leave your Rolodex behind for the new team if you would, and of course, I'll write you a decent reference in the event you find a decent position in Montana—or is it Nebraska?"

Juan, the head chef I'd coddled like a spoiled child for more years than I cared to think about, barely looked up from his boeuf bourguignon when I told him in the kitchen that I was leaving.

"Adios, amiga." He waved airily, which I took to be the Spanish equivalent of, "Don't let the door hit you in the butt on your way out."

Lulu's skating teacher seemed genuinely sorry that his promising little skater was leaving, and the neighborhood pizzeria we'd frequented for years gave us a free pepperoni by way of goodbye. I did make another few calls, but in truth, I was a little taken aback at how few people we knew who might even notice we were gone and more confident than I had been until now about my decision to make the move.

Penny wrapped towels around vases and knickknacks and packed them in a sturdy box. "You know," she said after a long silence, "I took the bar exam again last week."

"I know. How did it go?"

She sighed heavily. "Believe it or not, there are 112 days to go before they post the results. That's twice as long as it takes to sail around the world and thirty days longer than Kim Kardashian's first marriage lasted."

I couldn't help but laugh.

"It's not funny," she said. "I seem to be living in a perpetual state of limbo."

"Sorry, Penny, I shouldn't have laughed. Why don't you take some meaningless little job just to keep you busy while you're waiting?"

"I don't want a meaningless little job. To tell you the truth, I'm not even sure I still want to be a lawyer." She took a beat. "What would you think about my going with you to South Dakota?"

I looked up from my packing. "Are you serious, Penny? Why would you want to do that?"

"Why not?" She sat on an arm of the sofa. "You're going to need some help when you get there. I could keep an eye on Lulu while you start clearing stuff out and getting the house ready to renovate. If I pass the bar, I can always come back here, but meanwhile, I keep myself occupied and you have some help getting started."

The words spilled out in a rush, but the plan, in her mind at least, had clearly been well thought out and who was I to turn down the best offer I'd had in years?

"Besides," Penny said and grinned as if to seal the deal, "I can appreciate a guy in tight jeans every bit as much as the next girl."

It took five days to finish packing and load our stuff into a U-Haul trailer. Penny and I would take turns driving on the five-day road trip to Deadwood.

In a stroke of luck, my cranky landlord agreed to buy my mix-and-match furniture: an Ikea sofa, two mismatched armchairs, two beds including Lulu's trundle, a couple of assorted tables and nightstands and a ten-year-old TV. It gave me pause to realize how little I had anchoring me to my life in California.

I transferred my bank accounts to South Dakota, left our forwarding address with the post office, and ticked off the chores on my to-do list one by one until there was nothing left to do but drive.

Penny's mom packed a tin of homemade oatmeal cookies for us, "in case we got hungry in the desert," and stood at the curb, waving a teary goodbye as we pulled out into traffic. The skies were clear, and the days ahead seemed full of exhilarating promise, and except for an overheated engine in Arizona and a blown water hose that kept us overnight in Wyoming, the old Chevy behaved itself and the miles and the cities flew by.

We stopped at Mt. Rushmore, so Penny could have her first look at the national treasure, with Lulu now acting as guide, and our spirits were high as we made the last turn, in the gathering dusk, onto Route 14 into Deadwood.

I had called ahead to give Hannah an estimated time of arrival, but there was no way we could have been prepared for the greeting that waited for us when we got there.

The lights were on in every room of the house, casting a cheery glow, and a Welcome Home banner fluttered in the breeze from one end of the front porch to the other. Morgan came bounding down the front steps, her grandmother close behind her.

Hannah's daughter, Faye, and her grandson, Petey, hovered close behind, and at the top of the steps, a crooked grin on his face, stood Police Chief Charlie Banks.

I had not felt so warmed and welcomed since the first time I'd found myself folded into the loving arms of Marty's grandma, Bubbe Lou. But as it turned out, there was more than one reason for tonight's impromptu reception.

TWENTY-ONE

Lulu was exhausted and more than ready to fall into bed in my old room as soon as we'd polished off the refreshments and Sarah and her family had gone. I put Penny into Katy's old room, knowing full well I would sleep on the living room sofa tonight because I wasn't yet ready to move into the room that had been Aunt Sarah's.

I said good night and went downstairs to say good night to Charlie. Before I could say much, he drew me down to the sofa and took my hand in his.

"I have something I have to tell you," he began soberly, "and it won't be an easy thing to hear."

My heart did a funny little flip-flop.

"But I'd much rather you hear it from me than through the café grapevine."

"Okay."

He looked directly into my eyes. "Nancy Jamison is dead."

Once, in an early conversation with Charlie, I had shared my old, irrational worry that death seemed somehow to follow me. But of all the things I expected to hear, this one threw me for a loop.

Charlie went on, softly and patiently, before I could formulate a response.

"Apparently, she was up on her roof, sometime during the day before yesterday. From the tools we found lying around, she must have been up there pounding down loose shingles. Somehow, apparently, she lost her footing and fell. The mailman found her body yesterday. The coroner says her neck was broken. The death was ruled accidental."

I started to speak, but Charlie squeezed my hand. "I know. I know what you must be thinking. But this has nothing to do with you and everything to do with Nancy. She was fearless. There was nothing she wouldn't attempt, and this time, look, accidents happen . . ."

I was well aware of Nancy's do-it-yourself mindset. And yes, accidents happen. But Nancy was also Doreen's best friend, and Doreen, too, had suffered an accident only weeks ago. *Two young women in the prime of their lives.* It seemed more than a little odd.

"Charlie, Nancy was very intent on looking deeper into Doreen's accident, and she never believed, not for a minute, that Doreen had stolen any drugs."

"I know that," Charlie said. "As it turns out, the drug issue will probably just go away. No formal charges have ever been filed, and it's unlikely they will be. As for her accident, well, it's been deemed just that. There's no evidence of anything else. I don't know why Nancy couldn't accept that."

But something bothered me. "What if it wasn't an accident, Charlie? What if someone else took those drugs and tried to blame it on Doreen and arranged her so-called accident to cover it up and then killed Nancy to keep her quiet, too?"

His voice was soothing. "I know where you're coming from, but really, Julie, I think that's a bit of a reach."

His eyes met mine for a brief, searching moment. "Okay, it's not in my nature or my work habits to leave any stones unturned. If it will ease your mind, I will personally review every scrap of evidence again. If there's any rational connection between those two deaths, I promise you I will find it."

I nodded slowly, reminded once again how quickly a life could be ended, even a life so tethered to your own that the loss left you gasping for breath. Neither Doreen nor Nancy fit into that category, and maybe I was overthinking things. But I felt their ghosts slip silently into the long line of souls that had somehow imploded in my wake.

At four in the morning, Penny was snoring softly in what I still thought of as Katy's bedroom, and Lulu lay spread-eagled on top of the flowered quilt in the bed that had been mine when I was her age. I knew because I checked on them both in the light of a three-quarter moon.

Sleep eluded me. Too many questions and unbidden images were sparring in my travel-weary body. Unwilling to referee them, I threw on my robe, made a cup of tea, and headed out to the new back porch, where I sat heavily in an old camp chair and stared into the middle distance.

I listened to the crickets and tried to fill my senses with the familiar and glorious landscape in front of me. The Black Hills crouched in stark relief against a slate-colored night sky, backlit by a wash of mauve and silver moonlight unlike anything you can see in the city.

Whether I liked it or not, I felt I was home again, in the place where I'd spent more years of my life than I had in any other place, and despite the sadness that always evoked, there was still the grounding of family. Lulu was my family now, and my heart spilled over at the thought of her. We could grow together here and build something new that would be here for Lulu long after I was gone.

I began to feel a little better, and as if on cue, the first light of a pink sunrise crept up over the hills. I willed away the darkness, ready and eager to see what life had in store.

By the time Lulu came bounding down the stairs, I was mixing a bowl of pancake batter, Aunt Sarah's old cast iron griddle heating on top of the stove.

"If you look in the cupboard under the sink," I told Lu, "you should find an old tin bucket. Take it out back, to the right of the porch, and I bet you'll see some blueberry bushes. If we're very lucky, this early in the summer, there'll be enough berries for these pancakes."

She came back with a third of a bucketful, more than enough for breakfast. I had rinsed the berries and was mixing them into the batter when Penny came downstairs. Twenty minutes later, we were seated at the table, heaping our plates with pancakes.

My table. My family. My whole new life in the country.

I wondered briefly if there was a place for Charlie in this new family picture. He was caring and kind, always solicitous, a strong and comforting presence, but apart from that first unexpected kiss and the brush of his fingertips grazing my cheek, there didn't seem to be anything more. Maybe he was shy, or just as badly scarred as I was, and reluctant to move too quickly.

But it didn't matter. What I needed now were friends, and I seemed to be making those and debating a plan that, for the first time in years, actually seemed to have a future. I dug into my pancakes.

First order of business: get the U-Haul unpacked, start settling in, and set a date to meet again with Nate Miller and Harrison Palmer.

The thought had barely walked through my head when the kitchen wall phone jangled. It was Harrison.

"Good morning, Julie. Glad to have you back. How are you?"

"I'm fine, Harrison. It's nice to be back. I was going to call for an appointment."

"Good," he said. "Because something has come up. Can you come in around noon?"

TWENTY-TWO

Harrison's outer office was empty when I got there, and no one was sitting in Nancy's place at the desk. I stared at the empty place and said a sad, silent goodbye before knocking on the door to the inner office.

The door, which had been slightly ajar, swung open in front of me. Harrison smiled, less broadly than usual, and ushered me into the room. He sat across from me in the pair of guest chairs instead of behind his desk.

"Sorry," he began. "I should have left my door open. Being here in the office alone is a little hard to get accustomed to."

"I'm sure it is. I can't begin to tell you how shocked and sorry I am. I didn't know Nancy all that well, but it's hard to believe she's gone, and I have to say I'm reeling a little over this odd string of unexpected deaths."

He nodded. "I know what you mean. What a tragic accident. Not that it was unusual for Nancy to be tinkering on her roof, or anywhere, for that matter. But right on the heels of Doreen Hastings . . ."

"Not to mention my aunt . . ."

He looked at me.

I shrugged. "Maybe it isn't in quite the same category, but three quick deaths in such a short time in this little town . . . I have to say, it makes me a little uneasy to be back here."

Harrison managed a wan smile. "I can understand that, and I hate to add this to everything else, but this could complicate things for you even more." He picked up a thin folder from his desktop. "Julie, do you know a Hanover Welty?"

I repeated the name. "No, I don't think so. Who is he?"

"I've just received a letter from him . . . from his attorney in Kansas City, actually. Welty claims to be the son of Pauline Lacey Welty who's allegedly an estranged and now deceased sister of both your mother and your Aunt Sarah."

I blinked, stunned. *A third sister? Talk about family secrets!* It was hard to believe, but if it was true . . . "That would make him my first cousin."

"It might," Harrison said, "and that's where things get a little murky. First, it will take a little research to determine if any of it is true, if there ever was a third sister, and if Welty is actually her son. Because if it is true, and that's the purpose of his letter, he wants to claim a share of Sarah's estate."

I grappled first with the possibility that I had a cousin I never knew existed. But in the next instant, I began to consider the implications of that, including the prospect that my unexpected inheritance might no longer belong to me.

"Can he do that?" I asked. "If he is a relative, can he claim a share of the estate?"

"It depends," Harrison sighed, drumming his fingers on the desk. "In a way I feel somewhat responsible. When Sarah was ready to discuss her financial options, I suggested she put everything into a trust, like the trust she had already set up to fund her family foundation. If she had done that, there wouldn't be much of a chance that anybody could successfully challenge it. But Sarah thought that was more protection than she needed, because the rest of her estate, as you know, was pretty simple and straightforward. Sarah wanted a will leaving everything to you, which I prepared according to her instructions."

"So, she didn't know about the possibility of other relatives?"

He shrugged. "If she did, she never mentioned it. If she'd had any idea that someone else might come forward, we could have inserted a phrase into the will to indicate that you were to be the sole inheritor no matter who might challenge her wishes."

I nodded.

"But we didn't do that, so there may possibly be a window of opportunity for Welty, or any other relative out there, to challenge."

Harrison must have read the conflict in my face.

"Let's not jump to conclusions," he said. "We have yet to determine who this Welty is, or whether a claim might be valid. At this point, I'd be curious to know how this guy knew not just where Sarah had been living all these years, but that I was her attorney of record."

He flashed what I saw as a smile of encouragement. "And it's important to know that even if there's a chance of a legitimate claim, we may be able to negotiate a settlement."

I took a breath, my mind spinning. "What about the house? The renovation?"

"Julie, this is a lot to take in, and it will take some time to resolve. But at the very worst, no matter how it turns out, you will likely retain at least half of Sarah's bequest at minimum, more than enough, I would think, to go ahead with your plans, especially since you've uprooted yourself and your daughter to come back home to Deadwood."

I visualized images of the empty apartment we'd left behind in California. Then I tried to focus on the present. "Actually, I thought that's why you wanted to see me—to talk out the details of coming to some agreement with Nate Miller."

"Secondarily, I guess that's so," Harrison said, picking up a second folder. "Nate has submitted a completed set of plans, along with an estimated time frame for completion of the work and a breakdown of estimated costs. In addition to contributing all the labor, and in lieu of a down payment per se, he is offering to ante up a third of the anticipated costs of the remodel."

He handed me the folder. "I've gone over the numbers, and it seems to me you have enough capital to proceed with this if you want to, even if Welty is successful in his bid, and even if you retain only half the equity in the house."

I nodded.

"You may want to have a financial advisor crunch the numbers before you make a decision. I can give you the name of someone in Rapid City. Anyway, look these over and call if you have any questions or just call ahead, leave a message on the machine, and come on in if you like."

He stood up. "Sorry I don't have anyone yet to answer the phones, but I listen to the messages every couple of hours."

I mustered a smile. "Thanks, Harrison. Why isn't anything ever easy? I'll look this over and be in touch."

He walked me through the empty reception area and opened the front door. "I guess I never realized how much I counted on Nancy until one day she just wasn't here. Worse yet, to tell you the truth, I haven't been rushing to replace her. I almost can't bear the thought of getting accustomed to somebody new."

I pondered that and my own suddenly shaky position, as I stepped out into the street. I debated stopping for lunch at the café and decided it wasn't a bad idea. Might as well get the news out around town that we were back. Hopefully to stay.

Shading my eyes against the sun, I glanced across the street. I thought I caught a glimpse of Nate Miller lounging against the side of a building. I checked the streetlight and looked back again. Now there was nobody there.

I crossed the street and looked both ways through knots of meandering tourists, but I caught no glimpse of Nate Miller or anyone else I knew.

Why, I asked myself, would Nate have been watching Harrison's storefront office?

I must have imagined it, I told myself, heading toward the café. But the man seemed to have an uncanny knack for giving me a case of the willies.

TWENTY-THREE

When I got back to the house, Penny and Lulu were unpacking the last of their suitcases, having feasted, Lulu informed me, on a sumptuous lunch of cheese crackers and peanut butter, the only decent edibles in the kitchen.

"Okay, I get it," I said, dropping my bag on the sofa. But the time had come to steel myself to move into Aunt Sarah's old room. "Give me an hour to get my bags unpacked and then we'll hop in the car and go for groceries."

My suitcases stood at the side of Aunt Sarah's bed, where Charlie had dropped them the night before, but I wasn't yet ready to tackle them. My head was still full of the scary possibilities my meeting with Harrison had uncorked and my uncertain feelings about forging any deal with the puzzling and inscrutable Nate Miller.

I looked around the big room, bounced a bit on the big bed, and ran my fingers over the ornately carved oak headboard. I didn't remember the headboard from my youth, and I tried to recall if I'd ever once been invited into this room as a child. Try as I might, I couldn't remember that I had. This had been Aunt Sarah's private space, off limits to me, for sure and maybe even to Katy.

It occurred to me then that my aunt had probably drawn her last breath in this bed. So, I started by stripping off the linens and remaking the bed with a set of well-worn, pine scented sheets I found in the hall linen closet.

Then I moved to the oak dresser and methodically emptied every drawer, stacking flannel nightgowns, sturdy underthings and aprons into nice, neat piles. I set them aside in a corner of the room to be donated to the nearest thrift shop.

I opened a suitcase and refilled the drawers with my own pajamas, underwear and socks, along with a couple dozen T-shirts, some shorts and capris, and a few pairs of folded jeans.

In another suitcase were my dresses, skirts, suits and blouses—working clothes, most of which, I realized now, would likely get little wear in Deadwood. Anyway, I told myself, they would need to be pressed before I hung them in the closet. So, I put aside the suitcase along with another one full of shoes, handbags, and odds and ends, figuring I would empty the walk-in closet tomorrow and put my things away.

I sat on the bed and opened the nightstand drawer, where I planned to stash a little cash, the pearls I'd found in Aunt Sarah's bank box and the only other good jewelry I owned: the little diamond earrings and bracelet Marty had given me on our wedding day.

I rifled around, hoping to find some photos, old photos of people I might be able to recognize. But what I pulled out was a box of stationery, a tiny book of daily prayers, a couple of opened letters, and some old receipts. I glanced at the letters, from people whose names meant nothing to me, and they turned out to be thank-you notes for help they had received from Katy's Legacy Foundation.

Running my hand around the back of the drawer to be sure I hadn't missed anything, I pulled out a little square, blue book—an old diary, from the look of it, with a stained leatherette cover and a locking clasp from which a tiny key hung on the end of a short, soiled string. The once gilt-edged pages had clearly been water-damaged, leaving them rumpled, clumped unevenly together, and unable to lie flat.

I turned the little key and the lock sprung open. To my surprise, the inscription on the first page read, "To Katy on her 16th birthday—Love, Brenda."

I vaguely remembered a Sweet Sixteen party for Katy not too long after I came to town and a tall, dark-haired girl named Brenda who shortly afterward moved with her family to Texas or somewhere else out West.

I began to smile as I turned the damaged pages. Some of the ink had blurred and run, but I saw that Katy had written in the diary every two or three days, faithfully recording her moods and hopes along with everyday events.

"Mo-om!" Lulu's voice, clearly impatient, climbed the stairs and barreled around the corner. I glanced at my watch, surprised to realize it had been well over an hour since I'd come upstairs.

Feeling guilty, as though I'd been caught eavesdropping, I turned to the back of the book, eager to know when the last entries had been made. The last dated page said April 6, 1994. I calculated quickly. It had been some six weeks before Katy was murdered. But a handful of succeeding pages, maybe half a dozen or more, had been ripped out of the diary, leaving nothing behind but ragged scraps of paper in the binding.

"Mother!"

I sighed. "Okay, Lu. I'll be down in just a minute."

Dying to read more of Katy's diary, I jammed it back into the drawer. I pulled myself together. Tonight, I promised myself, after we were all in bed, I would bring in a cup of tea and take time to peruse the pages.

Downstairs, Penny was on the sofa, texting, probably with her mom.

Lulu was playing solitaire at the dining room table. "Can I have an iPad?"

"No."

"Can I have an iPhone?"

"You don't need one."

"Boy, you're bossy."

"Lu!"

Lulu huffed. "I'm almost twelve! Everyone I know has a smartphone."

"In time," I told her, gathering up my bag and making a mental note to surprise her with a phone when her birthday rolled around in December.

Penny stowed her phone in her purse. Lulu pulled on her sneakers. By the time they came through the front door, I was already in the car.

I drove first to the produce stand I'd seen at the edge of town, and we loaded up on salad greens, home grown cucumbers and tomatoes, big dark cherries and tree-ripened peaches and apricots. We added a couple of melons, some local honey and homemade pickles, and it took the three of us to load it all into the car.

We drove slowly past the Open Cut, and I gave Penny a short history of the mine. "You should go to the visitor's center," I told her. "You might want to take a tour."

"Humpff," Lulu groused from the back seat. "You're not missing anything. It's creepy. They kill canaries."

At the grocery store, we filled in the basics and loaded up on milk, juice, and cereal.

"Can we stop for a frozen yogurt?"

I looked at Lulu. "Sure. Why not?"

So, we stopped at the yogurt shack and sat on a bus bench, slurping cones and watching the world go by. It was warm and sunny, not a cloud in the sky, and the sun felt good on our shoulders.

Tourist season, I noticed, was now in full swing, the restaurants and the casinos busy and the street crowded with people. We made a game of trying to distinguish the local folks from the tourists.

A dapper little man who looked slightly familiar paused and turned to look at me. "Ms. Goldman. I heard you were back."

I couldn't place the face.

"Malcolm. Rennie Malcolm, Director of the Lacey Foundation."

"Of course. I'm sorry. This is my daughter, Lulu, and our friend, Penny Jason."

He nodded perfunctorily, looking at neither of them. "Will you be joining us at Wednesday night's board meeting?"

"I wasn't aware there was a board meeting," I said. "I don't really expect to be involved."

Malcolm studied me. "Oh. Well, good then . . . we'll carry on as usual."

Something in his tone rubbed me the wrong way. I paused. "When and where is the meeting?"

"Seven thirty Wednesday evening in the meeting room of the library."

"I see. All right, thank you."

He looked at me, as though waiting for more, but all he got was what I thought of as my Mona Lisa smile. After an awkward pause, he nodded curtly and was gone.

"That lowered the temperature," Penny said.

Lulu looked up, curious, but I ruffled her hair as I swallowed the last of my cone. "Time to go if you guys are done. We've got all those groceries in the car."

We'd been gone no more than a couple of hours, but the sun had begun to set, turning the sky a fiery red and casting a dusky glow on the landscape. So, it wasn't until we pulled into the driveway that I saw it and slammed on the brakes.

The big front window of the house had been shattered. I stared at the gaping hole.

TWENTY-FOUR

Charlie had left the station for the night, but he was at the house within twenty minutes of my call. He had already dispatched two on-duty officers, a very young and clean-shaven kid named Brian Reyes and his older, bearded partner, who introduced himself as Officer Ken Downey.

They bagged for evidence the good-sized rock that had landed in the middle of the living room and were combing the shrubbery just outside for shoe prints or who-knows-what else.

"Don't anybody walk barefoot in here for a while," I warned, sweeping up glass shards so Penny could begin to vacuum.

Lulu sat cross-legged on the sofa. "Duh," she mumbled softly.

I shot her a look, and she smiled sheepishly.

"Sorry." She rolled her eyes.

Charlie knocked and let himself in. He was dressed in a T-shirt and cargo shorts. "Everyone's okay?"

"Yes," I said. "It happened while we were out, sometime in the last couple of hours. Ticks me off." I continued sweeping. "I can't begin to think who would do this."

Charlie took a long look around and went out to talk to Reyes and Downey.

"It has all the earmarks of a stupid prank," he said when he came back in. "Kids, probably, it's hard to tell. What bothers me is this is a quiet little cul-de-sac. No reason for kids to be out here messing around."

I nodded from my chair at the dining room table. Penny turned off the vacuum.

"My guys will check with the nearest neighbors, see if anybody saw anything, and we'll let you know if anything turns up. Are you okay being here overnight?"

I shrugged my shoulders. "Sure."

"It's after hours, but I can call Ralph Neiman at the hardware store. If he can't get the glass replaced right away, he can probably get out here and get the window boarded up until he can."

"No need," I assured him. "It probably was just some kid. I'll call the hardware store myself. We'll be fine."

The two officers asked if there was anything more they could do.

"No," I told them. "Thanks for getting out here so quickly."

Lulu jumped up from the sofa. "Anybody hungry? What's for dinner, anyway?"

I looked at Charlie and gestured toward her. "Clearly, she's not worried. Have you eaten?"

He smiled. "I was about to throw a steak on the grill at home when you called."

"We don't have steak, but we can rustle up some burgers. Can you stay and join us for dinner?"

He hesitated, but in the end, he stayed. We ate out on the new back deck. It was an opportunity for him to get to know Penny, and he was surprised to learn she was a law student.

"Really?" he said. "Will you be practicing here in Deadwood?"

Penny shrugged. "Not likely. I'm waiting, for the third time, to see if I passed the California bar."

Charlie nodded, spooning baked beans on his plate. "Just thinking ahead, I guess. I had lunch today with Harrison Palmer, one of our lawyers here in town. Julie knows him. He told me he's looking for a front office assistant, somebody with enough of a legal background to do some paralegal work for him."

He took a big bite out of his burger. "Might be worth checking. It could be right up your alley."

"Maybe," Penny said. "But I'm actually here to help Julie with Lulu while she gets the remodeling project up and running."

"I'm hardly a baby," Lulu muttered, "in case nobody noticed."

At this point, I wasn't sure there would be a remodeling project. At Harrison's suggestion, I'd set up a meeting with an accountant in Rapid City. But apart from that, it seemed to me I wouldn't need much help minding Lu, and Penny's helping out at Harrison's office might be a good thing for both of them.

With dinner over, we cleared the dishes and got an assembly line going in the kitchen. It was nearly nine when Penny and Lulu headed upstairs to find an old movie on TV.

"Thanks for dinner," Charlie said at the sink. "I really enjoyed tonight."

"You're welcome. We did, too. It's almost like you're part of the family."

He smiled, seeming to ponder the thought. "Yes. It would be really easy . . ."

Then he put a hand around my waist and leaned in for a kiss, and I had to admit it sent a little shiver down my spine.

"Hey," Lulu called from upstairs. "*You've Got Mail* is on! It's a cool movie! Anybody interested?"

We broke apart. "Sure," I called. "Give me a minute, and I'll be there."

Charlie smiled. "I'm glad you're back."

I nodded. "So am I."

"Look," he said after a moment, "are you sure you guys will be all right? I could sleep here tonight—on the sofa, just to be sure you're all right . . ."

I shook my head and walked him to the door. "We'll be fine. Really. Thanks."

It was after eleven when the movie ended and another half hour taking turns in the bathroom before we were ready for bed. To be honest, I had zoned out a time or three during the movie to reflect on that near kiss in the kitchen, but by the time I closed the bedroom door behind me, I was ready to put it on the back burner and have another look at Katy's diary.

I ran my hand over the front of the book, its leatherette cover dulled over the years to a stained and faded blue-gray, and I wondered where on earth it had been in the twenty-plus years since Katy's death. Surely not here in Aunt Sarah's night table, where it would have been protected from the elements. From the condition of the pages, the book had been wet, even waterlogged for a time, before it came into Aunt Sarah's hands.

I read the first few blurred pages, written in the upward slant I remembered as Katy's loopy handwriting. Shopping with friends . . . hanging out with the boys . . . a birthday poem for me. I remembered the poem. It brought tears to my eyes. Test grades . . . dances . . . barbecues.

I moved forward, turning pages, reading random entries. Her eighteenth birthday . . . senior prom . . . longer gaps of time between the entries.

Once as I read in the quiet room, I thought I heard a noise downstairs. I froze for a moment and listened, finally forced myself to creep down the stairs, to move slowly toward the broken window.

But the house was still and mostly silent, except for the ticking of the old cat clock in the kitchen. After a minute, I climbed the stairs and resumed reading the diary.

Eventually, I got to where the pages ended, and I ran my fingers along the thatch of tattered shreds in the binding. I had to wonder what had become of the missing pages and if they might have revealed whom Katy had been seeing before she was so cruelly murdered.

Again, I wondered how and when the diary had come into Aunt Sarah's hands. I tried to imagine her, maybe sitting in this bed, reading it just as I had and wondering if Katy would be alive today if she had not kept her secrets to herself.

For the first time, I felt a kinship with my aunt I had never felt before. If nothing else, we forever shared the loss of the girl we had both loved.

If Charlie was right, my aunt's bequest was proof that she had long since forgiven me for failing to confront Katy when she left home that night and for whatever other grudges she might have held. But the little nub of guilt that had never gone away lodged stubbornly in my consciousness.

I lay back on the pillows, still holding the diary, thoughts and memories competing, my early years in Deadwood, all the years since, a bed and breakfast, of all things.

At some point, I guess I must have fallen asleep, because the next thing I knew, daylight was streaming in the windows and the doorbell was sounding incessantly. I struggled awake and looked at the clock. Five minutes past eight.

Too groggy to distinguish between anxiety and annoyance, I threw on a robe and padded downstairs. The doorbell rang again, and without thinking, I pulled the door open and blinked.

A face I didn't know grinned wryly back at me. "Cousin Julie, I presume."

I stared.

"A late sleeper, it seems. Sorry. My name is Hanford Welty, your cousin Hanford. Good morning."

He was tall and slim, with a long, thin face, unreadable dark eyes, and a hint of red in his longish hair.

I was beyond stunned, but I found my voice. "How—what are you doing here?"

"I got here yesterday. Stayed the night in town. I thought it was time we met."

He smiled and gestured toward the broken window. "Not a moment too soon, it turns out. I don't know, Julie, it seems to me you should be taking better care of our property."

TWENTY-FIVE

I took in the stylish cut of his clothes, the expensive leather loafers. If I were inclined to look for a family resemblance, I probably could have found it. Instead, I recovered from my stunned surprise long enough to tell him to come back later.

"Better yet," I amended, getting my head back on my shoulders, "why don't you contact me through my lawyer, Harrison Palmer? I believe you know where to reach him."

My newfound cousin, if that's who he was, flashed me another sardonic grin. It was enough to put a lid on any familial feelings I might have had. I slammed the door in his face.

"Who was that?" Lulu asked, standing at the bottom of the stairs.

"I'm not sure. He says he's my cousin."

It occurred to me he might also be the joker who threw a rock through the window.

"Your cousin?" Lulu pushed hair out of her eyes. "I didn't know we had any cousins."

"Well, I didn't think we did. We're looking into it. Anyway, I didn't like his attitude. What kind of person comes banging on your door at this hour of the morning?"

"He wasn't banging on the door," Lulu said. "He was ringing the doorbell. It woke me up."

I ruffled her hair on my way up the stairs. "Well, I guess it's time to be up, anyway. Put on some clothes and tell Penny breakfast is in fifteen minutes."

After a Cheerios breakfast, I called Harrison, who answered on the first ring.

"Hey, Julie, I was just getting in. What's up?"

"My blood pressure," I told him. "I just had a visit from my alleged cousin—Hanford Welty. He was at the door early this morning. Said he got into town yesterday."

"Really?"

"Which is interesting, in that someone threw a rock through the window here yesterday while we were out shopping."

There was a short pause. "That *is* interesting. What did you tell this guy?"

"That he could contact me through you."

"Perfect. That's exactly what you should have done. I'll let you know if he calls me. Meanwhile, go about your business. If he turns up again or bothers you in any way, give Charlie a call right away. Meanwhile, I'll get hold of this Welty's attorney. This is absolutely unacceptable."

I decided to take Lulu and Penny with me into Rapid City. It would give them a chance to see the sights while I met with the accountant Harrison had recommended. Before we left, I made a quick call to the hardware store and made arrangements to have the window repaired. Then I took a few minutes to gather up all the paperwork I thought I needed for my meeting.

As we piled into the car, I noticed a beat-up gray pick-up truck parked across the narrow road. No one was in it, and looking both ways, I spotted nobody as far as I could see.

"Wait here," I said, more curious than anything else as I stomped around to the back of the house.

Nate Miller, on his hands and knees in the scrub, was measuring a section of the foundation.

I watched him for a minute. "What are you doing?"

He didn't flinch. "Re-checking some numbers."

"This is private property, Mr. Miller, and I would appreciate it if you stayed off of it unless and until you have permission."

He looked up, his dark eyes smoldering. "Look, Ms. Goldman, you may own the property, but the labor I plan to commit to the remodel is every bit as valuable in terms of profit."

My temper flared. "*If* there is a remodel. If I *consent* to a remodel, and by the way, if I may ask, where were you yesterday afternoon? You wouldn't by any chance have any idea how that front window of my house was shattered?"

"No. I noticed it this morning, though, and I resent the implication. Why would I want to vandalize something I expect to have an interest in?"

It was a valid question. My anger sputtered.

"But I'll be happy to put in a new glass."

"No, thanks. I have a workman coming." I stifled what was left of my outrage. "But until and unless we have a signed agreement, please stay away from the property."

I swiveled on my heel to find Penny and Lulu watching. I shooed them back to the car.

"That went well," Penny murmured.

"Pretty bossy, Mom."

I glared at her and got into the car, backing out of the driveway with more speed than was called for.

The two of them had the sense to keep their voices down, and my anger, which probably was a little over the top, cooled as we neared Rapid City.

"See that bronze statue of John. F. Kennedy on the street corner?" I asked as we approached the center of town. "There's a whole series of life-size statues of the presidents scattered throughout the downtown area, all created by local artists. Plus, there are some interesting little shops and stuff to wander through. I shouldn't be more than an hour or so."

We agreed to meet where I dropped them off, half a block from the address I was looking for, and I grabbed my briefcase full of bank statements and building specs and headed up the street.

Jen Howard was about my age—a pretty blonde with a ready smile, a discerning ear, and a patient but no-nonsense attitude. She offered coffee, which I accepted, and took fifteen minutes to read through my assorted paperwork.

"I can see why you don't want to be hasty signing on for this project," she said. "Your financial position has been greatly improved by this inheritance, and you are right to want to protect it."

She approved of the decisions I had already made to earmark funds for Lulu's education and establish a modest nest egg and emergency fund.

"Of course," she went on, "the house in Deadwood is your most valuable asset, and the fact is, the proposed remodel would likely increase its market value."

I nodded.

"The big question is how committed you are to turning your home into a bed and breakfast because you don't need the additional space unless you plan to use it for that purpose."

I was well aware of that, but I was also aware there weren't too many other ways for me to make a living here if Lulu and I stayed in Deadwood. So, I guessed maybe I was more committed to the idea than I had been ready to admit.

Jen Howard looked again at the preliminary proposal Harrison had hammered out with Nate Miller.

"As this is written," she said, "fifty percent of the equity in the property would be reserved for Lulu no matter what. Of the other fifty percent, you would retain half, and if he completes the remodel, Mr. Miller would own the other half. He would also be entitled to compensation if his costs are substantially higher than expected, and your portion of any profit accrued over time would revert to him upon your death, should that occur."

I nodded again. *Upon my death.* "Does that seem fair?"

"I think so, on the face of it. Your daughter's interest is protected in any case. If you want to start this business venture, and you're comfortable that Mr. Miller will make good on his end of the bargain, then yes, I would think it seems to be a win-win investment opportunity."

I sat there for a moment, owning up to the fact that any reluctance on my part now probably had less to do with the proposal itself than with my mixed feelings about Nate Miller, which fluctuated wildly between respect for his workmanship and some antagonism I couldn't quite explain.

"Thanks," I said finally, getting up to go. "I really appreciate your input."

I left, assuring her I would contact her again if I had any further questions. Penny and Lu were coming around the corner just as I reached the car.

"Cool little town, Mom," Lulu said. "The ice arena converts to a concert hall in the summertime!"

"Really?" I kissed the top of her head. "How interesting!"

We stopped for lunch on the way out of town. Penny tried a buffalo burger and quickly pronounced it fab. Lulu and I did not regret we had opted for grilled cheese sandwiches.

Back in the car, we buckled ourselves in for the half-hour drive back to Deadwood. I consulted with myself and made a conscious decision to let my head rule the day.

"Hey, you two," I looked back. "Would you mind a quick stop before home?"

Hearing no objection, I stopped the car in front of Harrison's office. The three of us piled in and I called Harrison's name as I peered into the inner office.

"Hey, Julie, come on in." Harrison ushered us inside. "This must be Lulu." He stuck out a hand. "Glad to meet you. Harrison Palmer. I've heard a lot of good things about you."

He turned to Penny. "And you must be Penny. Nice to meet you."

His smile was warm, and he seemed to appraise her as he offered an outstretched hand. "Charlie tells me you're waiting for results of the bar exam in California."

Penny smiled back. "Not for the first time, sad to say. I know the law. I know I do. I'm a nervous test-taker, I think."

Harrison nodded. "A lot of people are. You probably did fine this time."

Motioning us to sit, he took the only place left behind his well-ordered desk. "Actually, I was going to call you, Julie. I connected with Welty's attorney in Kansas City. He had no idea his client was here in Deadwood, much less that he'd turned up uninvited at your house. He agreed to advise him to keep his distance while the case proceeds."

"Great, thanks. I hope he listens."

I looked at Lu and Penny. "Could I ask you two to wait for me out in the reception area? There's something I want to go over."

"I just came from Jen Howard's office in Rapid City," I told him after Lu and Penny had gone. "She reviewed the agreement and basically said this is a reasonable investment for me if I'm sure I want to open a bed and breakfast."

"And do you?"

I took a deep breath. "I have to tell you, Harrison, something about Nate Miller just gets under my skin. It's probably silly, but that's the way it is. That's really what's been holding me back."

Harrison nodded. "I understand. He's a hard nut, and maybe it's best to trust your instincts."

"I know, but on the other hand, my instincts haven't always been on target, and in many ways, if I'm going to stay here in Deadwood, it seems silly to let them get in the way."

Harrison said nothing.

I took a deep breath. "I've reviewed the plans over and over. I know Nate can do the work, and I think the remodel is a good opportunity for both of us, and I also think," I said, feeling more confident, "that my Aunt Sarah would want this."

He waited.

"So, I've made my decision." I plunged ahead. "I'm ready to sign the agreement."

TWENTY-SIX

In the mail when we got home were my first utility bills, a "Welcome to Deadwood" letter from the Chamber of Commerce and a copy of the agenda for tomorrow night's meeting of the Katy Lacey Family Foundation.

I scanned the agenda: acceptance of a gift of one thousand dollars, the proceeds from a Rotary Club fundraiser; a board review of two applications for assistance; and discussion and recommendation for the position of part-time foundation director to expand into a full-time position at double the current salary.

I bristled. Not that it was any of my business, but really? What was that all about?

On a whim, I called Hannah at the flower shop.

"Hi, Julie. I'm glad you caught me. I'm closing a little early today. Petey's working on his Eagle Scout project, and believe it or not, he wants his grandma to help with something at the Senior Center."

"Fun," I said. "I won't keep you. I was just wondering . . . what do you know about Rennie Malcolm?"

"Rennie? Not much. He's the director of your aunt's charitable foundation."

"Yes, I know, and apparently, he's lobbying the board to take on additional control."

Hannah paused. "I wouldn't know about that. He's a snippy little guy, I know that much. Cocky, I guess you'd call it. No time for anybody else unless it suits his purpose. Even his wife . . . ex-wife, I should say. She left him a couple of years ago."

"Mmm," I said.

"They had a horse ranch, not far from Chief Charlie's, just outside of town. Rennie sold it after his wife left. Call Helen Kovich if you want to know about Rennie. She's on the board. She should know."

I remembered the kind-hearted Mrs. Kovich from the luncheon after Aunt Sarah's funeral. But I debated how politically correct it would be to discuss the agenda, or the foundation director, with a board member prior to the meeting. In the end, I decided it didn't matter. I would go to the meeting. I had a bonafide right to be there.

"By the way," Hannah said, "I don't know if you've heard the news. It looks like poor Doreen and Nancy can finally rest in peace. My sister, the one who works at the hospital? She tells me the drug theft charge against Doreen has been officially dropped."

"Well, that is good news. Nancy would be gratified. What kind of drug was it, anyway? It must have been something pretty potent."

"Something unpronounceable . . . s-u-c-c-h, something or other. I don't suppose it really matters now. How are things coming along for you?"

I blew out air. "Well, I took the plunge and signed the contract to get the remodel going."

I could feel Hannah's smile. "That's wonderful, Julie! Congratulations!"

I was tempted to ask her more about Nate but was too late to matter anyway. We set up a play date for Lulu and Morgan on Friday, and I let it go at that.

I had barely hung up when the phone rang. The window guy, who had apparently been out earlier to measure, would be back in an hour to replace the glass.

I left Penny, bless her for her patience, playing Scrabble with Lulu at the kitchen table and went upstairs to finish organizing my things. I had opened my second suitcase to sort through my old work clothes when I heard the telephone ring again.

I heard Penny answer it. "Oh, hi, Harrison. Hold on. I'll get Julie for you. Oh. Really? Well, sure, why not? Hold on just a second anyway. I want to be sure I can get away."

She met me on the landing. "Harrison is on the phone. He'd like to talk to me over dinner, if it's okay."

"Of course it's okay. You don't need my permission."

"I just thought if you were planning to go out . . ."

"Well, I'm not, and anyway, you can probably use some time away from Lulu."

"I don't—"

"I know. And I appreciate you, Pen. But go and have a good time."

She was upstairs changing her clothes when the phone rang yet again. This time, it was Charlie. "I've still got those steaks I didn't grill the other night. Are you ladies free to come out here for dinner?"

"Lu and I are available," I told him. "Penny's going to dinner with Harrison."

"No kidding," he chuckled. "That was fast. I didn't know they'd met."

"This afternoon in Harrison's office. I went over there to sign the agreement for the remodel."

A pause. "Well, you've been busy. Congratulations. I guess we'll have some champagne with the steaks."

The front window good as new again, I went upstairs to change. I traded in my pantsuit for jeans and a tank top and was playing with my hair in front of a mirror.

"What's that all about?" Lulu stuck her head in.

"What?"

"You hardly ever care about your hair."

I shrugged. "That's because it hardly ever cares what I think. Go and change your shorts for jeans. We've been invited to dinner at Chief Charlie's."

"All right!" She turned and headed to her room. "Maybe I can ride Sparkle!"

As it turned out, it was too near dusk to ride when we got to Charlie's ranch. But he was just about to feed and water the horses.

Lu brightened. "Can I help?"

He showed her what to do, left her with the buckets, and joined me at the barn door to watch her. "She's a quick learner."

"You may be sorry you got her started."

"Why? She's welcome out here anytime and you, too." He grazed my left cheek. "It's nice to have women around the place."

I smiled. "I understand you lost one of your neighbors. Rennie Malcolm had a ranch near here?"

"Yep. He sold it. I don't think he ever liked it much, anyway."

It was hard to imagine the nattily dressed Malcolm mucking around on a horse ranch. "Do you know him pretty well?"

"Malcolm? Not really. He directs your aunt's foundation, doesn't he?"

"Yes," I said. "And apparently, since he no longer has the ranch, he wants to do it full time."

Charlie raised his eyebrows. "Can't blame him for that, if there's enough work to keep him busy."

We watched Lulu put the buckets away and turn on the tap in the trough, resting her hands on her narrow hips as she watched the horses drink. The hay was fragrant, and the night was warm. We watched in easy silence.

"I wish I had some news for you about that busted window," Charlie broke into the quiet. "No usable prints, nothing from the neighbors. Some kid, I guess, taking target practice."

"Maybe," I said, not fully believing it. "Although I can think of a couple of other suspects."

His eyebrows rose. "Who?"

I shook my head. "I don't want to get into it—"

"Julie, if there's something I should know—"

"No," I said. "I'm not accusing anyone at this point . . ."

Charlie turned to face me full-on. "Listen, if you're feeling threatened, Julie . . . I remember how uneasy you were your first couple of nights in that house."

"That was when I was there by myself. I have Lu and Penny there now—"

"All the more reason to keep you safe. If there's something you're not telling me . . ."

I shook my head again. "We'll be fine, Charlie. If there's anything you need to know, I'll tell you."

He took a beat. "Promise me."

"I will. I do."

"I'll schedule a patrol car to do a drive-by once or twice in every shift."

"Not necessary."

"I'll do it anyway."

I smiled sheepishly. "Thanks. It isn't necessary, but I appreciate your concern."

He looked deeply into my eyes. "It's more than just professional, you know."

"Is it?"

His face was inches from mine.

"Hey." Lulu came running up alongside us. "How do I get Sparkle to share? She's hogging everything in the trough!"

Charlie grinned. "Don't you worry about Henry. He'll get his share of dinner."

Lulu didn't look convinced.

"And you, you must be starving. Who's ready for a steak?" He turned on his heel and led us back to the house.

TWENTY-SEVEN

Penny was sprawled on the sofa in her robe and slippers when we got home at a little after nine.

"Hey, Pen. Did you have a good time?"

She put down her magazine. "I think so."

"You think so?"

She shrugged and grinned a Penny-like grin. "I don't know what I was expecting exactly, but it turned out to be as much a job interview as a date."

"Really?" I shooed Lulu up to change for bed and sat in the chair across from Penny." Harrison wanted to know where I had studied, if I was leaning toward a legal specialty, and if I had any interest in trying some paralegal work here while I'm waiting to see if I passed the bar."

I considered. "Well, if we're going to start construction, I'll be here with Lu most of the time, and if you don't need to be here to babysit, it might be kind of fun for you to help Harrison out. I know he misses his assistant."

"Yes, he mentioned it. What was that all about?"

"It's a really sad story. Apparently, she fell off the roof of her house while she was up there replacing some shingles—"

"What?"

"I can believe that much," I said. "Nancy was young and active, and I know for a fact she was a devoted do-it-yourselfer."

I paused. "What does seem a little odd is that her best friend—someone I used to know—died in an accident, a car accident, on the night I got back here to Deadwood."

I wasn't sure how much more to say. I'd been trying not to think about any of it. But I couldn't help remembering Doreen's call. Something she had wanted to tell me.

"Well," I said finally. "It doesn't matter now. But one thing I know for sure. Harrison needs help, and you may be just the right person to step in and do the job."

"Maybe," Penny said. "It could be kind of fun. Maybe I'll stop by the office tomorrow."

We checked the locks, turned out the lights, and headed upstairs for bed. Lulu was already under the covers, staring into space.

"Hey, Lu. Ready for a hug?"

"I was thinking. I need a new bike. Chief Charlie said I could go out to the ranch anytime."

"I don't know about that. You will not be at the ranch unless one of us is out there with you. But a bike isn't a bad idea. Let's look for one in the next few days."

It seemed to satisfy her. I sat on the bed, and we cuddled for a long minute. She was growing up, no doubt about that, but for the moment, she was still my baby.

In Aunt Sarah's room, *my* room, I corrected, I brushed my teeth, got ready for bed, and settled back on the pillows. I needed to spring for a new comforter. Maybe even paint the room—something to make it seem like mine, that I wasn't intruding on my aunt.

I opened the nightstand drawer and took out Katy's diary. Idly, I read through the pages, some of them water-damaged almost beyond distinction, but I heard Katy's unmistakable voice: *January 9—Today we ditched school an hour early to beat the crowd to the lake. I'm determined to get Julie up on the ice, but the poor little thing won't even try if anyone else is watching. . . .*

I'd forgotten how shy I had been as a kid about dancing, or skating, or doing anything in public until I had worked up some confidence and how hard and patiently Katy had worked to get me up to speed.

I smiled, realizing how unlike me Lulu was in that regard and how glad I was that she was up for anything, rushing headlong into life.

She was much more like Katy. I fingered the ragged edges of all that was left of the diary's final pages. How different all our lives might have been if Katy had not been torn away.

Would I have left Deadwood at the age of eighteen? Met my husband, Marty, in New York? Had my precious, precocious little girl?

And what of Katy? What would she have done? She had talked about being a veterinarian.

I put away the diary, turned out the light, and settled in under the covers. I must have fallen asleep pretty quickly, because when I was awakened, abruptly, the bedside clock read just after midnight.

At first, I was annoyed. It was the second time this week I'd been awakened from a deep sleep. I sat up slowly and listened.

I heard something that sounded like pebbles being tossed against the window. *On the second story? Get a grip. Unlikely at best. . . .*

I struggled out from under the covers, drew back the curtain at the window. Of course, there was nothing. I squinted into the darkness. But all I saw were the trees against an inky sky and a small sliver of moon.

For a moment, I thought I detected movement, a quick, shadowy form. Then there was nothing, just an eerie quiet. I guessed I must have imagined it.

I went back to bed and pulled the covers close, but sleep was slow in coming back. I could not remember feeling so on edge since my first weeks without Marty, when every noise in the night was magnified, and I couldn't seem to find my place in bed.

Before I knew it, a jumble of images played themselves out in my brain, and sleep, no matter how I tried to capture it, slipped further and further away.

Eventually, I guessed I must have dozed, because I woke to the smell of coffee. It was eight thirty when I slipped on my robe and padded down the stairs.

Penny and Lulu were at the kitchen table, working on a panful of scrambled eggs.

"Hey, Mom." Lulu spread jam on a piece of toast. "We thought we'd let you sleep. Want some toast?"

"I made you coffee." Penny sipped at her tea. "Did you sleep well?"

"Actually, no. For some reason, it was hard to doze off, and then I couldn't seem to stay asleep."

I poured myself coffee, joined them at the table, and accepted a piece of toast. "Yum. I love this blueberry jam. Perfect for a bed and breakfast. Hey, Lu, what do you think? I wonder if we could learn to make it."

Lulu shrugged. "Maybe tomorrow. How about today we go bike shopping?"

"Maybe on Friday. You have a date to see Morgan. Maybe we'll all go then."

"I do? Wow. Penny, you come, too. I need to decide between burgundy red and a really sleek silver."

I sipped my coffee, hearing their chatter but not really listening. After a minute, I hauled myself up and headed for the front door.

"Be right back," I heard myself mutter. "I just want to check on something."

There was nothing unusual on the back porch, and nothing in the driveway out front. I walked around to the back of the house. Nothing there, either.

I scanned the road both ways before going back into the house. My imagination was running amok, or else I was a certified wimp.

I went back inside and sat at the table. Lulu had run off somewhere.

"Everything okay?" Penny asked.

"Yes, so Pen, what did you decide? Are you going to go in and talk to Harrison?"

She smiled. "I think so."

"Good for you!"

She shot me a shy grin. "You're right, Julie. The man needs help."

I had a feeling there was something more.

"And there's something about a guy in bun-hugging jeans that makes a girl sit up and take notice!"

TWENTY-EIGHT

Nate Miller called on Wednesday, just after lunch.

He wasted no words. "You signed our agreement."

I waited for the "thanks," but it did not come. "You're welcome," I said anyway. "If our advisors are right, it should be profitable for both of us, assuming we make a go of the bed and breakfast if and when the remodel is finished."

"There's no 'if,'" Nate said shortly. "The remodel will be finished. As for when, I expect in three to four months, assuming decent weather."

"So, what happens next?"

"Well, now, I presume, I have your okay to be on the property when I need to."

His tone was sarcastic, but I didn't bite. "Anytime between eight thirty and five thirty. Regular daytime work hours. If you need to be here before or after that, I would like to know in advance."

There was a short silence on his end. "I want to get started as soon as possible. I'll be ready in the next few days. But there are things you'll need to do first—clearing the decks, moving furniture, getting stuff out of my way."

My orderly nature balked at the thought of the house all torn apart.

"If you want, I'll come over this afternoon and block out some alternative traffic paths, move some of the furniture out of the way, and lay down some plastic sheeting."

It was a reasonable offer. "That would be fine. I'd appreciate it."

"Okay, good, then. I'll be there within the hour."

By four o'clock, the living and dining areas had been turned into something of a war zone—carpets ripped out and stacked against the walls, the big dining table jammed into the living room, chairs overturned on top of it, and a narrow swath of plastic-covered floor the only path to the stairway.

Penny had taken the car into town to meet with Harrison at his office. Lulu followed silently in my wake, watching the merciless dismantling.

"Yikes," she muttered at one point. "I might have to move in with Morgan."

Nate ignored her. "At some point, I'll have to get upstairs, too," he said. "I have to tear down a couple of walls and reconfigure the bedroom space."

I wasn't happy to realize that this surly stranger would be up there rummaging around among our personal things. I still wasn't a hundred percent sure it wasn't Nate who'd thrown that rock through the window. But I'd signed the agreement, and there was no way to keep an eye on him all the time.

He had nodded curtly when I'd met him at the door, not even a hint of a smile. I wondered yet again if I was making a mistake, but I tried my best to be pleasant, and to be fair, even while he tore things apart, he did make an effort to be considerate, carving out a livable space for us in the suddenly cramped quarters.

"Listen, Nate." I looked him squarely in the eye when he stood at the door to leave. "I know we haven't always been on the best terms. At least some of that is my fault, and I want to apologize for any misunderstanding."

I handed him a key to the front door. "Since we're going to be working together on this project, I will do my best to be cooperative."

He nodded tersely, but if I expected anything more, it was clear I wasn't going to get it. He shoved the key into his jacket pocket and took his long frame down the porch steps. "I'll be stopping by sometime tomorrow," he said. "I'll be doing some preliminary work."

I gritted my teeth. No apology, no olive branch. It was going to be an interesting three months.

* * *

The Deadwood Library was a salmon-colored building fronted by four imposing columns. Katy and I had spent a lot of time inside years ago, discovering a treasure trove of teen novels to take home and read on rainy afternoons.

There were four people seated at a scarred oak table when I made my way to the community room; Helen Kovich, in a flowered housedress, who I recognized right away and surprisingly, Father Ruggio seated next to her. Another man, in shorts and a plaid shirt, looked familiar, too, probably someone I'd met at the funeral, and Rennie Malcolm, in a blue linen jacket and tie, who looked at me coolly from his place at the head of the table.

"Ms. Goldman," he acknowledged, his ruddy face expressionless, but ice dripping from his voice. "How nice you should decide to join us."

"You invited me," I reminded him, though it was not quite accurate. He had only asked if I planned to be there.

I offered a hand to Father Ruggio, who shook it enthusiastically and welcomed me back to town, and to Mrs. Kovich, who got up to give me a hug.

She introduced me to the portly, gray-haired man seated on the other side of the table. "Frank Anderson," she prompted me. "You may remember he was one of the fellows who carted all that food to your house after the repast."

Anderson stood up to shake my hand. "Ms. Goldman—"

"Please, it's Julie."

Mrs. Kovich informed him I was back to stay, living in Aunt Sarah's house.

"Is that so?"

Clearly, Mr. Anderson was not a regular at the café.

"Well, great!" he boomed. "Glad to hear it. Sarah was a wonderful woman."

"Thank you." I took a seat at the far end of the table as two newcomers came in.

Rennie Malcolm did the honors. "Roy Bachman and Gert Solomon," he snapped.

I nodded at a smiling woman of indeterminate age and a burly, bearded fellow who held out a seat for her to take.

"This is Julie Goldman," Rennie went on. "As Sarah's heir, she has inherited the right to oversee foundation business, or so Harrison Palmer informs me."

I remembered the first time I had been in Harrison's office and Rennie Malcolm rushing past me in a huff before we could be introduced. I smiled at the newcomers and thanked them quietly for their work at the family foundation. I lapsed into silence when Malcolm pounded the table with a small, wooden gavel to bring the meeting to order.

The minutes and financials were read without discussion and approved. I was stunned to realize, once again, how much money was in the foundation's working account, which had been fattened, Mrs. Kovich said, by a recent grant from a charitable trust—a grant, Malcolm was quick to explain, that he'd been working toward for many months.

Gert Solomon read the Rotary Club letter accompanying their enclosed donation. It was accepted with gratitude by the entire board. Gert would generate a thank-you note.

Frank Anderson passed around copies of the two letters requesting assistance from the foundation. The facts and circumstances were in process of being verified, reports and recommendations to be made the following month, followed by questions and a vote. I have to say, I was pretty impressed with the board's seeming efficiency.

Finally, Malcolm cleared his throat and read his proposal for full-time director's status and adjusted salary.

Mrs. Kovich began the discussion, reminding the board, to my surprise, that Sarah had been opposed to such a move. "We all know she thought the foundation could be adequately overseen on a part-time basis."

"And let's not forget," piped in Father Ruggio, "Sarah believed in tight purse strings. Her goal was to keep foundation expenses at a fraction of expected disbursements."

Malcolm, supported by Roy Bachman, spoke at length about the hours he was putting in above and beyond the time he was paid for, writing grant requests, soliciting donors, and managing foundation business.

"I don't know," Mrs. Kovich maintained. "Until recently, Rennie, you were spending a lot of time squiring a pretty young woman around town after you gave up the ranch."

Malcolm's face turned a mottled red. "What I do in my personal life is no concern of this board. As for the ranch, it's long gone, and I resent the implication that it ever kept me from performing my foundation duties."

"I never said that," Mrs. Kovich said mildly. "Only that nothing has changed much in regard to foundation business. I can't see that you suddenly need to put in so much more time now."

The discussion grew louder. I just listened. Malcolm continued to press his case.

After a while, he called for a vote. "You, Ms. Goldman, are not permitted to vote," he reminded me. "Unless a tie-breaker is needed."

From his tone, I had the distinct impression he expected his proposal to pass. But it didn't. The vote was deadlocked three to three, Mrs. Kovich, Father Ruggio, and Gert Solomon lined up squarely against it.

Clearly exasperated, Malcolm glared at me. "And what have you to say, Madame tie-breaker?"

I surprised him. "Actually, I'm not ready to vote. I'm afraid I don't have all the facts."

Everyone at the table looked at me.

I smiled the way I smiled at my brides when they made impossible requests of the hotel. "I'm going to ask the foundation director to document his time and duties over the next thirty days—tasks and administrative duties performed and the hours spent on each task. I would also request a detailed proposal stating his goals for the foundation and the additional tasks he expects to take on in the event his hours are extended."

The room went quiet. Eyes blinked. Avery would be proud.

TWENTY-NINE

I opened the front door of the house to find Hanford Welty sitting in my living room. He was lounging in a club chair that had been wedged firmly between a bookcase and the upended coffee table.

"I told Penny she shouldn't have let him in." Lulu, ready for bed in an *I Hate Justin Bieber* T-shirt, peered out from the middle of the stairwell.

Penny shrugged. "I guess I wasn't thinking, Julie. He introduced himself as your cousin."

Penny had been asleep when he'd appeared the other morning, but she should have known better than to let a stranger into the house just because he claimed to be a relative.

Still, the better part of my anger was directed firmly at Welty.

"What on earth do you think you're doing, turning up here again?"

"Checking up on my half of the property," he said. "I see you replaced the broken window."

I could feel the flush rising to my cheeks. "I would like you to leave, now. I expressly told you that if you needed to contact me, you should do it through my attorney who informs me that your attorney is in full agreement that you are to stay away . . ."

He got up slowly. "As it happens, my guy is faxing your guy, even as we speak. I have every right to keep a close eye on property in which I have an interest."

He looked around the messy room and flashed me a laconic smile. "Clearly, somebody should be keeping an eye on what you are doing to this house."

I opened my mouth, but he was moving to the door, and discretion seemed the better part of valor. I held my tongue, opened the door, and gave it a swift and satisfying push as his back disappeared down the steps.

I looked up at Lulu, who stood on the stairwell. "Time for bed. I'll be up in a minute."

"Bos-sy," I heard her grumble. But I turned my attention to Penny.

"For heaven's sake, Pen, I would have thought you'd know better than to let some stranger into the house."

"I know," she agreed. "He said he was your cousin. Is he?"

"I don't know. Maybe. . . . Either way, anybody could have said that."

"You're right. I'm sorry. It won't happen again." She looked totally crestfallen.

I gave her a hug. "I know. It's okay. I just, I don't know why I'm so jumpy."

She gave me a wan smile. "I can't imagine. New home, new life, all these decisions to make . . . I'm glad I decided to come with you, Julie. One familiar face in a town full of cowboys and bogey men."

I looked at her—really looked at her. There was barely ten years difference between Penny and me, but I tended to think of her as a teenaged sitter or an ever-present younger sister. But in fact, she was a functioning adult and one with a fairly logical mind, given her years in law school.

For a moment, I was tempted to blurt out everything that had been weighing on me since my return to Deadwood: the puzzling string of deaths, the missing diary pages, the fear that the future I thought I was building could be yanked out from under my feet, and the vague but never far away feeling I was living my life smack in the center of some great, cosmic dartboard.

But in the end, I just smiled. "You're right. I guess I was just a little rattled. Sit for a minute before I go upstairs and tell me what happened with Harrison."

He was eager to start her helping out at his office with twenty hours or so a week, she told me. It was enough time to help him get his practice back on track and still help me out at home when I needed her.

"That's great, Penny," I said without hesitation. "I'll pretty much be here during construction, anyway, and this can be great experience for you, if you want to do it."

"Why not?" Penny grinned. "Who knows, maybe I'll decide to make this a permanent move. If I do, this could be a great jump-start on learning South Dakota law."

She did a little dance step and smiled shyly. ". . . And anyway, I think the man's a hottie!"

I laughed, gave her a high-five, and headed up the stairs, where Lulu was sitting up against her pillows reading Judy Blume's *Forever*.

I had bought the book for her months ago, primarily because, while we had talked about sex, and although Lulu's eye for boys seemed slow in developing, I felt the characters in this story about teenagers in love were especially true to life and a good lesson in making good decisions even in the flush of first love.

"Good book?" I asked her.

"I just started it."

"Oh. Well, you know you can come to me any time if you have any questions . . ."

"I know."

I nodded. "Good."

I watched her for a long moment, this woman-child I loved so fiercely. How proud Marty would have been of her!

I sat on the bed and hugged her tightly. "Love you."

"Love you more."

It wouldn't be long before she wanted a driver's license. But for the moment, she wanted a new bike. I didn't know why I found comfort in that, but I did.

I thought about going back downstairs, but it had been a tiring day, and the sleep interruptions I'd been having lately were doing nothing to help me rest. I took a long, slow, lavender-scented bubble bath and crawled into bed with my eyes already at half-mast.

I resisted the urge to look at Katy's diary and curled into a ball beneath the covers. But it seemed as though I had barely tumbled into sleep when an odd sensation of light passed across my eyelids. I struggled up, startled and confused, but frankly angrier than scared.

I threw off the covers, marched barefoot to the window and shoved the curtains aside, raising the window and leaning halfway out into the darkness. I saw the moving beam of a flashlight. It must have been what had awakened me.

"Who's there?" I shouted to a shadowy figure who turned the light in my direction.

"Ms. Goldman, is that you?" The figure came closer. "Gosh, I'm sorry if I woke you."

Perplexed, I watched through narrowed eyes as the figure quickly took shape. It was one of the officers who'd been the first to respond when the living room window had been smashed.

I squinted again. "Officer Reyes, is that you?"

"Yes, ma'am."

"What are you doing here?"

He turned off the flashlight. "Patrolling, ma'am. Chief's orders. He instructed us to keep a regular watch on your property."

"Uh huh. Does that include aiming your flashlight through my window?"

There was just enough moonlight to make out his self-conscious smile.

"No, ma'am. That was careless. I'm really sorry if I woke you."

I took a deep breath. "Okay, thank you, Officer. Everything's fine here, thanks and thanks for keeping an eye on the place."

I closed the window, rearranged the curtains, and sat on the edge of the bed, wondering if I was turning into Chicken Little, waiting for the sky to fall. But sleep was gone, at least for the moment. I pulled Katy's diary out of the drawer.

Choosing a page at random, I read the entry she had written the day our kitty-cat disappeared. Katy had been fairly certain he'd been caught by some hungry coyote. But she'd wanted to keep that from me. "*Just as well,*" she had written, "*for Julie to be a kid for as long as she possibly can.*"

I sighed. *Oh, Katy, how different things might have been if you hadn't tried to shield me from the truth . . . if we knew who it was you'd been so eager to meet in the middle of that long-ago night. . . .*

I closed the diary and took a long look at the water-stained cover. *Where had it been to incur such damage? Where had Aunt Sarah found it? And when?*

I turned to the back of the book, to the tattered remnants where pages had been ripped from the spine. For the first time, the realization hit me that it might not have been Katy who'd destroyed them. *Why would she, when she had no idea she might never see the diary again?*

What if Aunt Sarah had torn the missing pages out later? Why, and where were they now?

Not for the first time, I thought about Doreen wanting to tell me something, and as I sat there ruminating, something else came to mind, lighting up the corners of my mind like headlights on a foggy day. Mrs. Kovich telling me, after the funeral, that my aunt had been wanting to contact me.

Why, after so many years? Could it have had something to do with the missing pages? Something Doreen wanted to tell me? Something to do with her sudden death?

I put away the diary and huddled under the covers, but my eyes remained stubbornly open, and the ghosts I had lived with for most of my life marched across my field of vision. My parents . . . Katy . . . Marty . . . Bubbe Lou. . . .

I reached deep to find the sense of well-being I had worked so hard to build.

But now Aunt Sarah marched in behind them, along with Doreen and Nancy Jamison.

I stared into the night. *Some bizarre Karmic prank?*

Try as I might, I couldn't think so.

THIRTY

In the morning, after breakfast, I picked my way through the narrow pathway we'd cleared through the dining room and made two calls from the living room phone. The first was to Charlie at the police station. I wanted to tease him about the Keystone Kop he had sent to watch over my house, but he stopped me in my tracks.

"Hey," he said. "You saved me a call. I was thinking maybe tomorrow night—best ribs you ever ate, a little place just north of Lead."

"Yum. I love ribs."

"Great, so do I. You're welcome to bring Lulu." It was almost an afterthought. "Penny, too, if you like or maybe . . . just the two of us this time. Totally up to you."

It was my turn to smile. "I pick just the two of us this time . . ."

"Perfect." I could almost see a smile on his face. "I'll pick you up at seven."

I decided to save the teasing for later. "Sounds good," I said. "I'll look forward to it."

"Me, too. But wait a minute. It was you who called me."

"Right," I said, thinking fast. "Um, I told Lulu we'd go bike-shopping. Is there someplace local we can go?"

"Yep, there's a bike shop in Hill City, I know, and I think there's one in Spearfish. Hold on a sec. I'll look them up."

But I already knew as much, thanks to a brief search on my phone.

"Thanks, no need. I'm sure I can find them, and thanks, too, for the invitation, Charlie. I'll see you tomorrow at seven."

My second call was to the coroner Charlie told me had signed Aunt Sarah's death certificate. I found him in the phone book, J.D. Rafferty, M.D., listed twice, once under "Physicians" and again under "County Offices, Coroner."

He wasn't available at either number, but I was able to make an appointment to see him in his medical office later in the afternoon.

Penny and Lulu were playing Battleship at the only clear surface available in the house—the kitchen table. I was on my way in there when the phone rang.

"Hey, Julie, it's Harrison. Good morning."

"Hi." I wriggled my way back into the same small space I'd just left, on a pile of sofa pillows jammed haphazardly into one corner of the living room. "I hear you have a new employee. Do you want to talk to Penny?"

"So I do, and I'm delighted. Thanks for bringing her to town! I know she'll be just the help I need. I think we'll be getting her started on Monday. But actually, at the moment, it's you I need to speak to. I have some faxes here that came in overnight from Hanford Welty's attorney. I'd like to go over them with you."

I made a sour face. "He was here again the other night—Welty, that is. He was waiting for me when I got home from the library. I ushered him out and told him again he was to contact me only through you."

"You did the right thing. There's no reason for him to be on your property."

I nodded. "So, we still don't know . . ."

"Not conclusively, no. But if you have some time today, can you drop by my office for a few minutes?"

I checked my notes for Rafferty's address. I thought it was not far from Harrison's office. "I have an appointment at one this afternoon. Can I see you sometime after that?"

"Sure, I've got a Rotary meeting till two. Any time after that is fine."

"Good." I wriggled up from the nest of pillows. "See you sometime after two."

"Say hi to Penny. Tell her I look forward to seeing her bright and early Monday morning."

"Will do." I headed back to the kitchen. "That was Harrison," I announced.

Penny looked up.

"He's looking forward to seeing you on Monday morning."

Penny made a show of studying her Battleship board, but her mind was elsewhere. I could tell.

I sat at the table. "Listen, guys, I've got a couple of appointments in town this afternoon, and Nate Miller will probably be here to get some work started." I looked up at the noisy cat-clock. "What do you guys have in mind for today?"

"Well," Penny said, "if I'm starting work on Monday, I'd like to have some fun today with Lu. Maybe take a picnic out to the lake."

I considered the logistics and realized for the first time that having only one car between the two of us could definitely become an issue. But Penny didn't have much money, and the unaccounted-for expense was more than I thought I could afford.

"Look." I opened the refrigerator door to take stock of the pickings. "Go ahead and pack your picnic lunch. You can drop me downtown whenever we're ready and then head out to the lake. I can either catch an Uber, or you can pick me up when you're ready."

"Yay," Lulu said, scrambling to pack up the game.

"Sounds good to me." Penny got up to help. "We can always keep in touch by cell."

Amazingly, we were ready in half an hour and headed out the door, Lu and Penny swinging a picnic basket filled with sandwiches, fruit, and bottled water. But we all stopped dead in our tracks and stared. My car stood on an ominous tilt in the driveway.

"Nuts," I muttered, making a circuit around it. The left rear tire was flat. "Back in the house, guys." I shooed them in. "I could probably change it if I put my mind to it, but it might be faster to call a garage."

I sighed heavily, kicking the tire. *Another juvenile prankster?* Fuming in spite of myself, I checked my phone and called the nearest garage. They promised help in a matter of minutes. So, I gave the old porch swing a workout until a tow truck turned into the driveway. The girls came out to take over the swing when I headed down the front steps.

The driver was a cheerful older man in bibbed overalls, with rosy cheeks, a balding pate, and an unruly walrus-like moustache. "No worries," he bellowed. "Just your standard flat, looks like. We'll have you on the road in minutes."

I checked my watch as he grabbed a jack and headed toward the offending tire.

"Sam DiSpano," he told me, bending down for a closer look. "New here, aren't you? There was an older lady who lived in this house, I—well, hello!"

He looked around and reached to his left to pick up something from the ground.

I walked over to see what he was holding.

"This here's the cap to the valve stem."

I peered at it, knowing full well what it was and feeling my frustration turn to fury.

"This wasn't no leak," Sam DiSpano said, confirming what I already knew. "Prob'ly nothing wrong with the tire. Looks like somebody let the air out."

THIRTY-ONE

I backed out of my driveway, steaming, within minutes after DiSpano's tow truck pulled out of it. Getting the air back into my tire was easy. Figuring out who had let it out in the first place was apt to be a whole lot harder.

There was no way this was some random prank, not this close on the heels of the shattered front window. More likely, somebody was making some kind of statement, and I was determined to find out who and *why*.

Officer Reyes had presumably seen nothing suspicious when he was making his rounds of the property the other night. But nights could be long, as I was finding out, and dark. It would have taken only seconds for someone to yank the cap off the valve stem and take off into the night. By car? On a bicycle? On foot?

I wondered if it was worth calling Charlie again, asking him to send someone around to look for bike treads or tire treads other than mine.

But several vehicles had pulled in and out of the driveway in the last few days alone: police cars, the guy from the hardware store, the tow truck, and Nate Miller. There had even been a kid on a bicycle taking subscriptions for the local paper.

Nate had arrived a few minutes earlier, just before the tow truck left. He parked his dusty pick-up across the road and walked past us to the front door. He didn't bother to ask what had happened. *Was that because he already knew?*

And what about Hanford Welty, my erstwhile cousin? He could have popped the cap off the valve stem in seconds on his way out of the house. Come to think of it, I hadn't noticed another vehicle in my driveway when I drove in after the board meeting. *How the heck did Welty get there, and just how brazen was he?*

Then I thought about Rennie Malcolm, who was clearly seething by the time I left the library meeting. *Was he angry enough, childish enough, to stop by my house in the middle of the night and let the air out of my tires?*

It was a short stretch to realize that each of three had, or thought he had, good reason to resent my coming back to town. Every one of them had had something to gain by Aunt Sarah's death—more, perhaps, if I were out of the picture. But a broken window and a flat tire were pretty juvenile ways to show their anger.

It was something to consider, I told myself as I pulled up in front of the medical offices of J.D. Rafferty, M.D. I'd been so lost in thought I had hardly been aware that Lu and Penny were in the car. But now I slid out from behind the wheel so Penny could take over.

"I'll call you when I'm done here in town, and we'll figure it out from there, okay?" I blew a kiss to Lu and patted Penny on the shoulder. "Have fun. See you later."

Rafferty's outer office was assembly-line efficient; a U-shaped grouping of green tweed chairs anchored together by corner tables stacked with assorted magazines. A couple of tired green plants stood sentry in the corners, and a small cubicle fronted by frosted glass hid the receptionist from view.

The office was empty, and I moved directly to the window. The glass slid open and a gray-haired woman with several chins looked up from her lunch.

"Sorry," she said, moving her lunch aside. "I shouldn't be eating at my desk."

"No problem," I assured her. "I'm Julie Goldman. I have an appointment to see Dr. Rafferty."

"So you do," she agreed, running a manicured finger down the page of an appointment book. "May I ask why you need to see the doctor?"

I blinked. "Oh, I'm not a patient," I told her. "I made the appointment to consult with Doctor Rafferty in his capacity as county coroner."

The woman managed a toothy smile. "Ah. Well, please have a seat."

I sat, looking across the empty space at a seascape on the far wall, which seemed like an odd choice of artwork for an office in the Black Hills of South Dakota. But the thought barely registered before the inner door opened and the receptionist called my name.

She led me down a short hall and into the doctor's inner sanctum, a narrow space just large enough to accommodate a desk, three chairs and a file cabinet.

"Have a seat," she directed me again. "The doctor will be with you shortly."

I supposed it was possible he was with a patient, though I heard no voices or movement. But in a moment, a stout, balding man in a starched white jacket strode into the room. He sat behind his desk, leaning in toward me as closely as his paunch would allow.

He stuck out a hand. "Ms. Goldman, I presume. Pleased to meet you. Tell me how I can help you."

He looked directly at me, which I found reassuring. I smiled and shook his outstretched hand, taking in pale but alert blue eyes and a pinkish face that clearly never saw much sun.

"I don't know if you've made the connection, Dr. Rafferty, but I'm Sarah Lacey's niece. I'm hoping you remember my aunt. She passed away some weeks ago."

"Well, of course," he assured me. "Everyone here knew Sarah. She was quite a special lady. Half the city turned out for her funeral after she died so suddenly."

"Yes." I nodded. "And that's why I'm here. My aunt and I had been . . . estranged for a while. But from what I've been told, her death really was quite sudden."

"Acute myocardial infarction, as I recall. I can look back at my notes if you like. But it was, plain and simple, a heart attack. It happens sometimes, quite suddenly, especially in people with risk factors."

"What risk factors?"

The doctor hesitated. "I don't like to discuss the state of my patients' health, even with family after they're gone, but I can tell you that Sarah was overweight. She had a history of elevated blood pressure and cholesterol, which was not unusual in a woman her age. Statistically, you know, the most common cause of death is cardiovascular, and as I said, these things happen all the time."

I thought it over. "I see . . ."

Rafferty looked at me.

"What about an autopsy?" I asked. "Would an autopsy have been your decision?"

His back stiffened. "Absolutely. But in this case, there was no reason to order one."

I waited.

"Sarah's body was found, still warm in her bed, by our chief of police, Charlie Banks. She was seventy-seven, showed no signs of struggle, and nothing seemed out of the ordinary. The chief himself examined the premises for any sign of forced entry or foul play, and I was there to examine the body within the hour. Given Sarah's medical history, there was no reason to think anything else but a heart attack and no indication for autopsy."

The doctor looked pointedly at his watch. Clearly, he was getting impatient. His reasoning seemed sound, and to question him further seemed useless.

I got up to leave, no closer to any answers than I had been before I came. "Thanks for seeing me, Doctor Rafferty. I hope I haven't taken too much time."

I walked out into the bright sunshine deflated, wondering if my half-baked theories were delusions or an overblown reaction to a couple of mischievous but likely meaningless shenanigans.

It was just after one thirty when I left the doctor's office. It was too early to see Harrison. Anyway, I was starving. I decided to stop in at the café.

As I walked past the Midnight Star Casino, a man came storming out of the place and nearly knocked me down. He didn't appear to notice me, but I recognized him right away. I watched Hanford Welty move quickly down the street before I went on to the café.

It was late in the lunch hour, and the place was half empty. Earlene greeted me as if I were an old friend.

"Julie, how are you? How's Lulu?"

"Fine," I said, taking a seat at the counter. "She's growing up faster than I'd like."

Earlene smiled, handing me a menu. "They sure do have a way of doing that."

I ordered a tuna sandwich and an iced tea with lemon and handed the menu back to her. "The mountain air seems to agree with her, though. She doesn't seem to miss the beach."

Earlene grinned, scooping ice into a glass. "Well, good! Your aunt would be happy."

Would she? Would Aunt Sarah be happy to know I was back here in Deadwood? I shivered. I had a soul-shaking premonition there was something she wanted me to know.

"The word is," Earlene said and set a sandwich in front of me, "you've started rehabbing the old house."

"Yes." *The Deadwood pipeline at work.* "Nate Miller is doing the renovation."

"Mmm." She nodded. "He wanted to, real bad. Don't know that Sarah was ready, though."

"Really?"

"Mmm. She had some reservations, for sure. But she was a good sort, Sarah. She would have hated to throw a wrench in his plans. Nate was so eager to remodel the place."

And now she was gone, and here I was, caving in with hardly a fight.

I picked up the sandwich and took a bite, but my appetite was strangely gone. I managed to eat half of it.

"Got to go, Earlene," I said. "I'm on my way to an appointment."

"Do you want a takeout box?" Earlene called after me.

But I was halfway out the red door.

THIRTY-TWO

It wasn't quite two, but the "Open" sign was faced forward in the storefront window. The outer door to Harrison's office was open, and his inner door was ajar.

"Hey, Julie," he said, hanging his jacket on a coat rack. "Your timing is perfect. Come on in."

He was casual but business-like in dark jeans and a checked shirt with a bolo tie at the neck. He looked chic and with it, a true country professional. I could understand why Penny seemed smitten.

"Hi." I took a seat in my usual chair. "I can half-guess why you wanted to see me."

Harrison nodded, pulling a thin file out of the stack piled on his desk. "I have to tell you," he said, "based on all the material faxed to me by his attorney, it appears Hanford Welty is who he says he is."

He handed me a copy of a birth certificate.

I looked at it. Hanford Eugene Welty, born April 6, 1977, at Women's Hospital, Columbus, Ohio. The mother was listed as Pauline Lacey Welty, the father as Joseph A. Welty, deceased.

"How do we know for certain that Pauline Lacey was a sister to my mother and Aunt Sarah?"

He handed me another fax, a copy of another birth certificate. Pauline Jean Lacey, Springfield, Missouri, March 9, 1948. My mother would have been about eight years old then, Aunt Sarah ten or eleven. Pauline's parents were listed on the certificate as Kathleen Emerson and Franklin Emerson. My grandparents. I recognized their names.

I looked up at Harrison, trying to make sense of what I was feeling.

"I don't know what to say," I told him. "These certainly do seem genuine. It seems my family was very good at keeping secrets. Or maybe I was just too young to understand."

I sat back in my chair. "I was ten years old when my parents died. Shortly after that, I went to live with Aunt Sarah, who I'd never even heard of until my grandmother sent me here. I don't think anyone, even my grandmother, knew that Aunt Sarah had a daughter, and I don't remember ever discussing family with anyone all the years I was growing up."

"I understand," Harrison said. "Families can be a tricky business. But at this point, anyway, you're absolutely right. These do appear to be legitimate."

I nodded. "So, I have a living cousin. Hanford Eugene Welty . . . I'm not sure how I feel about that. He's been anything but friendly or interested in anything except the possible value of the house."

Harrison said nothing.

"What does this mean in terms of my inheritance?"

Harrison cleared his throat. "Well, several options come to mind. The first is to acknowledge him as a bonafide claimant and hand over half the estate."

I blinked.

"But I don't think it will come to that. Welty may be a legitimate nephew, but he had no relationship with Sarah during her lifetime, that I'm aware of, and there is no evidence that she even knew of his existence or if she did, that she wanted him to inherit. Her instructions were pretty clear about that."

"So, what does that mean? Will he just pack up and go away?"

"No, I don't think so. He seems adamant in his intent to challenge her will, and while I don't think he could make a winning case in court, there may be no need to let it go that far."

I waited.

"I think we need to investigate a bit into his background and finances. I know someone who can do that for us. Welty's retained representation thus far, but who knows whether he's got the funds to press on? If it's just a quick little killing he's after, I'd recommend another option: offer him a settlement. One that's small but attractive enough to make him back off from any further claim on the estate."

It seemed sensible, and I trusted Harrison.

"Go ahead and do what we need to do. It seems a shame that I can't pursue a relationship with my only living cousin. But he's really being obnoxious. He may have gone so far as to let the air out of one of my tires just to remind me that he's out there watching."

"You did the right thing, letting him know in no uncertain terms that personal contact is unacceptable at this time. I'll remind his attorney to make that clear to him, and if Welty continues to badger you in any way, we can get a restraining order against him."

I'd worked with a woman at the hotel in Dana Point who had a restraining order against her former husband. It didn't keep him from accosting her in a parking lot and breaking her arm and several ribs.

I shuddered at the thought, but I managed a smile. "Thanks, Harrison. I appreciate your help."

He walked me to the door, and I suddenly remembered I didn't have my car. I could call for an Uber, but the afternoon was lovely, and I was in no hurry. I decided to walk the mile and a half from town.

I stopped for an ice cream and turned the first corner toward home. Pulling out my cell, I called Penny. "Hey, it's me, Pen. Where are you?"

"Still at the lake. We waded in to our knees. It's cold, but it's very pretty here, and there are lots of people out today. Lulu's made a couple of new friends."

"Great. Well, don't hurry. I'm walking home from town. Did I tell you I have a dinner date with Charlie?"

"All right," Penny chuckled. "Good for you! We'll be home in a couple of hours. There's leftover pasta from the other night. That'll be fine for us."

"Perfect." I stopped to watch a bushy-tailed squirrel shinny up a towering oak. "I'm sure you'll be home before I leave. Have fun! See you later."

A cool breeze filtered through the afternoon sun. I loved the sound of it rustling through the trees. It put me in mind of lazy afternoons when Katy and I would ditch the school bus and take the long walk home.

Eventually, I made the turn into Bluebird Hill Lane. Nate's pick-up was gone. But I had to say, I felt a little uneasy as I got closer to the house. I half expected to find another broken window or a big, red X painted on the door.

Nothing seemed amiss, but it occurred to me suddenly that a dog might be a good idea. Lulu would be thrilled, and it wouldn't hurt to have a dog on the property.

To be on the safe side, I walked down the slope and around to the back of the house. I had to smile. Big, brave me. What did I expect to find?

Nate had apparently cleared some brush in preparation for pushing out a wall. Amid the debris were a pile of rotting boards and what looked like some rusted pipes.

In a flash, I recalled a narrow little outbuilding that had sat not far from the house—a shed of some kind, or maybe the remains of what once upon a time had been an outhouse. I remembered it was dirty and smelled like wet socks, and Aunt Sarah had yelled at me more than once to stay away from it. Now I approached the pile of debris with caution.

The brush was tinder dry, and the rusting pipes left a powdery film on my fingertips. But the rotting boards, when I reached out to touch them, felt vaguely damp to the touch, as if they had been subject over the years to the steady drip-drip of water, and it came to me with a fleeting certainty that this was the place, in the damp remains of the old shed, where Katy might have hidden her diary.

Maybe she put it there for safekeeping, hidden away from prying eyes if she began to write about a lover. But she never retrieved it, and at some point, who knew when or why, Aunt Sarah must have discovered it water damaged, but still readable, just as I had found it in her night table.

But she wouldn't have had any reason to tear out the last few pages. *So, the question was, who had and what secrets had been revealed in them?*

More importantly, where were they now? Whose eyes had been the last to read them?

THIRTY-THREE

Charlie arrived in a jacket and slacks just before seven o'clock, with flowers for me, a pretty desk clock "for Penny the working girl," and a book, *An Introduction to Grooming Horses*, for Lu.

"If you're going to ride Sparkle," he told her soberly, "you're going to have to know how to groom her afterward."

Lulu's eyes were wide. "All right! When can I ride again?"

Charlie shrugged. "Up to your mom. We'll discuss it."

He drove us to a place called Chez LeBlanc, somewhere just out of Spearfish, a faux brick building set with strings of twinkling lights and set far back on a wide, green lawn.

"I'm not much on this continental stuff," he said. "But they tell me the ladies ~~like it.~~ like it—and the ribs are good."

The interior was subdued but inviting, with lacy half-curtains at the windows, pale watercolors on the walls, and flickering tea lights on every table. Soft music blurred the voices of half a dozen couples around the room.

"Nice," I said, as we slipped into a booth. "I'm betting the food is great."

Charlie looked at me from across the table. "You look nice. Really nice."

I was wearing my all-purpose little black dress, the same one he'd seen a couple times before. But I'd tied on a soft, silvery scarf, my hair was piled on top of my head, and at Penny's insistence, I'd taken more time than usual on my make-up.

"Thank you," I smiled. "So do you."

We ordered a white wine suggested by the waiter and a small log of brie with crackers.

"So," Charlie said when the wine was poured. "How have you been? Settling in?"

I shrugged. "I guess so." I wasn't sure where to begin. "I haven't been sleeping terribly well."

"Why's that?"

I had planned to tease him about his Keystone Kops waking me up with a flashlight. But that was hardly the only thing keeping me awake, and this didn't seem the time for a ribbing.

I took a deep breath. "To tell you the truth, I'm beginning to get the feeling that somebody doesn't want me back in Deadwood."

Charlie frowned. "Why?"

"It may not seem like much, but the broken front window, for openers, and then the flat tire." I filled him in on the latest incident. "It seems childish, I know, but it's more than just that. It's a feeling, I don't know, an attitude. Sometimes it seems wherever I am, I can feel hostility coming at me."

Charlie sat up straighter. "What are you saying? You think somebody is threatening you?"

Now I felt silly. "Not directly, Charlie, it's hard to explain . . ."

Then I blurted it out. "I know it sounds silly, but I'm beginning to think there might have been something fishy about my Aunt Sarah's sudden death."

He started to say something, but I stopped him with a gesture. "I spoke to Doctor Rafferty, and he assured me, just as you said, that she died of a sudden heart attack."

I hesitated. "But I think maybe she might have learned something about who Katy was seeing before she died and that somebody else knew that, too . . ."

Charlie listened, his brows knit together. "Who?"

"I don't know. I don't know. But in the back of my head, I have this crazy feeling there's something I'm not seeing."

"Julie, I was there that night . . . the night your Aunt Sarah died. Granted, I don't know why she had called me earlier, but there was absolutely no reason to think her death was anything but natural."

"I know, I know, and I have to say, my track record on trusting my feelings hasn't always been great. I just, I think there are some people in town who may have had a lot to gain if Aunt Sarah was out of their way, and now here I come to complicate the issue . . . I don't know. It's just a feeling—all these silly little signs—that somebody wants me gone, too."

Charlie looked at me sternly. "Who are these, 'some people,' Julie? Can you name them?"

I shook my head. "I'm still not ready to point fingers. Maybe I'm way off-track . . ." I tried a smile. "Poor Charlie. All you did was ask how I was doing."

He reached across the table and took my hands in his. It made me feel safe and cared for. It was a feeling I wasn't accustomed to, but I knew I could learn to like.

"Julie," he said, "thank you for trusting me with that much. I think you know I care about you—on more than one level. As a cop, I'll do anything in my power to keep you safe from harm, but I ask you not to keep anything from me, or you'll make my job that much harder."

I nodded.

"If I need to, I'll camp out on your lawn every night just to make sure you're okay."

I smiled and was about to make some smart remark, when Charlie's face grew serious.

"And there's something else," he said quietly. "Something you need to know . . ."

There was no mistaking the emotion behind his words.

"It's been a long time since I let myself daydream about having any kind of a family life, but since I met you, I find myself daydreaming again. I hope I'm not making a mistake."

I felt a prickling behind my eyes. I tried to blink it away. I was trying to formulate some kind of response when the waiter appeared at our table.

Charlie gently let go of my hands. "To be continued," he said, looking directly into my eyes as he took the menu from the waiter.

We passed on the ribs and ordered vichyssoise, a cold potato soup the waiter recommended, and duckling a l'orange, which I recommended, with duchess potatoes and asparagus. The waiter left, and there was an awkward moment. As usual, I jumped right in.

"You better have meant it, giving Lulu that book. She'll haunt you till she gets to ride again."

"She won't have to. It's fine with me. I'm off duty this Sunday."

I told him I thought that might work, that I was looking forward to the three of us spending more time together. I hoped that might satisfy his unanswered question, and apparently it did, because the soup arrived, and Charlie seemed content to settle in and enjoy the meal.

We talked about the renovation going on at the house, with no reference to my concerns about Nate. He mentioned the county fair coming up in a few weeks and the strain it would put on his already stretched-thin department.

We talked about the bike I planned to buy for Lu, how glad I was it wasn't a car, and my reluctance to see her fly faster and farther than I was ready for.

"I can't imagine anything harder," Charlie said, "than looking at your child's back as she struts out into the world."

I told him I was thinking of adopting a dog and how much Lu would love that. But mostly, I let myself relax enough to enjoy the wonderful dinner.

"Never had duck before," Charlie mumbled between bites. "I wouldn't have believed how good this is."

We finished with a shared dish of crème brûlée, dipping our spoons beneath the crackling sugar glaze and smacking our lips over the custard.

There was an awkward moment as we got back into his car and Charlie asked me back to his place for a nightcap. But I wasn't ready, and for all I knew, the girls would be waiting up for me.

I squeezed his hand. "I don't think so, Charlie. Not yet. But thanks for asking."

The drive home was slow and quiet, and when he pulled into my driveway, I thanked him profusely for a truly memorable evening.

"My pleasure," he murmured, leaning in for a slow, tender kiss. I found myself caught between simple pleasure and something a lot deeper.

To my relief, Lu and Penny had gone to bed, leaving a light on for me, so I could make my way across the living room. I picked my way through the obstacles and plopped down onto a couple of overturned sofa cushions. I was not ready to go upstairs, and I sat there for a long moment, leaning against the wall and replaying the evening.

Then I opened my eyes and looked around at every inch of the living room, trying to picture the space transformed into a sleek but comfortable multi-functional space. It might never have the grace of the Stevens Point Hotel, but I hoped it would be and warm and welcoming because despite what anyone else might have in mind, it was going to be my home and my daughter's.

It was hard to believe how my world had changed in the weeks since I'd left the hotel. Maybe it was time to stop thinking so much and simply let my new life happen.

As a matter of routine, I picked myself up and detoured into the kitchen. Dishes done, oven off, cupboards closed. The message light was blinking on the answering machine. Odd that no one had answered the phone.

I lifted the receiver, pressed the button, and listened to a series of clicks and beeps. Then a strange voice, oddly distorted. . . .

"Julie, Julie . . ." A strangled sigh. "When will you get the message?"

THIRTY-FOUR

I asked Penny, casually at breakfast, if anyone had called the night before. She told me she thought she'd heard the phone ringing sometime after she'd dropped off to sleep, but she didn't think it was worth getting up for.

"I figured if it was you," she said. "You would call me back on my cell phone. Anyone else could just leave a message."

I nodded, spooning jam on my toast. "Everything okay here, then?"

"Yep. Quiet night." She lowered her voice. "So, how was your date?"

"Very nice," I told her as Lulu charged down the stairs. I turned to my daughter. "How would you like to go riding at Charlie's on Sunday?"

She let out a whoop. "All right! And today I get my bike, right?"

I smiled, nearly as excited as she. "I'm going upstairs to get dressed. Morgan will be here at ten."

She arrived on the dot, with Faye, her mother. I could see Petey in the front seat of his mom's Explorer.

"It's wonderful you can take Morgan today," Faye said. "Mom's at the shop, and I need to run some errands with Petey, some stuff he needs to finish up his Eagle project."

"No problem," I assured her. "Take as long as you need. We're going bike-shopping. Morgan can help Lu choose."

I debated calling Charlie about the message on my machine. I had listened to it twice last night and gone up to bed without deleting it. Once again, I had not slept very well, but now, in the light of day, it seemed ridiculous—another childish prank, maybe more inconsequential than the first two. I marched into the kitchen, pushed the delete button, and very nearly scrubbed the pattern off the few dishes in the sink.

By eleven, the four of us were strolling the aisles of the bike shop. The array of colors, styles, and accessories was almost more than the human eye could register.

"Hey, Morg, which do you like better?" Lulu was a study in concentration. "The red one or this cool silver number?"

It was a moot question because Morgan was inspecting a snazzy electric blue cruiser, and Penny and I watched silently as the two girls flitted from one model to another.

Choosing a new bike was a rite of passage I had never experienced for myself, having inherited Katy's outgrown Schwinn shortly after I arrived at Aunt Sarah's. But Penny assured me it was only a little less significant, in the scheme of things, than picking out your first new car.

"I wouldn't know about that, either" I told her. "I've never bought anything but 'pre-owned.'"

Penny laughed and moved ahead to put her two cents into the decision. I stared in wonder at a never-ending display of saddles, grips, bells, and baskets, caught between resolve to let my daughter choose whatever she liked and a lifelong habit of pinching pennies.

Eventually, the three of them reached consensus on the burgundy model, duly outfitted with custom grips and a white wicker basket "guaranteed to withstand weather damage."

I flinched when the bill came to more than I had paid for my bus ticket out of Deadwood, but I hadn't seen Lulu this excited since her first afternoon on the ice. She watched, clucking like a mother hen as the store manager loaded her baby into the trunk of my car and tied a red flag on the portion that stuck out.

We stopped for burgers on the way home, Lulu keeping a watchful eye on the back end of the car, and I have to say I was prepared for most anything when I made the last turn into Bluebird Hill Lane.

Nate's pick-up was parked in the middle of the driveway, which I thought was pretty territorial of him, but apart from that, nothing seemed amiss. We unloaded the bicycle—carefully, lest we dare to leave a scratch— and Lu hopped on for a short spin around the cul-de-sac.

When I opened the front door, a cloud of plaster dust hit me in the face and the noise was all but deafening, as though a giant jackhammer was making short work of the walls. I motioned Penny to stay outside and picked my way through the cloud. Nate Miller, in plaster-covered overalls, was manning the ear-splitting machine.

He hit a switch and the noise level dipped. "Sorry," he shouted over the din. "This won't take more than a couple of hours."

"What are we supposed to do in the meantime?"

Nate shrugged. "Had to be done sometime. Why don't you head out somewhere for a couple of hours . . . the park, or the community pool?"

I'd heard about the pool, but we'd not yet been there. It sounded like a good idea. I nodded. "Can I go upstairs for a minute?"

He nodded, bending over the jackhammer. "Let me know when you're out of here."

I climbed the stairs to what was left of Lulu's bedroom and pulled a couple of swimsuits and extra T-shirts out of the bureau. I found a bikini and a cover-up in Penny's room, and I grabbed a swimsuit and shirt out of mine.

Stuffing them all into an oversized beach bag, I gathered a stack of towels from the linen closet and headed back downstairs.

"Okay, I'm leaving," I shouted to Nate. "What time will you be out of here?"

"Not sure," he shouted back. "I'll try to be out by five."

Muttering, I headed back outside in time to see Lulu cruising smoothly up the driveway.

"Put the bike in the garage," I told her. "We can't get in the house right now for all the noise and plaster dust."

I held out the beach bag. "Who's up for the community swimming pool?"

We got back in the car and headed out to the pool. In the parking lot, I pulled out my cell phone. I couldn't reach Faye, but Hannah answered at the flower shop.

"We're locked out of the house this afternoon because of the construction," I told her. "We're headed for a dip in the community pool. Tell Faye to pick up Morgan at your house. I'll drop her off when we're done here."

Hannah insisted we stay for dinner. "Nothing fancy, but it won't be covered with plaster dust."

The weather was warm in the heart of summer, and the community pool was large and inviting, surrounded by colorful umbrella tables and chairs set out on a wide concrete deck. At a table in the shade, I spotted Rennie Malcolm, looking distinctly out of place in a business suit, deep in conversation with Roy Bachman, whom I recognized from the foundation board meeting.

Rennie made a point of ignoring me. When I walked past him and said hello, he grunted something unintelligible and turned away. I continued walking to the deep end of the pool, then dove in with a satisfying splash.

The four of us played around and swam a few laps in the sparsely populated pool. I was pleased to see Lu could keep up with Morgan, who was a good, strong swimmer, and pretty much with Penny, whom I didn't know until now had lettered in water polo in high school.

By four, exhausted, we climbed out and sunned on the nearly deserted deck. Malcolm and Bachman were gone. At quarter to five, we changed into dry clothes and headed out for Hannah's.

She had stopped on her way home from the shop and picked up a big bucket of chicken, and we all pitched in to set the table.

"It's Friday," I reminded Lu. "But the candlesticks are at home."

"Candlesticks. Not to worry." Hannah set a pair on the table and rummaged in a drawer for candles and a couple of linen napkins.

We draped the napkins over our heads.

"Do we know the prayer by heart?" I asked Lu.

She raised her eyebrows questioningly, but we surprised ourselves, reciting it from memory with ease.

I tried my best to let everything fall away and steep myself in the quiet of the Sabbath. But I couldn't seem to let go of the tension that was settling deep into my bones. I felt as though I was waiting for something . . . like another shoe to drop.

THIRTY-FIVE

As it turned out, I didn't have long to wait.

We'd spent much of Saturday cleaning up after Nate, and while Penny lounged in the tub on Sunday making herself beautiful for work the next day, Lulu and I had a lovely afternoon at Charlie's ranch.

It was the best kind of mountain day, warm and sunny with enough of a breeze to dapple the leaves of the treetops. I watched Charlie help Lu tack up, and they headed out for a trail ride. The dogs slept under an oak tree, and the ranch was so quiet, I could hear Lu's voice and the clop of the horse's hooves even after they'd disappeared into the woods.

They were gone for nearly an hour and a half while I slouched in a rocker on the porch, sipped a glass of cold lemonade, and worked the Sunday crossword.

When they came back, Charlie let Lu help him remove the saddles and blankets, and he gave her a lesson on cooling down the horses and grooming them with a curry comb and brush. He was patient and encouraging, and Lulu's brown eyes literally shone with excitement.

"I don't know, Lu," I teased. "You may have to choose between ice skating and horseback."

We roasted hot dogs and marshmallows over the barbecue grill, and Lu taught us a *SpongeBob SquarePants* campfire song as the sun dipped below the hills. Charlie pretty much kept his distance, with Lu privy to our every move, but the ambience was easy and familiar, and it was well past her bedtime when we got home.

I fell asleep that night without much difficulty, but at a little after two in the morning, something jolted me awake.

I threw on a robe and padded to the window, half expecting to see Charlie camped out on my lawn, making good on his word to keep watch. But it was quiet outside. I saw nothing, and I told myself I was being an idiot.

Then on Monday morning, the phone rang just minutes after Penny took the car and left for work.

"Good morning, Julie, it's Harrison."

"Hey, Harrison, good morning to you. Penny's on her way to the office."

"Great. I came in a little early to get some stuff ready for her. But actually, I need to talk to you."

I sat down on my little nest of sofa cushions. "Okay, what's up?"

"I have a preliminary report here from the investigator we hired. He didn't have to do much digging to find out that Hanford Welty is in over his head financially, mostly to a couple of Chicago card sharks."

I remembered seeing him storming full tilt out of the Midnight Star Casino.

"He owes something like eleven thousand dollars," Harrison said. "Could be more by now, who knows?"

I nodded. "For what it's worth, I happened to see him the other day barreling out of the Midnight Star. He was in a huff. Maybe he's not having much luck here, either. But what does that mean for us?"

"If he owes money, he may be looking for a quick way out. I still think a good option is to offer him a settlement in return for relinquishing any further claim on the estate. Maybe twenty-five thousand, enough to pretty much clear his debt and give him a head start on some kind of future."

It was a lot of money, but more than that, I had a sinking feeling it might not be enough to get him out of our hair. But we had to start somewhere.

"Okay," I agreed. "Let's do it."

"I'll draw up the paperwork," Harrison said. "He doesn't get a cent without signing away any further interest in the estate."

Lulu, amazingly, was still asleep. She was exhausted, I guessed, from sheer excitement over the new bike, the long trail ride and the campfire. I poured a cup of coffee, grabbed my checkbook, and decided to use the quiet time to pay a couple of bills.

When I was finished, I took my coffee mug outside and set it next to the porch swing, where I thought it might be nice to sit and enjoy the morning sun until Lu came downstairs. With the stamped envelopes in one hand, I headed down the path to the mailbox and yanked open the little metal door.

I jumped back a few steps when I saw a field mouse inside. Then I realized the creature wasn't moving. Cautiously, I bent for a closer look, fully prepared to leap back again if it moved. But it didn't. It simply lay there.

I stood up straight. There was a dead field mouse in my mailbox. I sincerely doubted it had clambered up the post under its own steam to yank open the door and drop dead inside. But if it hadn't, then someone had put it there.

I didn't know whether to be angry or scared or whether to laugh it off as just another stupid prank, except the stupid pranks were piling up faster than dirty socks in a locker room. Anger won out, and I found myself hopping mad, clamping my lips together to keep from screeching.

Dropping my envelopes to the ground, I rushed back to the house, grabbed a couple of paper towels, and ran back with them to pick the critter up by its tail and dump it into a trash can at the side of the house.

I wiped out the box, deposited the envelopes inside, slammed the door shut, and jerked up the faded red metal flag.

By this time, my adrenaline had mostly dissipated. I walked to the porch, picked up my coffee mug, plopped down on the porch swing, and promptly burst into tears—big, rolling tears of frustration, not so much because I was angry, but because once again, it was pretty clear that none of these little annoyances were random. Someone wanted me out of here, and maybe it was time to pay attention.

I ticked off all the ways things might be different around here if I had never responded to that first early-morning call from Charlie after my aunt's death.

Nate Miller might have worked out a deal with Harrison allowing him to use my aunt's house as collateral while he remodeled it, retaining primary interest in the new, income-producing property.

Rennie Malcolm might have manipulated the board into giving him full-time stewardship of the foundation, not to mention direct access to its funds.

And Hanford Welty, who for all I knew had been keeping tabs on the state of Aunt Sarah's health and finances for years, might have been able to stake his claim as the sole heir to her estate.

I, on the other hand, would still be living in Southern California, unemployed and with no financial cushion in the bank but with my equilibrium fairly intact and no more to worry about than paying the rent on time and getting Lulu to her skating lessons.

I would not be concerned with missing pages in a twenty-year-old diary. I would not be toying with forging some connection between Katy's death and my aunt's, much less with the accidental deaths of two women I barely knew.

And I definitely would not be stressed out over a smashed window, a flat tire, an enigmatic message on my answering machine, and a dead mouse in my mailbox!

"Mom!"

My daughter thumped her way down the stairs. Licking-my-wounds-time was over. I took a big gulp of the now-cold coffee. What was I going to do?

THIRTY-SIX

The answer to that, like so many other unanswered questions, was never far from my mind. I went about my daily life like I was stuck in a revolving door, minding Lu, keeping up with the bills, watching the house take on a new configuration right before my eyes.

But if I was wrestling with whether or not to stay, Lulu seemed to be flourishing. She was growing up before my eyes and relishing all the new experiences she'd had since we'd arrived in Deadwood. She adored Morgan and the whole notion of a Best Friend Forever, and the two of them spent hours tooling around on their bicycles, pining for nothing except maybe winter and a frozen lake to skate on.

Penny, too, moved blithely through the days with a new air of purpose and self-confidence. While it was only part time, she seemed to love the work at Harrison's, although I suspected it might have as much to do with her crush on him than on any newfound passion for the law.

On the surface, at least, we fell into a sort of routine. When Penny didn't need the car, we shopped, took day trips, sometimes picnicked at the lake or swam in the community pool. Three mornings a week, when Penny was up and out early, Lu and I arranged play dates with Morgan, Hannah, Petey, and the family, or with Charlie, when he had a day off. Or Lu and I read or played board games on the porch while Nate plugged away inside.

The hammering and sawing got to us sometimes, and it hadn't been easy sleeping in rooms where the walls sometimes didn't reach the ceiling. But the bedrooms had now been reconfigured and the new living/dining/reception room was beginning to take recognizable shape.

One morning, Nate confronted us in the middle of a Scrabble game. "I'm out of cash," he announced. "If you can pitch in a couple thousand dollars, I think I can have this finished by Labor Day."

I looked at him.

"Maybe twenty-five hundred," he amended, "for some crown molding, paint and flooring. Look, I'm flat broke. Every dollar I had has gone into this remodel, and you've got more than enough equity in the place to come up with a couple thousand dollars."

Equity that might have been yours, if I had not shown up to snatch it from under your nose.

As it was, I decided there was no point in bickering over a relatively small sum. "I'll get the cash for you," I said. "Just see that I have copies of the receipts. I'll need them all for tax purposes."

He made a wry face. "Yes, ma'am," he said, the only time he'd called me that since the first time he'd appeared on my doorstep.

He started to turn away, then turned back again. "One more thing," he said. "Once I'm finished, we're open for business, so we should get a little promotion going. You can handle that, I would think—some ads, maybe a press release. Anything to get the phone ringing and the paying guests coming in."

He paused. "I don't know about you, but I could sure use the income."

Maybe I was slow or had been too preoccupied with other things, but the fact that the bed and breakfast could be open for business in a matter of weeks caught me by surprise. Big time. I wasn't sure if Nate was being practical or condescending about my ability to do my part, but either way, he was right. I needed to get a start right now, not just on promoting the new business, but on breakfast menus, pricing, everything.

"You're right," I told him. "Thank you, Nate. I will. I'll get started right away."

He narrowed his eyes, surprised, that I didn't argue or get up on a high horse. He nodded curtly and made his way back inside.

"Can I put this game away," Lulu asked, "and maybe go for a bike ride?"

"Yes," I said. "But if you're alone, no more than a mile or two before you turn around for home."

"I know, I know, Miz Bossy." She was out of her chair, scooping Scrabble tiles into the box. "I'll call Morgan. Maybe she can meet me."

"Fine," I agreed. "But be back by dinner time."

I decided this was as good a time as any to dive into bed-and-breakfast plans. I went into the house, managed to dig up a yellow pad and pencil, and settled in the porch swing to work on some ad sketches. I had barely penciled in, "Bluebird Hill Bed and Breakfast" at the top of a page when my cell phone rang.

"Hey, it's me." I smiled at the sound of Charlie's voice. "What are you up to?"

"Well, believe it or not, as Nate just reminded me, I am about to become the proprietor of a business. He made it pretty clear I need to get off my duff and make some practical plans."

"Oh. Well, I'm down here at the mine for a safety inspection. I thought maybe you'd like to come down here and see me in the line of duty and then maybe head out for an ice cream or something stronger."

I smiled again. "I'd like to, Charlie, but this is one of my car-less days. Another time, maybe?"

"Oh right, I forgot. Well, here's another idea. How about I pick you up when I'm finished here and take you and Lu out to dinner?"

"By the time I'm able to get back in my kitchen, I will owe you eleventy-eight dinners."

"No problem," he said. "I'll put in my orders. We'll see just how good a cook you are."

I laughed out loud. "What time will you be here?"

"Not sure. Maybe five-ish."

"That should be fine."

"Well, great, then. I've got to get back. See you later."

I was working on a press release for the local papers when Lu came pedaling up the driveway. Though I'd never written one, my years at the hotel had made me familiar with the format, and if news of our opening made the local papers, it would be as good a start as we could hope for.

"Hey, Mom!"

"Hi, Lu! Have a good ride?"

"Yep. Morgan wasn't home, so I just went to the park and circled back. What are you doing?"

"Working on a news release to let people know our bed and breakfast will soon be open for business."

The idea seemed to take her by surprise. "There'll be a lot of strangers tromping around through our house."

"Yes, but they will be paying for the privilege, and it's as good a way as any to support ourselves."

Like most kids, Lulu had no real idea where our money came from or where it went. The phrase, "I can't afford it," had been a constant in her life, but that was about the extent of it. Now she looked at me and nodded soberly. "Can I help?"

I smiled. "In fact, you can. From now until school starts, you can help me test out recipes. We'll have to serve breakfast to our guests."

Her eyes lit up. "Cool!"

"Put your bike away and change your clothes. Charlie's taking us to dinner."

"Cool," she said again, walking her bike into the garage.

It was quarter to five, and I was changing my own clothes when the phone rang.

"Julie? It's Harrison."

"Hi, Harrison. How are you?"

"Fine. What a treat to have Penny here. Makes my day a lot more manageable."

His voice took on a sober tone. "Listen, Julie, I have some news. It's a letter from your cousin's attorney. Welty is turning down our offer. He wants to go to court and sue for half the estate."

My heart sank. "So, now what?"

Harrison paused. "I think he's bluffing, Julie. His attorney must surely be aware he won't pull much weight in a court of law. So, the choice is, stick to our guns, offer a larger payoff, or tell him we'll see him in court."

I considered. "Is he still in town?"

"I don't know. You haven't seen him?"

"Not since the day I saw him storming out of the Midnight Star. I was just wondering if maybe we should arrange to meet."

"I wouldn't advise it. Keep your distance. You don't want to confront him face-to-face. But as I said, we will have to do something. Stick to our offer, up the ante, or let him make the next move."

I tried to rein in my racing thoughts. "Let me think about it, Harrison."

"Of course. But you know, you gave me another idea. Let me check in with some friends around town, find out just how well-known Hanford Welty has become in our local casinos."

THIRTY-SEVEN

The night had been still and undisturbed for a change, although, thanks to Harrison's news about Welty, and what it might mean for Lulu and me, I tossed and turned for a good part of the night anyway.

Our dinner with Charlie had been uneventful—pasta at a local place he liked and a quick tour back at the house to show Charlie how the reconstruction was shaping up. He was duly impressed and equally impressed with Lu's snazzy new bike.

"You're in the country now," he told her. "I hope you know the rules of the road."

Coming from me, she would have rolled her eyes at getting a lesson about the rules of the road. But she took it from Charlie with more patience than I knew she had in her.

By nine, after we'd shared our take-home pie with Penny, Charlie left, and we made it an early night. It didn't matter. I spent too many hours trying out crazy scenarios to get any meaningful rest.

To boot, I realized, as I stumbled out of bed, this was Wednesday, four weeks to the day since the last foundation meeting.

I hadn't received notice of a board meeting tonight, and I had not seen

Rennie Malcolm, except for that one brief sighting at the swimming pool, since I'd sat across from him at the library meeting room.

Penny had left for work, and Lulu was working in a bowl of Cheerios when I joined her in the kitchen. She let the cereal fall from her spoon. "Can we try out some kind of food for the B and B?"

"I have to search the Internet for recipes," I said, pouring cereal for myself. "Some interesting muffins and coffee cakes, maybe, and some sort of breakfast casseroles and I'll check in with Hannah. She's a pretty good cook. I'll bet she has some secrets up her sleeve."

"So, not today . . ." Lulu sighed. "Okay, so Battleship or Yahtzee?"

She looked so crestfallen. I could hardly stand it, and in truth, I was getting as tired as she was of game days out on the porch. "Listen," I said. "Let me make a couple of phone calls. Then we'll see what we can do."

I checked in first with Gert Solomon, whose number I found in the local directory, and whom I knew from the last meeting was secretary of the foundation board. She confirmed the meeting tonight.

"Odd," she said, "that you didn't receive your notice . . . I thought I added your name to the mailing list, and I sent out the notices a week ago."

So, now what? Was somebody pilfering my mail?

I almost hoped that was the case, because if a culprit was ever found, that was a federal offense.

"No matter," I said to Gert. "Please check the mailing list again, but I'll be there tonight, at seven."

Nate, dressed in a pair of clean, faded overalls, came in without a word and went to work. I settled into my nest of pillows in the living room and called Hannah at the florist shop.

She liked the idea of trying out recipes. "It's a slow day here, anyway," she said. "Let me call Faye and see if she can cover for me this afternoon."

It turned out Faye was able to help. Hannah and Morgan would pick us up at noon and take us to Hannah's for a bake-off.

Lulu was thrilled.

"Get your clothes on and find something to do," I said, grabbing a banana. "I need a little time on my laptop."

In my bedroom, I keyed in my handwritten news release and emailed copies to every paper in the area, including the *Rapid City Journal* and every local paper I could find in Pierre, Sioux Falls and other cities dotted around the state.

I checked the advertising rates for a few national travel magazines where we might consider running an ad. Expensive, but probably worth a try. At least the cost would be tax deductible—assuming we had any income.

Finally, I Googled for breakfast recipes, plugged in the printer, and printed out a few that looked interesting.

I started to close the laptop, when an odd notion flitted through my head. I found myself entering into the search engine the first few letters of the drug Hannah had told me was the one Doreen allegedly had stolen . . . *s-u-c-c-i*. . . .

To my amazement, the name popped up big as life on my screen. It was almost unpronounceable. *Succinylcholine*, but beneath the name was a long list of references.

I clicked on the first one. The drug, I read, was a paralytic agent, a muscle relaxant used by physicians in surgery or sometimes in emergencies . . . it *can cause short-term muscle paralysis, heart arrhythmia, and/or circulatory collapse.* . . .

I reared back. I was no doctor, but it was pretty clear this was not a drug to fool around with. It could *choke off oxygen, deregulate body temperature, and result in cardiac arrest.*

Why on earth would Doreen have stolen such a drug—if, indeed, she

had stolen it? Was that what she had wanted to talk to me about on my first
night back in Deadwood?

"Mom! Hannah and Morgan are here! Are you ready?"

"Yes, Lu!" I snapped the laptop shut just as I heard the doorbell. I
snatched up the recipes, slipped my feet into sandals, and sprinted down the
stairs.

The girls decided that a B and B with wild blueberries growing out back
had to have blueberries on the menu. So, we combed Hannah's recipe books
for recipes and ended up having a delicious, if pretty unusual, dinner at
Hannah's house that night: two kinds of muffins, blueberry banana bread,
and a French toast casserole of bread, eggs, and milk with a blueberry sauce
on top.

Hannah pronounced every one of them a winner—"fit for the most
discriminating guest!"

It was past six when Hannah drove us home. Penny was nowhere to be
seen. I tossed my batter-spattered shirt into the laundry and stopped to take
a good look at the old washer and dryer in the laundry room.

They were probably, I figured, the very same ones that had stood here
when I was a girl. With the extra loads of sheets and towels a B and B would
require, I was afraid we would need some new, more efficient machines. Of
course, it meant more money out the door, which reminded me I needed to
stop at the ATM on my way to the library to take out the cash I'd promised
Nate.

As a result, I was the last one into the meeting room. Mrs. Kovich had
brought homemade oatmeal cookies, and the board was munching and
chatting.

"Nice of you to join us." Rennie banged his gavel. "The meeting will
come to order."

Gert Solomon passed me an agenda, and the items were checked off one by one. In less than half an hour, we arrived at "Old Business," topped by the issue of Rennie's bid for a change of status and salary.

Rennie cleared his throat, taking a long look into each face around the table. "Ms. Goldman has asked me to account for my time," he said, as though I'd asked him to strip down to his underwear. He passed around a stack of neatly bound sets of paper. "I have therefore prepared a full report and made copies for each of you."

"Thank you, Rennie," I said cheerfully, making a point of addressing him by his first name. "Since you've made it so easy, why don't we take a few minutes so that each of us can read it on our own?"

In the few minutes of silence, punctuated only by the occasional rustle of paper, I saw that Malcolm had accounted not just for the current thirty-day period I asked for, but for a period of the last several months.

In each of those months, he claimed he had put in between fifty and sixty hours of work a week, split between bookkeeping, grant-writing, telephoning, assorted administrative activities, and meetings or "personal appearances" before current and potential donor groups.

I wondered if his tête-à-tête with Roy Bachman at the community pool that day was counted among those meetings.

In any case, it seemed to me there was more posturing and "planning time" than actual substance to the long hours he claimed. I was debating just how to broach the matter when Mrs. Kovich jumped in.

"For pity's sake, Rennie, this is as much a bunch of meaningless frou-frou as anything I've ever seen. You've accounted for everything except emptying the trash can, unless that fits under 'administrative activity.'"

Father Ruggio cleared his throat and blinked his soulful blue eyes. "I'm afraid I'd have to agree. I have no idea who this Casper Cready is, but I'd be mighty upset if you'd spent seven hours on the phone with *me* in a single month."

An angry red began to creep up from Rennie's starched white collar. But before he could begin to sputter out an answer, Frank Anderson got to his feet.

"All right, all right, now, ladies and gentlemen. Let's not make this an attack. We all know Rennie's worked hard these past few years to help the foundation grow."

"Hear, hear," Roy Bachman chimed in.

Gert Solomon leaned forward. "No argument, Frank, but he's always done it on a part-time basis, and nothing he'd presented in these documents leads me to believe his position should be expanded to forty hours a week."

"Besides," said Helen Kovich, "as a full-time position, we'd need to include health and vacation benefits."

Rennie stood. "No benefits necessary. I can take care of myself."

Voices grew louder, words tumbling over each other. Finally, I stood at my seat until quiet was restored.

"Please," I said. "I never meant to start a civil war here. Why don't we just take a vote?"

The vote was four to two against Rennie's request, Frank Anderson moving to the "no" column so that I did not need to break a tie.

When no new business was introduced, Rennie brought the meeting to a close. It clearly took every ounce of restraint he could muster, and I watched him march stiffly out of the room like a kid who's been denied the family car.

Father Ruggio told me not to take it personally, and nobody seemed upset or surprised. My guess was this was not the first time they had seen Rennie's temper flare. I said a few quick good nights and headed out to my car.

I was just preparing to turn out of the driveway when a dark SUV pulled up beside me. Rennie rolled down his window. I rolled down mine. He glared at me with undisguised hostility.

"You are the most disruptive element to hit this town in years. Your aunt would be thoroughly ashamed of you."

THIRTY-EIGHT

I fumed all the way home, debating the truth of Rennie Malcolm's accusation. I had no idea what Aunt Sarah would think of the way I was handling her estate. But I thought she might be proud of the way I had stepped in to see that foundation business was carried out the way she would have wanted.

In the end, of course, there was no way to know. I was just glad to be home.

Lulu was in bed, but Penny was awake, poring over a tome on the South Dakota penal code. She'd moved an armchair out of a crowded corner into a circle of lamplight, and she looked up when I came in.

She pushed her glasses up higher on her nose. "Hey, Julie. How was the meeting?"

"Don't even go there." I sank into the nest of pillows I'd created in the corner. "Why on earth is it so hard to know if you're doing the right thing?"

Her pixie face relaxed into a grin. "Because life is a bar exam, and we're too stubborn to stop trying to get it right."

I had to laugh. "How's everything here?"

"Great. In fact, guess what?"

"I couldn't possibly."

"I've got a date Saturday night with Harrison. A real date, this time. He called tonight and made it very clear it is *not* business-related."

"Really?"

"Yep. He's taking me to dinner at a French place somewhere near Spearfish."

"Chez LeBlanc. I was there with Charlie. You'll love it. That's great, Pen. Have fun."

She sat back and stretched. "You know, Julie, I think this move to South Dakota was the smartest move I ever made. I really want to thank you for bringing me along, even though I know I haven't been much help to you since we got here."

I didn't tell her I wasn't sure it was the smartest move for me. "So far, I haven't needed much help, and it's fun for Lu and me just to have you here. You know you're part of the family."

"I know," she said. I appreciate that, and if things turn out the way I think they might, I may decide to make the move permanent, whether or not I pass the California bar. Harrison is helping me get up to speed on South Dakota law."

"So I see. Well, I hate to sound like a mother hen, but don't make too many moves too fast." I hated to take the wind out of her sails. "I hope it all works out the way you want it to."

"Me, too." She got up from her chair. I helped her push back into the corner.

"You know, I hate to admit it," she said, "but the renovation's looking pretty good, even if Nate is a pill."

I had to agree, and I looked around the room trying to visualize what it would look like when it was finished. I liked what I saw. I hugged Penny and turned around to switch off the porch light.

I rummaged in my bag for the cash I'd taken from the ATM earlier. I scrounged up an envelope, wrote NATE on the front, and laid it on top of the gray metal toolbox that had become a permanent fixture in the dining room.

Then I headed upstairs, looked in on Lu, and closed my bedroom door behind me.

In the big bed, I pulled out my yellow legal pad, propped it against my knees, and began sketching ideas for a magazine ad, something catchy but short, something that would fit without crowding in a small but distinctive display box.

In the background, I drew an outline of the Black Hills against a dark sky studded with stars. Over that, I printed BLUEBIRD HILL Bed & Breakfast and in smaller letters, "Find your place in the peaceful hills of Deadwood, South Dakota." At the bottom of the ad, I printed our phone number and my personal email address.

I sat back to look at it. *Find your place in the peaceful hills of Deadwood, South Dakota.* I wished I could take my own advice, but I did like the look of the little display ad. It was a good start, anyway.

It occurred to me like a bolt out of the blue that we'd need to have a webpage, too—something interactive, with graphics and photos and pricing information and a link for making reservations. Of course, I would have to find and hire somebody to create it, and that would be more money flying out the door!

I shook my head. There wasn't much choice. Everyone went to the Internet. It had to be done if we were going to compete in the crowded bed-and-breakfast space.

I hauled my laptop up on the bed, eager to check out the webpages and pricing of other B and Bs in the area. But when I opened the lid and connected with the Internet, something else came to mind. For the second time that day, I typed the first few letters of that unpronounceable drug into the search line.

I clicked on the entry below the one I'd been reading when I'd been interrupted this afternoon . . . *administered by syringe, stops the heart . . . brain cells turn off in minutes. . . .*

Another entry included *untraceable due to rapid dissolution . . . sometimes referred to as the perfect murder weapon, used in a number of documented high-profile cases. . . .*

The perfect murder weapon. I leaned forward and read another entry.

I read, clicked, read again, until a single phrase jumped out at me: *sometimes used by veterinarians as a humane way to euthanize horses . . .*

And in a moment of clarity, an odd scenario began to play itself out. What if Doreen had pilfered the drug just as the hospital alleged—a single dose, for a friend who asked her to help him put down a sick horse?

It didn't take much thought to realize that half the local population owned horses, but I remembered something Mrs. Kovich had said during my first foundation board meeting a month ago, something about Rennie spending too much time in the company of some pretty young woman, and I wondered if that pretty young woman could possibly have been Doreen, who took the drug as a favor to Rennie, who had owned and sold a horse ranch . . . ?

It was a stretch, I told myself, but easy enough to check out.

And the playbook kept running. *What if Doreen's friend hadn't wanted the drug to euthanize a horse at all? What if she suspected the dose she'd given him had been used to murder a human being?*

My skin felt chilled, and I rubbed my arms to warm them. *Aunt Sarah, who had taken a stand between Rennie and his self-centered ambition . . . Was that what Doreen had wanted to tell me?*

I shook my head. I was way ahead of myself. It was a heart attack in an elderly woman.

But the image of Rennie, hungry for control, refused to go away, and a drug that dissolved so quickly in the blood would have made Aunt Sarah's death appear natural.

I recalled Charlie telling me that my aunt had left a message for him on the night he'd found her dead. *Was she calling to tell him she felt threatened by the director of her charitable foundation? Was it possible Charlie had arrived only hours after Rennie had left her dead in her bed?*

I leaned back against the pillows. Aunt Sarah had never been one to lock her doors. I remembered that from the years I lived here as a kid. Rennie could have known that, could have gotten into the house easily enough and injected the drug as she slept. . . .

No wonder Charlie had found no sign of a struggle. She'd never had a chance to fight back.

I closed the laptop and slipped between the sheets, shivering in the summer night chill.

If it was true, then maybe Nancy had been right. Maybe Doreen's accident was *not* an accident, not if Rennie thought she was going to tell the truth and had found a way to keep her quiet.

Did that in some way connect to the missing pages in Katy's diary? Even to her death years ago? I turned off the light, pulled up the covers, and tried to close my eyes. But the pictures in my brain refused to quit.

Nancy had never for a single minute believed Doreen's accident was an accident.

I stared up into the darkness.

Was that why Nancy died, too?

THIRTY-NINE

The thing about morning is that it tends to make your worst nightmares seem like overblown fantasies, and as I watched daylight turn the curtains pink, the scenario I had put together in the darkness felt more and more outlandish.

For one thing, as Doctor Rafferty had confirmed, there was no reason to think that Aunt Sarah had died of anything but natural causes. For another, even the hospital wasn't certain where the single missing dose of the drug had gone, much less where it had ended up.

Maybe it *was* used to put down a horse, and even if Doreen had been involved, there were hundreds of horse owners in the area. Doreen had lived here all her life. She was a soft touch, and everyone knew it.

I threw my legs over the side of the bed. My eyelids felt like sandpaper.

And how could I convince myself that Rennie Malcolm wanted Aunt Sarah dead? He was an egotist and a control freak, but could I really think he would kill to get at foundation money?

I got up. The house was still. It was not yet six in the morning. I stood in the shower, letting the hot water sluice between my tired shoulders. Besides, Rennie wasn't the only one who saw Aunt Sarah standing in his way. *What about Nate, with his yard-long attitude and his serious designs on this house?*

Or my newfound cousin who, for all I knew, had been tracking the family money for years?

No doubt my move to Deadwood had put a crimp in their plans and I was still pretty sure it was one of the three who was now harassing me. But murder? I rubbed steam off the mirror and peered at my drawn face. I pulled on jeans and a T-shirt and silently padded downstairs.

The sun was rising over the mountains. How different things looked in the daylight. I picked my way through the cartons in the kitchen to get the coffeepot going.

On the rear deck, I was surprised to feel the promise of autumn in the air. I sat in a rocker while I waited for the coffee and gazed out at the landscape.

Mrs. Kovich could probably tell me, if I asked, who it was that Rennie had been seeing. Even Hannah might have some insight. I could call one or both of them, if for no other reason than to put an end to my late-night delusions.

I began to think it was also time to tell Charlie what I was thinking. I'd shared my concerns that the broken window and the flat tire were more than random vandalism. But he didn't know about the mysterious phone message or the dead mouse in my mailbox, and I hadn't told him the names of the people I suspected might be at the bottom of it all.

I could smell the coffee, and I went inside to pour myself a cup. Lulu, in a too-short old nightie, padded across the kitchen floor and wound her arms around my waist.

"Hey, Lu, good morning," I said, burying my face in her hair. It smelled clean and damp and vaguely like cinnamon and vanilla. "Mmm, you smell like muffins," I told her. "What are you doing up so early?"

"I had a bad dream," she whined.

Oh, no, I thought. *Not you, too.* "What did you dream about?"

"I dreamed I went to my new school, and I couldn't find any friends."

"But you already have a friend." I cupped her chin. "You couldn't have a better friend than Morgan, and you're smart and funny and nice to be around. I promise you it won't take long to make lots of other friends, too."

She twisted her mouth to avoid smiling. "What do you know? You're my mother."

"Right." I pulled her lips into a grin. "So, who knows you better than me?"

"I thought I heard you guys down here." Penny stood in the doorway. "What's all this snuggling going on without me?"

Lu and I separated to draw Penny in.

"That's better. Why is everyone up so early?"

I put water in the teapot for her. "It was a night of not-very-good dreams."

Penny closed the kitchen door to shut out the chill air. "Well then, I'm thinking we should do something fun. I'm not working today." She made a funny face at Lu. "How about we shop for school clothes?"

Lulu's eyes lit up. "Can we, Mom?"

"Sounds good to me. But I may need the car. I have some errands to run."

"No problem," Penny said. "We'll take the bus into Rapid City."

By the time we finished breakfast, it was after seven thirty, and Nate was already at work. He said nothing about finding the money I'd left for him, but that was no more than I expected.

"I placed a couple of good-sized display ads," I told him before he headed upstairs. "Can you be a little more specific about when you expect to be finished here?"

"I need you out," he said shortly. "A day or two at least. If the house is empty, I can finish faster. Can you all be out of here for the weekend?"

I thought about making a little joke about being kicked out of my house. But there was no humor in Nate Miller, so I simply nodded. "Sure, I'm not exactly sure where we'll go, but we'll be out of your hair for the weekend."

I thought for a minute and called Hannah. "Tell me I didn't wake you."

"You didn't. I need to be in the shop early today."

"Good. Hannah, I can't believe I'm asking, but could you possibly put the three of us up this weekend? If not, we can stay in a hotel downtown. It wouldn't be a problem. It's just that Nate says if we're out of the house, he can pretty much finish up here."

"Of course I can. What a good idea. We can fool around with a few more recipes. I'll see if Morgan can stay over, too. That'll make it fun for Lu."

At the bus station, I gave Penny a spending limit and handed over some cash. I asked them to buzz me when they were on their way back, and I stuck around long enough to watch them get on the bus.

At home, there was a message from Harrison asking me to stop by the office. I put down the receiver and picked it up again. I called Genevieve Kovich.

She answered on the first ring. "Julie, I'm glad you called."

"Why, Mrs. Kovich?"

"I've been meaning to thank you for the way you handled Rennie at the board meeting."

"I didn't do much. He kind of did it to himself. The report he prepared was simply full of holes."

"Still," she said. "It was you who asked him to put something on paper in the first place, and once he did, it was easy for most of us to see through his bluster once and for all. I'm delighted to know you have Sarah's spunk. She didn't take any guff from Rennie, and she didn't miss an opportunity to remind him she was his boss."

I started to say something, but Mrs. Kovich cut me off.

"And there's something else you should know, Julie," she said, taking a beat. "Sarah had plans to hire an outside auditor. She told me so herself. Rennie kept the books, and she wanted his accounts examined."

That gave me pause. "Are you saying she suspected him of mishandling the foundation's funds?"

"Well," she said, "I can't say I know that for sure, but he does have check-signing authority, and I think she was beginning to be suspicious."

I blinked. Maybe my midnight musings were not so outlandish after all.

"Well, thank you for telling me. I hadn't intended to become involved with Katy's Legacy, but maybe I need to rethink that, and Mrs. Kovich, can I ask you something?"

"Of course."

"Is Rennie an old-timer in Deadwood?"

"Well, he grew up here, if that's what you mean, but he went away to school, and we didn't see hide nor hair of him for years. Came back to town when he and his wife bought the ranch from the Dillards. That was six years ago this January. I remember exactly, because the Dillards were retiring to Florida. The auxiliary had a going away party for Henry and June, and I missed it because I'd just had my hip replaced."

"Ah, and when did he start working for the foundation?"

"Oh, right away. He had lots of credentials. Sarah and the board were impressed.

He'd been some kind of business manager—in Ohio, as I recall, where he'd been handling pretty large sums of money."

I wondered if his resume was in a file somewhere. Maybe in Harrison's office.

And then it spilled out. "One more thing, Mrs. Kovich. You mentioned once that Rennie was seeing someone here in town after his wife left. Do you happen to know who she was?"

"Well, of course, dear. It was that pretty young nurse, Doreen Hastings, the one who died in that terrible accident."

FORTY

With Penny shopping in Rapid City, there was no one sitting at the reception desk in Harrison's office. The inner door was ajar. I tapped lightly.

Harrison looked up. "Hey, come on in."

"Hi. It looks deserted out there."

"It is, and don't think it doesn't make all the difference." He motioned me to the seat across from him. "You wouldn't believe how much more work I get done on the days when Penny is here, not to mention, she's a quick study. If I didn't think it might put you in a spot, I'd ask her to work for me full time."

I smiled, thinking about their upcoming date. "Penny would like that, I think, and to tell the truth, once Lu is back in school, there won't be much that Penny can do for me at home. I'll be there most of the time, trying to make a go of the bed and breakfast."

"How's that coming along?"

"Okay, I think. The remodel is nearly done. I can't say I'd ever count Nate Miller as a friend, but he's doing a good job on the construction."

Harrison nodded. "Nate's a little grumpy, I know. But he's honest, and he's a hard worker."

"That he is, unlike some others I could mention, who appear to be looking for a handout."

He smiled. "Which brings us to your erstwhile cousin, who, it appears, is now trying to strike it rich at the card tables here in town."

I waited.

"Welty's running a tab at two casinos here in town, in addition to what he owes in Chicago. They're about to cut him off here, and he's probably getting desperate for money. As you already know, he turned down your settlement offer, which may or may not be enough to cover what he already owes."

"So, what happens next?"

Harrison sighed. "He's saying he wants his day in court, and my advice is to let him have it. His attorney will likely file suit here in South Dakota claiming Welty is entitled to half your aunt's estate. They'll probably add on funds to cover his court costs. Welty will assert you've dissipated a chunk of the estate and are conspiring to keep him from the rest."

I could feel the color draining from my face. "It isn't that I want to keep him from a rightful inheritance, and it's true, I have squirreled away a chunk of the money and signed away another chunk to pay for the cost of the remodel. We'll survive no matter what, I keep telling myself, but what scares me is that the money I invested for Lulu's education, which I thought was secure, well, even that, may be in jeopardy."

Harrison leaned forward, elbows on the desk. "Julie, whether or not your aunt knew of Welty's existence, she left explicit instructions that you were to be her sole heir. Under the circumstances, it isn't likely any court will allow Welty to breach that intent, even without a trust, especially when there is no evidence of any interaction between them."

Unless they had met in the dark one night when he injected a drug into her bloodstream. . . . I took a deep breath and let it out again. I had to stop inventing scenarios.

Harrison smiled. "Let me worry about it, Julie. You may never even need to appear in court. You've got plenty to keep you busy these days. Try to put it out of your mind."

It wouldn't be easy, especially when things I couldn't make sense of were happening all around me.

"Harrison," I said. "Change of subject, do you happen to know how or why Rennie Malcolm was hired as director of my aunt's foundation?"

"Not really. As you know, I inherited a kind of general oversight from my dad, who helped draw up the foundation's bylaws and the bid for tax-exempt status. But I don't serve on the board, and I pretty much stay out of the day-to-day unless they ask for legal help. Why?"

"So, you're not involved with audits or anything like that . . ."

"No. Not long before she died, Sarah asked for the name of a good accountant. I recommended someone in Rapid City, but I don't know if she ever called him." He swiveled to remove a file from a cabinet. "Do you want the accountant's number?"

I thought about it. "No, not at this point, thanks. But do you happen to have a copy of Rennie's resume in that file?"

His eyebrows shot up. "Gosh, I don't know." He rifled through the thick file. "Do you need it right away? I can ask Penny to look for it tomorrow. If she finds it, she can take a copy home to you."

"Perfect, thanks." I got up to go. "Thanks for everything, Harrison."

I stopped at City Hall to file for a business license for the bed and breakfast, then drove to an appliance store I'd seen in Lead. In short order, I whipped out my plastic for an energy-efficient washer and dryer, to be held until I called for delivery.

Right next door was a little secondhand shop gussied up to look like an antique store. Wandering through the dusty aisles, I came across some delicate English china, a service for twelve, hand-painted, with a small crack in one salad plate and a chip on the rim of a soup bowl.

I turned a teacup up to the light, admiring the tiny pastel rosettes and the way the light came through the thin china. It struck me as perfect for a bed-and-breakfast service, and since it was doubtful we'd ever be serving more than six or eight guests at a time, I could live with the two damaged pieces.

By the time the china was packed up and stored in the trunk of my car, I was starving. On impulse, I called Charlie at the station.

"He's investigating a little accident at the mine," the desk sergeant told me. "Some tourist took a header where he shouldn't have been heading and tore up a knee climbing out."

"Oh," I said. I started to leave a message but had a better idea. "Well, thanks," I said. "I'll catch him later."

I stopped at a deli, bought a couple of meatball sandwiches and some drinks, and drove to the old goldmine. Charlie was coming out of the office as I drove into the parking lot. I honked at him, and he looked up, his sober expression breaking into a smile when he saw me.

"Hey," he said. "I don't suppose you're here for a tour."

"No, thanks. I've already had one. I thought you might be hungry."

"Starved," he said. "Are you treating for lunch?"

"Yep." I motioned him into the car. "Are you up for a little picnic?"

I drove to the lake where I'd picnicked by myself on my first full day back in town. The leaves on the oaks were beginning to turn, and a stiff breeze riffed over the water. I took the bag from the deli and pulled a blanket out of the trunk, and we trudged to the nearest picnic table. We sat on the same side of the table and pulled the blanket over our laps.

Charlie ran a finger over my face. "There are dark circles under your eyes."

I shrugged.

"But you're beautiful. I mean that, Julie. The most beautiful woman I know."

It had been a long time since anyone called me beautiful. Come to think of it, my husband, Marty, might have been the only one who ever had.

"But you do look like you've been losing sleep. Why's that?"

I busied myself with the sandwiches. "It may sound silly, Charlie, but little things keep happening that are causing me some concern."

"Little things like what?"

I handed him a sandwich and a can of soda. "Well, you know about some of them . . . the broken window at the house and the sabotaged tire in the driveway."

He peeled back the sandwich wrapping. "Yep."

"Well, not long ago I had a phone message at the house. It came in late at night. A voice I didn't recognize, asking if I was 'getting the message.'"

I handed him a napkin. "And not long after that, I opened the mailbox one day and found a dead mouse inside."

Charlie looked as though he wanted to smile. "Well, we do live out in the country."

I unwrapped my sandwich. "Yes, I know that. I told you I know it sounds silly. But all things considered, I can't shake the feeling that somebody's watching me . . . wants me to know I'm not wanted here."

He took a bite of his sandwich. "Mmm, this is good. And why would somebody not want you here?"

I felt almost tongue-tied. "Because—I don't know . . . because I'm trying to solve some puzzles, because certain people might be . . . better off if I had never come back to Deadwood."

Charlie put down his sandwich and looked at me a moment. "You're serious about this, aren't you?"

I nodded.

"Do you have any idea who this 'somebody' might be? This person you see as a threat?"

"As a matter of fact, I do. There are several possibilities."

"Good. Who are they?"

I picked up my sandwich. "That's the thing, Charlie, I don't want to falsely accuse anyone. I'm checking a few things out, but I *can* tell you it's gotten to the point where I've always got my guard up. You asked me why I'm losing sleep, and that's the reason why."

Charlie took the sandwich out of my hand and laid it down on the wrapping. "Julie, I told you once, and I'll tell you again. I care for you. I'm still short-staffed with the county fair and all, but I offered to set up camp at your house myself if it will make you feel any safer, and I think you know I meant it. But short of that, there isn't much I can do until you *are* ready to point fingers."

I hesitated.

"Julie, look. Wacky phone messages get left all the time, and dead mice turn up everywhere in these parts. But maybe there is some sort of pattern going on here, and if there is, and if it continues, you know I'll do whatever it takes to keep you safe."

He cupped a hand around my cheek. "My gut feeling is you're reading too much into this stuff. But when and if you're ready to tell me who it is you feel threatened by, I promise I will do everything in my power to nab this guy."

FORTY-ONE

If there's one way to ruin a cozy little picnic, it's to turn the conversation to dead mice, unseen enemies, and things that go bump in the night. By the time I dropped Charlie back at the mine, I felt like a blooming idiot.

I waved goodbye and spit a little gravel as I turned the car toward home. It was bad enough I'd shut the door in his face when he'd just told me I was beautiful. On top of it, I hadn't even been able to come clean about who I was worried about . . . or why.

I knew Charlie would be more than ready to start investigating if I asked him to. But I already knew his manpower was short. I felt silly asking him to follow my hunches, and how ridiculous was I apt to feel if my suspicions came to nothing?

I was turning into the driveway when my cell phone chimed. It was 3:15 and Penny calling. "Hey," I said. "How are the shoppers?"

"Exhausted." Penny sounded breathless. "But victorious. We're getting on the bus."

"Great. I've just got a few things to do. I'll pick you up in forty-five minutes."

I carried the china into the kitchen, emptied the boxes, and stowed the pieces in the dishwasher, wondering idly if that, too, was going to need to be replaced what with all the extra duty it would be doing.

I poured myself a glass of lemonade, picked my way around the boxes of knickknacks Nate had added to the mess in the kitchen, and sat down at the kitchen table.

I listened to the whine of the old dishwasher. I was accustomed to worrying about money. But for the first time in my life, I had assets to protect, and that took me right back to the demons that were keeping me awake.

I was tied up in knots by the nagging feeling that all my uncertainties were connected, bits and pieces held together by a string I couldn't grab hold of.

I jumped when the phone rang and picked up the wall extension.

"Hey, Mom. We're back at the bus station."

I leaped to my feet, startled to realize that forty-five minutes had gone by. I reached for my keys, headed out to the driveway, and stopped. The garage door was wide open. I was sure it had been closed when I'd come home.

I peered in, wondering if Nate had opened the door, but his truck was nowhere in sight. I stepped inside to look around, but everything seemed exactly as it should have been—tools and garden equipment stacked to one side, some displaced furniture, dusty cartons and Lulu's new bike on the other.

Frowning, I pulled the heavy door closed, and though I rarely locked it, I did so now. But the lock was just a flimsy little gadget, and I found myself adding an electric garage door with a remote control to my list of unplanned expenses.

Lu and Penny waved from a bench when I arrived at the depot minutes later. They were surrounded by an alarming number of shopping bags, which they loaded into the trunk.

"Good grief," I said, "did you leave anything in the stores?"

Lulu laughed.

"Not much," Penny admitted. "I couldn't believe the good prices. Much cheaper than in California, and everything was on back-to-school sale."

"Fashion show!" Lulu announced as I pulled into the driveway.

I stared hard at the garage door, which once again stood open. I looked around, but there was no one in sight. I turned off the ignition.

"Something wrong?" Penny looked at me.

"I locked the garage door when I left."

She shrugged. "Maybe you only thought you did."

I pulled the heavy door closed again. The broken lock lay on the ground. *What if someone was in the house? What if they were still there?*

Wary, I hesitated. Then I did my best to shake it off. I picked up the lock and followed the girls inside, not for the first time angrier than disturbed that some demented jerk was so intent on upsetting me. Whoever it was, I gave him credit for *chutzpah,* as Bubbe Lou would have put it. It took a lot of nerve to be on and off the property twice in a short span of time.

It took the best part of an hour for Lulu to model her carefully selected new wardrobe, and I have to say I was well and truly impressed, not just at how much they had managed to buy for the money I'd allotted, but for how perfectly the leggings and skirts and jeans they'd chosen suited my pre-teen daughter.

"Penny, you are a marvel," I told her when Lu ran upstairs again. "When I grow up, I hope you'll take me shopping."

She looked right at me. "Julie, are you okay? You seem, I don't know, a little distracted . . ."

I shook my head. "There's just a lot to do around here, and some stuff going on I'm trying to piece together."

She looked at me closely. "Would it help if I stayed home from Harrison's office for a while, at least until you launch the B and B?"

"Thanks, but no. I'm working on it, Penny. One of these days, I'll get it figured out."

A thought I'd had before surfaced again as Lulu bounded down the stairs, changed now into shorts and an old T-shirt. I looked straight at her. "What would you think about getting ourselves a dog?"

My poor daughter was so excited, she nearly fell over an ottoman. "Are you kidding, Mom? When?"

"I'm not kidding. I think it would be a good idea and the sooner, the better, how's that? I'm putting you guys in charge of finding the nearest animal shelter. I think it would be great to find a rescue dog."

Lulu upended a stack of magazines, rifling through them for the Yellow Pages as though maybe I'd change my mind if she wasted a single minute. Penny pulled her phone out of her purse and started perusing the Internet.

"Maybe even tomorrow," I said, getting up to go upstairs. "But remember, we're leaving to spend a few days at Hannah's. We need to throw some things into a bag. And it's Friday. We'll want to say our Shabbos prayer before we head out for dinner."

In my room, I packed a nightgown and robe, a pair of jeans and couple of shirts. I threw in some underwear and my toothbrush.

A dog on the property would be a good thing. That it made Lu happy was a bonus. Penny was right. I was always on edge. A dog might make me feel safer.

I sat down on the edge of the bed, wondering what else to do, and when, if ever, I might find the answers to my questions.

Reason prevailed. Okay, I told myself, get real. I was weeks away from opening a business that could make or break our future. I'd managed to get caught up in foundation business I had hoped to totally avoid, and I was on my way to court to fight over money with a cousin who might be my only living relative. I had a right to be stressed, and maybe stress was fueling my overactive imagination.

But in my heart of hearts, I knew it was more. The question was how far to push it.

FORTY-TWO

Morgan moved in with us for the weekend at Hannah's, and with five females vying for one small bathroom, it was a little like the organized chaos I remembered from a long week I'd spent one summer when Aunt Sarah sent me to camp.

Hannah took it all in stride, planning a wiener roast dinner outdoors, and I took the morning as a timely opportunity to practice cooking breakfast for a crowd. On Saturday, I turned out a French toast casserole with fruit compote and bacon, bowing gratefully to the oohs and aahs and feeling only a little bit frazzled by the time the kitchen was clean.

By then, Lulu was pressing to go to the animal shelter, so the three of us and Morgan piled into the car and set out to find ourselves a dog.

In truth, we didn't so much choose a dog as we let ourselves be chosen by Rufus, a two-year-old, black-and-white Springer Spaniel with downy ears, a freckled chest, and I swear, a goofy smile on his face.

When Lu moved in for a closer look, he turned the smile full on, sidling against her with a satisfied sigh as if he'd known her in another life. Lu turned baleful eyes up at me and that was the end of my predisposed bias toward a strapping German Shepherd. My daughter was hooked, and I was done, and the only thing standing between the three of us was paperwork, a lot of paperwork.

Rufus, it seemed, had been abandoned some months ago right here on the steps of the shelter, in a dirty dog bed with his favorite toy, a mangy little rubber mouse. According to the shelter officer, he had yet to respond to anyone else the way he had to Lulu. But you would have thought we were trying to steal the dog for all the questions we answered, with Lu pitched forward at the edge of her seat, Penny and Morgan lined up behind her, and me rummaging for two kinds of identification and some proof that we were fiscally responsible.

In the end, we were told that if everything checked out, we could come back for Rufus mid-week after he'd had his "adoption examination." We felt disappointed to leave him behind, and if ever there was a time that called for ice cream for lunch, I figured this was it.

We went to the café to celebrate with hot fudge sundaes with extra whipped cream and double cherries. Earlene listened patiently to every nuance of our search for the perfect dog.

By three, we were back at Hannah's, where the story was retold detail by gory detail. By then, I was glassy-eyed, and the afternoon air had turned brisk, bordering on downright cold. I borrowed a sweater to wrap myself in and headed for the hammock that was strung up in Hannah's backyard. I might have dropped off for a welcome nap when the cell phone in my pocket woke me.

It was Charlie.

"Ms. Goldman." His voice was cool and professional. "This is Chief Banks, calling from the station here in Deadwood. Do you have a minute?"

I blinked, not sure what was going on. "What, yes, "What? Yes, sure."

"It's about a man named Hanford Welty."

I realized he must be calling on official business, and that someone else might be with him. I shouldered myself halfway up in the hammock. "Welty? What about him?"

"He's here at the station. He was brought in for assault. He has identification from Ohio and Missouri, but he claims to be in the process of moving to South Dakota. He says he's a cousin of yours and that you can vouch for him."

"Vouch for him?" I sat up straighter. "Hanford Welty wants me to vouch for him?"

Charlie paused. "That's what he says. Is he your cousin?"

"According to the research Harrison did, that might be the case, yes. But I don't know anything about Hanford Welty except that he has a sizable gambling debt and he's suing for half my aunt's estate."

"I see . . ." My guess was that maybe Welty was sitting across the desk from him. "I understand your position."

"What will happen to him?"

"That depends on whether charges are brought. Thanks for your help. We appreciate it."

I clicked off, throwing my legs over the side of the hammock and pulling the sweater closer. If that wasn't the most *chutzpah* I'd ever heard of, expecting me to vouch for his character while he was suing for half my inheritance.

Ominous-looking clouds had moved in overhead, and I made my way inside through the back porch as the first fat raindrops hit the ground.

Hannah was napping. Penny was upstairs, getting ready for her date with Harrison, and the girls were sprawled on the living room floor hassling over a game of Battleship.

"Did not," Lulu snapped, throwing plastic pegs into the box.

"Did, too," Morgan volleyed back.

It was the first time I had ever heard them argue, and it took me by surprise. I sat on the sofa. "Okay," I said. "Maybe everyone needs a time out."

Morgan marched upstairs. Lulu scooted backwards on her behind and parked herself firmly against the sofa.

"What happened?" I asked her.

"Nothing," she said.

"Maybe you need a nap."

"I don't need a nap."

"I think you do."

"You're being bossy again."

"I am not bossy." *Too much sugar. So much for sundaes for lunch.*

"You are, too!" Her eyes welled up, and she suddenly burst into tears.

I let her cry until she was finished, which took all of a minute. At that point, Morgan came down to apologize, and the next thing I knew they were running upstairs together, best friends again.

I watched them go. If only all of life's conflicts could be as easily resolved!

By then, the rain had asserted itself, and the wiener roast had to be moved indoors. But Hannah was nothing if not resourceful, and we ended up cooking hot dogs and marshmallows on skewers over a flame on the stove. It made for a kind of party-like atmosphere, and we laughed loudly and often.

I started to tell Hannah about Charlie's call and my cousin's unmitigated gall. But I caught myself up short, suddenly realizing that no one here, in fact, no one but Harrison knew about my newly minted cousin, much less that he wanted me to vouch for his character even as he was taking me to court.

I had been alone too long, I realized as I helped clear the table, solving my problems by myself because there was no one else I could turn to. No wonder my days were filled with suspicion and my nights with whys and what ifs.

I went to the window to watch the rain. I needed to get a real life.

FORTY-THREE

I got a good jolt of real life on Monday.

We trudged home from Hannah's at nine in the morning, tired and ready to spread out as much as possible in our own cluttered space. The moment we opened the front door, our jaws dropped in astonishment.

The jumble of displaced furniture and the narrow walkways we had lived with for so many weeks was gone, totally gone. In its place was a sleek, orderly and inviting space I nearly didn't recognize.

Crown molding set off the high-ceilinged living and dining rooms. The chandelier over the dining room table had been buffed to a crystalline shine, and the old rugs and furniture that had been here forever took on an almost stately air against freshly painted, cream-colored walls.

Green plants in graceful pots had been placed around the rooms, and in the open space between the living and dining areas was a polished oak reception table with a guest register, a plumed pen in a brass stand, and a Tiffany lamp filched from a bookcase in the upstairs hallway, where it had pretty much gone unnoticed for years.

Upstairs, where yards of plastic sheeting had masked off our view of the construction, we discovered two bedrooms and a connecting bath that had not previously existed.

To say we were floored would be an understatement. We had become so accustomed to picking our way around power cords and a changing succession of obstacles that the new space seemed grand and luxurious, a visual, larger-than-life realization of the plan Nate had rolled out on the coffee table to show me months ago.

"Wow," Lulu said it first.

"Amazing." Penny shook her head. "I never would have believed it."

Nate himself was nowhere in sight, but I was caught between admiration for his work and a guilty reminder that Lu and I would be the primary beneficiaries of the enhanced value of the house.

I decided that Lulu would stay in the room she was in, and I would stay in the one that had been Aunt Sarah's, leaving the new, light and airy bedrooms to be available as guest bedrooms.

Penny made a command decision to move into the smaller of the new rooms, leaving her old room—the one that had belonged to my cousin Katy—as the second and more central guest bedroom.

"Actually," she announced in a no-nonsense tone, "I will stay here only if I can pay you a rental fee, just as if I were a guest. I can afford it now that I'm working for Harrison, and I wouldn't feel right about taking a bedroom you could be renting to a paying guest."

I tried to reason her out of it, but Penny was adamant, and eventually we agreed on a number that she could afford and that would serve as the starting point of our bed-and-breakfast revenue. We decided we might as well get some boxes out of the garage, so we could begin moving our things.

"Since I don't have to move anything," Lulu said, "can I go out and take a ride on my bike?"

The skies had cleared, though it remained cold. "I guess so," I said, heading down the stairs. "Put on something warm and be back in time for lunch."

In the kitchen, I noticed the message light flashing, and I played back the tape. To my utter astonishment, someone had seen one of my newspaper ads and wanted to make a reservation.

"Oh my gosh," I yelled to no one in particular.

I got hold of myself, grabbed a pen and some paper, and sat down to return the call. That's when I realized I had made no decision on my bed-and-breakfast pricing.

I ran for my laptop to check the rates at B and Bs in surrounding areas. Feeling only slightly more confident, I picked up the phone and dialed.

"I found a dolly out there." Penny burst into the kitchen. "It'll make it easier to move our stuff."

"Sshh." I put a finger to my lips as someone answered my call.

"Hi," I said. "This is Julie Goldman returning your call to Bluebird Hill Bed and Breakfast in Deadwood."

Penny opened her mouth, raised her eyebrows, and took a seat across from me, clapping her hands without making a sound. I managed to negotiate a two-night reservation without sounding like a complete idiot.

I grabbed Penny, and the two of us did a silly little dance in the kitchen.

"We're open for business," I sang.

"This is great, Julie. This really was a good move! Good things are going to happen. I can feel it."

"I hope you're right." I wrote the date down for the arrival of our first paying guests, making a mental note to buy a reservations calendar and a receipt book. "Now let's get our stuff moved, so the guest rooms are ready for guests."

I called Nate, who didn't answer his cell phone, and left him a detailed message. I also made calls to Hannah and Charlie, primarily to share the news that the construction was finished and to invite them to see the remodeled space. Then I went upstairs just to marvel some more at the change.

It was past two when I realized I was starving and that Lulu wasn't home yet. *So much for being home in time for lunch.*

I headed downstairs, made some turkey sandwiches, and peered out the front door. "Lu, are you out there?"

There was no answer and no sign of Lulu or her bike. I went to the end of the driveway and looked down the road in both directions. She was nowhere in sight, and a curl of uneasiness snaked up my spine.

"Lu," I shouted. "Can you hear me?"

By now, the uneasiness was gaining traction. I ran to the kitchen to get my keys. "Penny," I shouted up the stairs. "I'm going out to look for Lu."

Beating back panic, I got into the car and peeled rubber out of the driveway. I was two miles up the main road when I spotted her, walking toward me with an uneven gait, her hair askew and the bike bumping along beside her.

I pulled over and slowed to a stop, literally shaking with relief. Her right knee was badly scraped, and she was grimy from head to toe, but she was all in one piece, navigating on her own, and that was enough to get my pulse nearly back to normal.

When she saw me coming, she burst into tears, let go of the bike, and came running. I held her until the tears stopped. "Are you okay?" I said into her hair.

"I don't know," she wailed. "My knee hurts."

"What happened?"

"I got run off the road," she managed. "I pedaled faster, and I hit a tree and I fell."

I reared back. "What do you mean you got run off the road?"

She nodded, sobbing out the words. "I didn't see the car. I think it was a truck, a little truck, like Nate's. It came up from behind. I thought it was going to hit me. By the time I crashed and got up again to look, it was gone."

For the first time in a long while, Lulu looked like the child she still was. Her dirty face was streaked with tears. "Mom, I was so scared."

The adrenaline that had been coursing through my veins turned suddenly to ice. It was one thing for someone to mess with me. Going after my daughter was taking things to another level, a level I would not tolerate.

FORTY-FOUR

The front wheel of the bike was mangled, but between the two of us, we got it into the trunk of my car.

At home, Lu undressed in the upstairs bathroom, so I could examine her from stem to stern. She had calmed down, and it didn't seem that anything was broken, but her sore ankle and scraped knee had already begun to swell, and purple bruises were starting to show on her left leg and right arm. I helped her run a warm bubble bath and told her to take a nice, long soak.

Penny brought in her iPod to keep her entertained, and I went downstairs to call Charlie.

He was at his desk. "Hey," he said. "I got your message. So, the house is done. When would be a good time to stop by?"

"Now would be a great time," I told him. "Lulu just got run off the road by some driver who didn't bother to stop."

"What?"

"You heard me. She was on her bike, less than a mile from home. Somebody, in a little truck, she thinks, drew up behind her, forced her into a tree and took off."

"Is she all right?"

"I think so. A scraped knee, a sore ankle, and some bruises that won't be pretty. Thank heavens it wasn't worse than that. But I'm so upset and so angry, I don't know what to do. Someone has a grudge against me. I told you that. Okay, I accept it. But going after Lulu crosses a line. Whoever it is has to be stopped."

There was a pause on Charlie's end. "Of course. I fully agree. But Julie, you haven't exactly been forthcoming. If you're ready to tell me who you think might be behind this, I will use every means I have to find and collar the creep."

I nodded. "I know, and you're right."

"Where's Lulu now?"

"Soaking in the tub."

"I'll be at your house in half an hour."

By the time he arrived, with a stuffed SpongeBob and a tin of cookies, Lu was in her bathrobe, nestled on the sofa under a hand-knit afghan Penny had brought from home.

"Hey," he said. "You don't look too bad for a girl who was thrown under the bus."

Lulu snorted. "Not exactly under a bus. Just chased into a tree by some jerk."

Charlie looked at me. "Why don't you give me a few minutes alone with Lulu? Then we'll talk. How's that?"

Penny and I moved into the kitchen. "Want something to drink?" I asked.

"No, thanks. Lu seems okay, and if you don't need the car, I'd like to go into the office. Harrison's working on some complex litigation. I'd like to do some of the research."

I nodded. "No problem. Home for dinner?"

"I think so. I'll let you know for sure."

I made coffee, poured a cup, and sat at the kitchen table, trying to put all the questions in my head into some sort of reasonable order. I was still struggling when Charlie came in and took a seat across from me.

"She's something," he told me. "Gutsy kid, like her mother."

It was scant praise, but I smiled.

"She'll be fine," Charlie assured me. "She's in there grooving to the music."

I poured him a cup of coffee. "She would have walked home, twisted ankle and all, if I hadn't come after her when I did. She's been asking for a phone, and I've been putting her off. But she'll have one tomorrow morning."

"Good idea." He looked at me. "The bad news is, it happened so fast she never got a good look at the vehicle. She thinks it was maybe a light-colored pick-up, but she can't be more specific than that. So, unless we can pin that to someone you know, I don't have a clue where to start. Could have been just some jerk yakking on a cell phone, passing through and paying no attention."

I nodded. "I know that, and I'm still not sure I'm ready to be placing blame. But frankly, Charlie, this whole string of dumb little incidents is keeping me awake at night. It's time to figure out whether I'm reading something into the tea leaves or whether someone is out to harm us . . ."

I looked him in the eye. "If I tell you who I suspect and the reasons why, it will all be confidential, right?"

He smiled. "Of course. If nothing else, it might put your mind at ease, and it will give me something to look into."

I knew he was right. I was tired of lying awake at night, spinning out suppositions. It was time to figure out how much of this stuff was deliberate and go after whoever was behind it.

I tried a smile. "Okay, Mr. Police Chief, I hope you don't wind up thinking I'm some kind of loony. But here's what I know, and here's some of what I'm guessing."

Charlie sat back in his chair and listened.

FORTY-FIVE

Once I started talking, it all tumbled out, every doubt, every suspicion, every motive I had ever imagined—the death of Aunt Sarah, my decision to come back to Deadwood, the accidental deaths of Doreen and Nancy, even the missing diary pages, and the string of odd little harassments that had dogged me since my return.

"It's all tied together somehow, like someone's pulling the strings," I said. "I've told you who comes to mind and why, but I think there's more, and I can't seem to get a handle on it, except I think it starts with the night Katy died and ends with Doreen and Nancy's accidents and maybe with my Aunt Sarah's death in between."

Charlie listened, his expression neutral. "We've sifted through a lot of suppositions, Julie, but no clear reason to think . . ."

I shook my head. "I know. But I also know there are at least three people who stood to profit by my Aunt Sarah's death . . . and I'm wondering if her death might have been helped along by that vial of stolen drugs. Whoever had that poison could have walked into her house that night and left the same way, just hours before you got there."

Charlie pressed his lips together. "I wish she'd been able to reach me when she called. I might have been there sooner."

He sat back in his chair, processing what I'd told him.

"But where do you come in? Why the harassment?" Charlie's frustration was clear.

"I don't know! Maybe just because I'm here, in Deadwood, asking questions and making a killer feel vulnerable."

I decided to put it out there. "If it's someone who's killed before, it's a short step from feeling harassed to doing something more permanent."

Put into words, the hypothesis sounded farfetched even to me. Maybe weeks of speculation and sleepless nights were finally taking their toll.

Charlie put a hand over his mouth. I could almost hear his mind working. "A surly vet with designs on your house, a business exec with a questionable resume, and a cousin looking for half your inheritance to get him out of debt," he said at last.

His hand moved down to rub his chin. "I know I don't have to tell you this, Julie. Murder is a serious allegation."

"I know that. But whether you can see it or not, it's pretty clear we're being harassed, and now, if Lulu is in his sights . . ." I looked directly at him. "I don't know what you can do, Charlie, but I will do whatever it takes to stop him."

The planes of Charlie's face softened, but I could see the doubt in his expression.

"You know I'm hearing you on two levels, Julie, as a cop and as someone who cares for you. I won't tell you I'm not having some problems with this, since I personally looked into every one of these deaths you think are suspect. But I promise you I will dig it all up again. There won't be any stones unturned. Either we'll zero in on some possible killer, or we'll prove your theories are baseless."

It was all I could hope for. We looked for a moment into each other's faces, and Charlie leaned slowly forward. Then Lulu burst through the kitchen door, and the moment vanished like smoke.

"Hey, you guys." She hopped, one-footed, to the table. "My bike is still in the car. It was brand new, and now it's ruined."

"It isn't ruined, Lulu," I assured her. "We'll take it in tomorrow to be fixed. Meanwhile, get back in there and keep that ice pack on your ankle. I want to show Charlie the renovations."

"Can I do it?"

"Get back on the ice pack!"

"There you go, being bossy."

I rolled my eyes. "Come on," I said, taking Charlie by the hand. "In spite of everything, Nate's work is impeccable. You have to see this to believe it."

I showed Charlie through the new living space. "It's hard for me to realize this is the same house I grew up in."

"It's great," Charlie said. "Efficient but comfy. I wouldn't mind staying here myself."

I took him upstairs. He was duly impressed that two new bedrooms and a bath had been created out of nowhere without cramping the original space.

"Have to give the man credit," he said. "Miller knows his stuff."

The irony was clear. *How could a man with this kind of talent also be a cold-blooded killer?*

Of course, one thing did not preclude the other. I knew I had already addressed that. The fact was, the house, this beautifully remodeled house, under different circumstances, might very well belong solely to Nate.

The phone rang. I picked up the hall extension. "Hey, Penny. . . . Okay, have fun. Thanks for letting me know. See you later."

"Penny's going to dinner with Harrison," I said. "I think they're becoming an item."

Charlie grinned, a far cry from the buttoned-down cop who had interviewed me. "Good for them. And that reminds me. We're overdue for another night out. Can we manage to make some time for us this weekend?"

"I don't know. I hesitate to leave Lu alone, but if Penny isn't around to stay with her, maybe I can arrange an overnight with Morgan."

"Sounds good to me."

I started down the stairs. "Okay. I'll do my best."

Lulu, to my utter surprise, was sound asleep on the sofa, Penny's iPod on the pillow beside her, inches from her ear. The stuffed SpongeBob Charlie had brought peeked out from under one arm.

"Every time I worry that she's growing up too fast," I whispered, "something reminds me she's still my little girl."

He smiled. "I wish I could stay, Julie. But I need to get back to the station."

I walked him outside. "I can tell you one thing. I'll be glad to have a dog on the premises."

I realized then I had not told him about Rufus, and I gave him the quick, condensed version.

"We'll bring him home from the shelter on Wednesday. He seems to be a lover on the surface, but I'm hoping he's a good watchdog."

"I hope so, too." Charlie stood at the door of the patrol car. "Save me from having to sleep out on your lawn."

I smiled, and he chucked me under the chin. "Good idea. I approve."

He leaned in, and I waited for a kiss, but Charlie was back in cop mode. "I made you a promise, Julie, and I will stand by it. I intend for you and Lulu to feel safe."

"I appreciate that."

He nodded stiffly and folded himself into the car.

Lulu was still asleep. I wandered into the kitchen to rinse out the coffee mugs and picked up the phone on the first ring. There was a hollow sound, and a rushing of air, and then a deep, distorted voice in my ear.

"Whose little girl are you, my dear, and whose little girl is nexxxt . . . ?"

FORTY-SIX

Charlie was still in the patrol car when I reached him. "You won't believe what just happened."

I could see his brows knit. "What?"

I told him about the phone call.

"What? Just now? Was it a voicemail?"

"No. It was live. The voice was distorted. They hung up before I could answer."

"So, there's nothing to trace."

"I guess not."

A pause. "Are you all right?"

"Of course I'm all right. Actually, as you may recall, this happened once before, except that last time he left a voicemail message, which I stupidly erased. To tell you the truth, I'm not nearly as scared right now as I am just totally pissed off. Who does this creep think I am, some swooning little belle from the last century?"

Charlie laughed. "If he does, he'd better think again. He doesn't know who he's dealing with. On the other hand, it may give us something to look at in terms of criminal profiling. Maybe we can find a behavioral pattern in one of these guys that goes back a ways. and if you should happen to get another voicemail message, save it. I want to hear it."

I nodded, and the idea of criminal profiling made me feel a little bit better. A history of broken windows, flat tires and leaving dead animals in the mailbox as a kid could help to narrow down my best guesses, although running my daughter off the road and into a tree didn't quite seem to fit the pattern of seemingly juvenile behavior.

"Listen," Charlie said. "I'm off tonight at six, and Lulu is in no shape to go out. How about I bring over a pizza and we'll have ourselves a cozy little dinner?"

"Lulu would love that."

"And you?"

"Why not?"

"Good. See you a little past six."

Lu was still sleeping, so I made use of the time to make a few phone calls from the kitchen to the appliance store to set up a time for delivery of the washer and dryer and to the bike shop to give them a heads up that we'd be in with a bike that needed repair.

I had just put down the phone when it began to ring. I snatched it up to keep from waking Lu.

"Hey, it's Hannah. I got your message. Congratulations! It's a milestone."

"Oh, thanks, Hannah. If it weren't for your encouragement, the project might never have gotten started."

"I don't know about that, but I'm glad it's finished, and I have to say, I'm anxious to see it! Can I stop by in an hour or so after I close the shop?"

"Of course! Oh, just a little heads up. Lu had an accident on her bike today. She's a little banged up, but she'll be glad to see you."

"What happened? Are you sure she's okay?"

"She's fine, maybe a little shook up. But she's fine."

". . . If you're sure, then I'll see you in a bit."

I was tossing a salad when Lu woke up. She came into the kitchen, afghan trailing behind her, and her lower lip stuck out to here.

"You look truly pitiful, Lulu Bear," I cooed, taking her into my arms. "Do you think you will live to tell the tale?"

She shrugged.

"Well, Hannah's coming over to see the remodel, and Charlie's coming back here with a pizza."

A short pause and Lu reared back, all smiles. "Yum! Can I show Hannah around the house?"

"I don't know," I said, inspecting her knee and ankle. Both seemed a little less swollen. "Do you think you can negotiate the stairs?"

She flexed her knee. "Yep, I think so." She put her weight on her ankle. "It hurts, but not as much as before."

"Well, good." I went back to slicing tomatoes. "Then I guess you can lead the tour."

Charlie arrived first, in jeans and a sweatshirt, with a pizza that made my mouth water. He was setting it in the middle of the dining room table when the doorbell rang again.

"I'll get it." Lulu hobbled to the door. "Hey, Hannah, come on in!"

Hannah paused when she saw Charlie and the pizza. "Oops, bad timing. Go ahead," she said. "I'll come back another time."

But we protested, and Lulu grabbed her hand. "Look at this," she crowed, showing her around the newly configured space. "And wait till you see upstairs!"

She drew her to the stairs and led the way up, favoring her bad leg.

"She seems to feel better," Charlie said.

"Pizza therapy, I think it's called."

Charlie followed me into the kitchen. "Just to put your mind at ease," he told me, "I've started the background checks with NCIC, the national criminal database, and I touched bases with a behavioral profiler I know, outside the department."

I nodded. "Thanks for that and for not just dismissing it out of hand."

We set the table in companionable silence, listening to the sounds of appreciation coming from upstairs.

"It's just beautiful," Hannah declared when they came back downstairs. "Everything looks so fresh and inviting. I may have to spend a night here myself, check out how you're doing on the breakfasts!"

"That makes two of us," Charlie said, grinning. "She says she can cook, but I wouldn't know . . ."

"She can, she can," Lulu sang. "We already tried out some recipes."

"Yes, we did." Hannah turned toward the door. "I think you'll be pleasantly surprised.

She paused, and I could almost see her contemplating the thought of Charlie and me as a couple.

"But now," she said, "I'm getting out of here, so you can enjoy your pizza." She was halfway out the door when she paused.

"Wait a minute." She rifled through her handbag and came up with a square white envelope. "This is an invitation for you and Lu to Petey's Eagle Scout Court of Honor. It's a week from Friday night at Friends Church. Petey wanted me to deliver this to you. He would love for you to be there."

I pulled the invitation out of the envelope. "We'd be honored to be there. I know how hard he worked for this."

"You don't know the half of it," Hannah chortled. "I have to say we're proud of him. He built a wooden patio cover at the back of the Senior Center and a storage cabinet with cabinets and drawers to hold all their games and craft supplies. Not bad for a kid who a year or two ago didn't know a hammer from a screwdriver."

She started out the door. "Anyway, there'll be refreshments after the ceremony, so we certainly hope you'll come."

"Wouldn't miss it," I assured her. "Tell Petey thanks for inviting us."

"I will," Hannah said. "And again, Julie, congrats on the new venture. Your B and B will be terrific, I know. Now, get to the pizza before it's cold."

Lulu didn't need to be asked twice. She flipped open the top of the box. "Double pepperoni! Double yum!" She scrambled into her seat.

"I know my customers," Charlie said, holding out a chair for me.

I had to admit it felt pretty good for the three of us to be together at the table.

FORTY-SEVEN

On Wednesday morning, I woke to the sound of hammering, the kind of eardrum-busting clamor I thought I was finally done with. When a pillow over my head did nothing to stop the racket, I got up out of bed and peered out the window.

Nate was pounding on the left side of the porch railing, which had been loose since the day we'd moved in. I called down to him, but he didn't hear me, so I pulled on a robe and trotted downstairs.

I wanted to ask him what he thought he was doing making such a ruckus before seven o'clock in the morning. But he had never returned my phone call, and he didn't look pleased to see me now, so discretion seemed the better part of valor.

I took a beat and tried for a smile. "Nate, the house looks incredible. I left you a message. Great job."

He favored me with a terse nod. "I've been over in Lead, converting some guy's garage into a playroom. But we gotta get this B and B business going, and the railing needed fixing before some tourist takes a header and sues."

I did not miss the proprietary "we." It irked me despite myself.

"I really appreciate your work," I told him. "And as a matter of fact, you will be glad to know, our first guest is booked in two weeks from this Friday."

He nodded as though he expected nothing less. "Good. You need to book in a lot more."

I held my tongue. "So, you're done here then, once the railing is fixed."

"Yep. Then we need to sit down with Harrison and figure out how I'm going to get my money out."

We had one reservation, and he was already looking to get his money out. I gritted my teeth. "You need to give it some time."

He gave me one of his no-nonsense stares. Then he turned his back and resumed his hammering.

I was not surprised the noise had wakened Penny and Lu. They lounged in the kitchen in their bathrobes. It was a workday for Penny, but I knew I would need the car, so I offered to make breakfast and drive her to Harrison's office before we ran our errands.

"Yes!" Lu said. "We get to bring Rufus home!"

"Yes, and take your bike in to be fixed. Then we have another little errand to do. I think it's one you're going to like. Meanwhile, go see if you can scrounge up any more blueberries out back. I'm going to make some pancakes."

By the time the girls were ready, I had checked to be sure the mangled bike was secured in the trunk. We dropped Penny off downtown and headed for the bike shop.

"Whoa, what's this?" The young man who'd sold us the bike scratched his head when we wheeled it on. "I remember you folks. What happened?"

Lu reeled out the story of being run off the road and hitting a tree head-on, trotting out her most dramatic voice and showing off her scrapes and bruises.

"Chief Charlie is going to find the creep," she asserted. "And I wouldn't want to be him when he does."

I smiled to myself, amused as much by her sudden show of fearlessness as her confidence in Charlie's police work.

The salesman hunkered down to assess the damage and gave me an estimate of the repair cost, which was nearly a third of the original cost of the bike.

Ah well, it was only money. We took our receipt and left.

Our next stop was the wireless store, where I told Lu to pick out a phone while I added her to my cell phone plan. If they didn't hear her shouting in the next county, it was not because she didn't try.

"I was going to wait until your birthday," I told her. "But that bike accident was a wake-up call. I don't ever again want you to be in a situation where you can't call for help."

She gave me a hug and nodded furiously all the while I was laying out the ground rules. Then she leaned over, planted a kiss on my cheek, and deliberated for less than a minute before picking out a hot pink phone.

As if she wasn't excited enough, we went on to the animal shelter, where Rufus carried on as though we'd left him in purgatory and miraculously showed up to snatch him back again.

Lulu was beyond ecstatic. "A dog and a phone in the same day! Wait till I tell Morgan!"

Two or three more papers to sign, and Rufus, newly washed and fluffed, was officially ours to keep.

They gave us a lightweight, feeble-looking leash, and we led him out to the car. It occurred to me we needed to make one more stop, for dog food and whatever else we might need.

Rufus rode quietly in the back seat with Lu, as though being in a car was second nature to him, and I drove to a nearby Petco store, where dogs were allowed inside. We were approaching the entrance when the doors slid open in front of us. We nearly collided with Rennie Malcolm, in his usual business suit and tie, behind a cart filled with big bags of kibble.

"Rennie." I gave him a courteous nod and stepped aside, so he could pass. But Rufus leaped up and pushed against the shopping cart, growling for all he was worth, and Rennie backed up into the store.

I took the leash from Lulu, wound it around my wrist, and managed to pull the dog back, though he continued to snarl, a low rumbling sound that was unmistakably unfriendly.

Rennie scowled and pushed past us. "Dog's as rabid as his owner."

My mouth dropped open, but before I could respond, he was halfway across the parking lot.

Lulu kneeled to pet Rufus, who reverted to his friendly self as though the incident had never happened.

"Sorry, Mom," Lu murmured, looking up at me as though it had been her fault.

"Nothing for you to apologize for." I shrugged. "Let's just hope Rufus isn't quite so fierce with every stranger he meets."

In a way, I meant that, because an aggressive dog could cause a lot of trouble. But I couldn't help but wonder what kind of vibes Rufus had picked up from Rennie. I reached down to ruffle his ears. *You go, boy. You look out for us.*

The best part of a hundred-dollar bill later, we wheeled our cart back to the car with more kibble, dishes, toys and treats than I ever knew existed, not to mention a sturdier leash and a dog bed the size of a bassinet.

Lulu busied herself all afternoon, finding a sunny spot in the kitchen for the dog bed, a place in the laundry room for the stainless-steel food dishes, and a dark corner of the overcrowded pantry for the bags of kibble and treats.

She called Morgan two or three times, busying herself while I sketched out ideas for our Bluebird Hill website and called from the house phone to set up a meeting with a web designer I found in the online Yellow Pages.

Charlie called at four o'clock. "I found out something interesting," he said. "Sarah surely must have done a background check before she hired Rennie Malcolm. But here's something somebody must have missed."

I waited.

"It seems Malcolm has an AKA. He's been known as Lawrence Manning. As Manning, he was suspected of embezzlement twelve years ago, by a charitable foundation he was working for in Maryland. They couldn't make the charges stick, so they let it go and Malcolm left the state—but not before the home of one of the more vocal board members mysteriously sustained some fire damage."

"Are you sure it was Rennie?"

"Can't be certain. This Manning person was never charged, and he seemingly dropped out of sight. What's more, if the fire really was arson, they never found the perpetrator."

I was stunned but not entirely surprised. I told Charlie about the incident at the pet store and the way Rufus had reacted.

"Maybe the dog's got good instincts," he said. "In any case, I'll be following up, I promise. Keep your chin up."

I was just off the phone when it rang again, and I took a reservation for October, a honeymoon couple who'd seen our ad and were looking for a little peace and quiet with access to the gaming in Deadwood.

Things *were* looking up, I told myself, at least for the B and B venture, and they were bound to improve when we had a website. I should have thought of that sooner.

By the time I picked up Penny at five, I was feeling pretty good. We'd had a productive day, we had a guard dog on the property, and Charlie, true to his word, was deep into fact-checking mode.

"Guess what?" I asked Penny, as she slid into the car. "We've got another booking for the B and B!"

"That's great," she said, looking fresh and crisp in slacks and a sky-blue silk blouse.

I looked down at my jeans and sweatshirt. Avery should see me now.

Penny's eyes danced. "I won't be home for dinner, Julie. I hope you don't mind. Harrison's picking me up at six."

"Why would I mind? Rufus will want to get reacquainted with you, but then you're on your own."

"Oh, by the way." Her smile faded. "I hate to be the bearer of bad news. Harrison will be sending you documents in the mail. But he asked me to give you a message. There's a court date set for the adjudication of Hanford Welty's claim against your aunt's estate. It's December second at District Court in Rapid City."

I looked behind me, checked the mirrors, and pulled away from the curb.

"Okay, thanks." I nodded.

So much for keeping my chin up.

FORTY-EIGHT

Lynnie Kurtz was a graphics design major at Western Dakota Tech in Rapid City, a dark-haired little ball of energy who was more than happy to take on the task of designing a website for the Bluebird Hill Bed and Breakfast.

We worked together for a few hours on Thursday. Mostly, I'd told her about the property and the rates while she moved around photos and images on the page and tried out some links and booking options. So, I was amazed when she called me on Friday morning and told me to turn on my computer.

I ran for my laptop, set it on the kitchen counter, and typed in what she told me to. Up came a series of rotating images: tall pines against an azure sky, a sylvan lake with the Black Hills as the backdrop, a dining table groaning under steaming platters of pancakes, and a cheerful blue-and-white checked gingham bedroom.

I watched as some cheerfully rustic lettering flew in from the edges of the screen, spelling out our name and logo. Behind that, the images rotated—Mt. Rushmore, the Crazy Horse Monument, bright lights and busy casinos, and a young couple riding horses at sunset along the pine-strewn Mickelson Trail.

Lynnie had used stock photos, I knew, but they painted an inviting picture. I played for a minute with the booking option just to be sure it worked.

"Lynnie, you're amazing," I shouted into the phone. "How did you do that so quickly?"

"I'm glad you like it, because it's ready to go live if you are."

"I like it."

She took a beat. "Good. Now go to a search page and type in 'Black Hills Bed and Breakfast.'"

I did, and we came up seventh on the search list. I knew from my days at the Stevens Point Hotel how critical coming up near the top of the search list could be.

"Wow!" I was really impressed. "How did you manage that?"

"Friends in high places," Lynnie giggled. "It's called search optimization. Keep playing with the links. Be sure everything you want is there and it's just the way you want it to look. We can make changes anytime, so don't hesitate to ask."

"I'm floored, Lynnie, and really grateful. I'll get a check out to you this afternoon. There's only one thing wrong."

"What's that?"

"I don't know where my head is! I'm looking at an image of a checked gingham bedroom, and I realize, better late than never, that our first guests are already booked and the new guest rooms are still empty!"

Lynnie laughed. "Can't help you there. But I'm glad you like the site."

"It's perfect. Let me play with it a little more, and I'll call you if I need to."

I couldn't believe how inept I was. I called Penny at work. "I need the car."

"No problem," she said. "I'll drive it home, and you can drop me back here."

I wrote Lynnie's check while I waited for Penny and tried to convince Lulu how much fun it would be to help me pick out furniture.

She looked seriously doubtful, but she didn't have much choice, so she stuffed her bad ankle into her new short boots and followed me out when Penny honked the horn.

Rufus watched us from behind the living room curtains.

"Bye, Rufus!" Lulu waved. "We won't be long, I promise!"

"How are things going?" I asked Penny as I slid behind the wheel.

Although neither of us had mentioned it, Penny had not come home for a couple of nights this week, and while I knew I had no business asking personal questions, I had to admit I was curious.

"Everything's great," she said with feeling. "Couldn't be better, in fact, I'm thinking I may go back home pretty soon and arrange to make the move here permanent."

"Really? Are the California bar results in?"

Penny shook her head. "They will be soon. But it doesn't matter that much to me now. Whether I passed it or not, I'm planning to take the bar exam here. You know I've been studying South Dakota law, and Harrison says he thinks I'm ready."

I nodded as I pulled up in front of the law office. "Wow. I'm happy if you are, Pen, and you know I think the world of Harrison." I was not her mother, but it spilled out anyway. "Just, well, just don't move too fast. Be sure you think things through."

I had thought of asking Penny to stay with Lu on Saturday night, so I could plan a night out with Charlie, but under the circumstances, I decided to check into an overnight with Morgan instead.

It took ninety minutes and half the balance in my checkbook to furnish the two new guest rooms, but I got home with the promise of a Saturday delivery and the surprising realization that my teenaged daughter had an eye for color and design.

"I couldn't have done it without you," I told her. "Not as quickly, anyway."

Lulu shrugged, though I could see she was pleased. "It was fun. I actually liked it."

When she went upstairs, Rufus trailing behind her, I called Faye, Morgan's mom, to check the possibility of an overnight, but it turned out Morgan's father was in town for the weekend, and Morgan and Petey would be with him.

I debated for a moment. At nearly twelve, it was reasonable to leave Lulu by herself for a few hours in the evening. But after her recent so-called accident, and with everything else going on, I wasn't ready to chance it.

I called Charlie. "I'm afraid I can't get out tomorrow night. But I do have a reasonable alternative. Why don't you come here for dinner and I'll prove that I really can cook?"

He didn't miss a beat. "Six o'clock?"

"Perfect. We'll see you then."

Lu and I went through our Friday night ritual, then ate a dinner of mac and cheese and curled up on the sofa with Rufus between us to watch an old favorite, *The King and I.* By the time it was over, Lu was ready to hit the sack. She tucked Rufus into his bed with a blanket before I tucked her into hers.

I played for a while with the prototype of the Bluebird Hill website until I was satisfied it was just what we needed. By that time, my eyes were at half-mast, too, so I turned out the lights, trudged upstairs, and peered in at Lulu.

At some point, I saw Rufus had left his comfy bed and padded upstairs to Lulu's. He was stretched out across the foot of it, his full weight on her legs. I was tempted to chase him back downstairs, but Lulu didn't seem to mind, so I decided to let it go.

I fell asleep arranging the new furniture in my head and thinking, not for the first time, how much fun it could be to spend money and that if I didn't call a halt to the spending pretty soon, I would end up as broke as I'd ever been.

The next thing I knew, my eyes flew open. I sat up straight and listened. It took a moment to realize that what I was hearing was a low, soft growl. I got out of bed and peered into the hallway. Rufus was at the top of the stairs.

He stood stiffly, looking down and growling deep down in his throat. Before I could react, he leaped down the stairs and stopped at the front door.

I followed him down, my heart racing. "What is it, Rufus? What do you hear?"

He looked up at me as though I had lost my senses and turned back to the door. I hesitated, then opened it a crack, and the dog barreled out into the night.

A light mist obscured my vision, but Rufus raced down the driveway, barking furiously and chasing down the road after something or someone I couldn't see.

I stood there, shivering, but after a minute or two, Rufus came trotting back, appearing at my side through the deepening mist like some returning knight to the Round Table. He stepped through the door and shook himself off as though he'd simply had a midnight stroll, and he looked up patiently as if to let me know it was okay to close and lock the door.

I ruffled the damp fur at the back of his neck. *What on earth had alerted him?* "Good dog, Rufus," I said, and he followed me up the stairs and padded into Lulu's room without so much as a backward look.

I nestled under the covers, but sleep was gone. I wrestled with the same old images. Finally, I sat up, turned on the light, and reached for Katy's old diary. I thought of Aunt Sarah, in this very same bed, reading these pages for the very first time . . . and in a flash of insight, I saw it.

The diary had been intact when she found it weathered but still whole. The final pages, the now missing pages, revealed who Katy had been seeing and who, Aunt Sarah must quickly have realized, had very possibly murdered her.

That was the reason she'd called Charlie that night to tell him what she'd discovered, and that was the night she was murdered her in her sleep before Charlie could get there.

FORTY-NINE

At four in the morning, I crept downstairs and made myself a cup of tea. I sat in the kitchen until I couldn't sit there anymore, and then I went back upstairs and waited under the covers until the first light came through the curtains.

I had no idea what time Charlie woke up, and I wasn't even sure anymore that I hadn't gone completely bonkers. But when my clock finally read six o'clock straight up, I dialed Charlie at home.

There was no answer. I left a message saying that I needed to reach him.

I tried him on his cell phone. He didn't answer that, either. I listened to his recorded voice.

"Charlie," I said. "It may sound crazy, but I think I figured something out. If someone did murder my aunt in her sleep, it may have been the same person who murdered Katy years ago. I'll tell you why I think that when I see you. Call me when you pick up this message."

I was filled with the kind of restless energy that came from a lack of sleep. I set the dining room table with a damask cloth and Aunt Sarah's best china and glassware. By that time, Lu was awake. I made oatmeal and cinnamon toast.

She was still at the kitchen table when Charlie called. I took it on the living room phone, but there was a limit to how much I wanted to say with Lu only yards away.

"Katy kept a diary," I told him. "I think Aunt Sarah found it shortly before she died. I think she knew finally, after all these years, who Katy had run out to meet that night—"

"A diary . . ."

"Yes."

Lu came into the living room and curled up on the sofa, pulling Penny's afghan around her.

I was sure Charlie could figure out where I was going with this. "Listen," I said. "This isn't a good time. But think about it. We'll see you tonight."

I was beating the heck out of egg whites for a soufflé when the new furniture arrived in the afternoon. Lulu let the delivery guys in and supervised three trips up the stairs while I got the soufflé ready for the oven.

I ran upstairs in time to see that everything was in place and in mint condition before I signed for the delivery, and Lulu and I did a little dance in the hallway as the truck pulled out of the driveway.

We had chosen what the salesman called, "Country French" bedroom suites, light oak with mirrored dressers and fluted bedside lamps, and we raided Aunt Sarah's bountiful linen closet for pillows, linens, blankets and comforters that seemed to lend the new bedrooms with an air of well-worn gentility.

"They look beautiful, Mom," Lulu assured me. "Anyone who wouldn't want to stay here is nuts!"

"Well, thank you." I gave her a quick little curtsey. "Now change your clothes while I finish downstairs. Charlie will be here any minute."

I had thrown myself into preparing what I hoped would be a fabulous dinner: a roast of beef, medium rare, with scalloped potatoes I'd learned to make from Juan, fresh asparagus, and—if I'd estimated the timing right—a chocolate soufflé to come out of the oven just as we were ready for dessert.

I glanced around the newly renovated space, my home now, mine and Lulu's. Despite the animosity of the man who had transformed it, it had a graceful and welcoming aura. The thought of leaving it made me sadder than I had been in a very long time.

The doorbell brought me back to earth. I was wearing a lavender washed silk blouse over form-fitting black pants, and I checked to be sure I wasn't wearing any chocolate before I ran to open the door.

Charlie looked great in a deep teal shirt that brought out the blue of his eyes. He had a huge bouquet of roses in one hand and a bottle of wine in the other. My first impulse was to kiss him roundly, but I settled for a kiss on the cheek. Just as well, because Rufus came running to check out the new human.

He started to growl.

"Stop it, Rufus. Charlie is a good friend."

"Wow, you look terrific," Charlie told me, handing over the flowers and reaching down to scratch the dog's ears.

"This is Rufus."

"All right," Charlie said. "Hey, Rufus. Take care of my girls."

"He's already doing that. He heard something or someone outside last night, and he took off down the road like a shot."

"Great. Good job, boy. Keep up the good work." He got up and sniffed. "Hey. Something in here smells wonderful."

He followed me into the kitchen and stood close behind me as I put the roses into water. I could smell his after shave, a spicy pine scent, and I felt the fingers of his right hand close gently around my waist. I might have turned if Lulu hadn't chosen the moment to come bounding into the room.

"Hi, Charlie! My ankle's better. Did you find the guy who ran me off the road?"

Charlie turned to her. "Not yet, dang it. It isn't easy with as few sketchy details as we have. But we're doing our best, and you can bet that anyone dumb enough to go after you again is going to have to go through me first."

Lulu looked mollified. "Okay. Mom made a fabulous dinner. Scalloped potatoes, my favorite."

"And it's going to get cold if we don't get to the table." I hustled them into the dining room.

"I do have a bit of interesting news," Charlie said, taking a corkscrew to the wine. "I got a call from a colleague this afternoon. It seems your cousin, Hanford Welty, is serving thirty days in the Rapid City jail for failure to pay a hefty bar bill."

"Really?"

"The sentence was in lieu of payment plus a fine, which he apparently couldn't come up with."

I wasn't surprised, but it didn't make me feel better. "Well, it seems I'll be seeing him in court in December. If he wins his case, he could be paying his debts with half of everything I inherited."

Charlie squinted. "Reason enough to want you out of the way so he can win his suit by default."

I decided that was enough of this conversation with Lulu, big-eared, at the table.

"The good news is, we have our first bookings for the B and B," I said. "And the website just went live. I'm hoping more people will find us now, especially as we get into ski season."

Charlie heaped potatoes on his plate. "Well, you've worked hard—you and Nate both. I hope this works out well for you."

"Me, too. Nate is already looking to start drawing out cash, and I'm not sure how that can happen unless we have some reasonable income."

"School starts next week," Lulu said, worming her way into the table talk. "Me and Penny went shopping—"

"Penny and I."

"Penny and I. And I get to take the school bus."

"You'll be the prettiest girl in school by far. And likely the smartest, too."

"I don't know about that." I passed the gravy. "But she's a pretty good little decorator. She helped me furnish the new bedrooms, and they look pretty good, I have to say."

"I'll show you after dinner."

"Sounds good to me." He helped himself to more beef. "I'm stuffed, but Julie, this is really good."

"See?" Lu chimed in. "I told you she could cook."

The oven bell went off in the kitchen. I excused myself to peer into the oven.

The soufflé was beautiful, rising high over the sides of the dish and smelling deliciously chocolate. I set it on a china platter and toted it into the dining room, where a silver bowl full of freshly whipped cream was waiting on the sideboard.

Charlie's eyes were as big as Lu's. "And I thought you were just a pretty face!"

We cleared the table and loaded the dishwasher as though we'd always done it as a team. I wanted to talk to Charlie, but Lu suggested a game of Cranium, and I figured it could wait for a while.

We acted out scenes and twisted clay into tennis shoes until we split our sides laughing, and wouldn't you know it? Charlie's cell phone sounded off just before nine o'clock.

"Emergency," he told us after a short exchange. "Some idiot tourist in the mine shaft."

"At this hour?"

"You'd be surprised. Happens all the time."

Lulu volunteered to put the game away while I walked Charlie out to his car.

"Have you thought about what I told you on the phone?" I asked.

"I have. I still am . . . you realize, if what you're suggesting is remotely feasible, it eliminates Rennie Malcolm as a suspect. To my knowledge, he wasn't anywhere in the area when Katy was killed twenty odd years ago."

I nodded. "Not so. According to Mrs. Kovich, he left the area sometime after college. He could have been here. Can you check it out?"

He cupped my cheek. "Interesting. I will check it out. Julie, I really do have to go. But I can't tell you how much I enjoyed tonight. I owe you one whenever you can get away."

He leaned in and kissed me in a way I knew I would not soon forget.

FIFTY

The doorbell rang at ten o'clock the next morning as Lu and I were finishing breakfast. To my utter surprise, it was Penny, rosy-cheeked and smiling broadly, with Harrison standing behind her.

"I would have used my key," she said. "But I wanted to be sure you and Lu were awake and ready for company before I brought Harrison in."

"We are," I said, swinging the door open. "Come in. The coffeepot's on and I'll put up some water for your tea."

"We'll just be a minute," Penny said, as I led them into the dining room.

"Whatever," I said. "Have a seat. I'll be right out with the pot."

I heard them whispering as I got out the coffee mugs, and I would have been glad to give them a minute. But Lulu had no time for courtesies.

"Penny!" She gave her a great big bear hug, as though she hadn't seen her for weeks.

"Hey, Lu. You remember Harrison, don't you?"

Lulu nodded. "Hi."

Harrison reached for her hand. "Hi, Lulu. Nice to see you again."

Lulu grinned and bounced into a chair, the more perceptive of the two of us. I poured the coffee while visions of court dates danced around in my head. Sunday or not, I debated whether this was, at least in part, a business call.

Penny set me straight. "I have good news and better news," she said, beaming.

Lu and I waited.

"The good news is I'll soon be moving out. You'll have another bedroom that can be rented out for bed and breakfast."

I finally guessed what was coming next.

"And the better news is," Penny linked her right arm through Harrison's and held her left hand out for us to see. On her fourth finger, a sparkling diamond ring made Lulu squeal with delight.

"Oh, Penny," I said. "Congratulations! You, too, Harrison. That's wonderful!"

"You're engaged!" Lulu danced around the table. "Wow! Can I be in your wedding?"

"Can a duck quack?" Penny laughed. "How could I get married without you?"

After a long round of hugs and kisses, Penny quit her dancing around, and we settled down to talk.

"In a way, Julie, this is all your doing," Harrison said. "I can't thank you enough for coming back to Deadwood and bringing Penny into my life, and I hope you're okay with my acting as your attorney even though I will soon be practically part of the family."

I gave him another hug. "I couldn't be happier, Harrison, on a personal or professional level. To tell you the truth, in more ways than one, I'm not sure this was the best move for me and Lu. But if it brought you two together, and you're both happy, I guess it was a good thing after all."

Harrison looked perplexed, but this wasn't the time to let him in on some of the stranger things that had happened since we'd come here. I knew with certainty I could count on him to represent my interests in the most professional way possible when we faced Hanford Welty in court.

"By the way," I told him, "I heard from Charlie that Welty is in jail in Rapid City. Non-payment of a bar bill, or some such thing."

"Yes, I know. I heard it from a friend who works in intake, and I can assure you this arrest, never mind his previous record, will not speak well for him in court. But this isn't the time for this." He squeezed Penny's hand. "We'll get together soon to talk."

I nodded. "So! What are your plans? Do you have a wedding date in mind?"

"Not really." Penny put an arm around Lulu. "Sometime in the spring, we think. I want to take the South Dakota bar exam in November and that will take some study time. Meanwhile, I plan to make a quick trip home, spend some quality time with my mom and pack up the rest of my ~~things,~~ things—which reminds me, Julie, can I borrow a suitcase or two for the clothes I'll be bringing back with me?"

"Of course. My suitcases are out in the garage. Help yourself to whatever you need."

More hugs, more oohs and aahs over the ring, and the two of them took off to drive to Harrison's hometown, nearly fifty miles away, to break the good news to his family.

Lu and I felt honored to have heard it first, though Penny had been practically part of our family for more years than I cared to remember.

I was happy for her, but I had to admit, it made me wonder about my relationship with Charlie. Last night's kiss was nice, but I was debating how I felt about anything more lasting when the telephone broke into my thoughts.

Lulu's bike was ready for pick-up. She let out a whoop. "Can we get it?"

She was so excited, she got Rufus in a snit. He ran around in circles, barking.

"Okay, okay," I said finally. "Get a jacket on and we'll go."

Fall had settled into the Black Hills, deep, heavy, and dark, a stark reminder that the snow I remembered was not far away. Lulu would be thrilled to take her skates out on the lake, but I drove the few miles to the bike shop thinking about the bone-chilling cold I'd been away from for so long.

Lu wrangled with Rufus in the back seat while I tried to keep myself from sinking into memories I'd left behind with the cold.

The bicycle was good as new, as shiny and perfect as the day we'd brought it home. We packed it carefully into the trunk, held snugly in place with a bungee cord and a couple of old blankets.

Of course, Lu wanted to test it out the minute we unloaded it in the driveway, apparently not the least bit concerned about the possibility of another "accident." I wished I could say I was just as unconcerned. I told myself I was being ridiculous.

"Be sure you have your phone," I told her, "and don't go more than a mile or two from home." I checked my watch. It was nearly half past twelve. "Be home for lunch by one fifteen latest and let Rufus tag along after you."

I stood there and watched the bike and the dog disappear from view, unable to shake the restless unease that was settling deep in my stomach.

To my vast relief, she was home on time. We made grilled cheese sandwiches for lunch, and when she sat on the sofa wrapped in the afghan to watch, I Love Lucy re-runs, I told her I would be in my room.

I stretched out on the bed hoping to sleep, but the memories that had plagued me on the ride to the bike shop refused to go away. I found myself thinking about my cousin Katy, and the next thing I knew, I had reached into the bedside drawer and pulled out the damaged diary.

I rifled the pages, reading here and there, examining the faded handwriting, and finally fingering the rough edges where the last pages had been torn away.

Once again, the shrill of the telephone snapped me back to the present.

"Hey, it's me," Charlie said. "Are you busy?"

"Not really," I muttered, resting the diary on my chest. "Just having a bit of a lie-down. I didn't sleep too well last night, and it's been a funny kind of a day."

"I called to thank you again for last night. What kind of a funny day?"

"For one thing," I rolled over on my side, "Penny and Harrison are engaged."

"No kidding! That's great. Good for them. Nothing funny about that."

"What happened to the guy in the mine last night?"

"He took a pretty good dive. Could have ended up a miner's canary, but we got to him in time. He'll be okay."

"I'm glad."

He paused. "You sound a little low."

"I am, a little, I guess." I reached over and put the diary away. "Aunt Sarah would have said I'm having a case of the melancholies."

Charlie chuckled. "And she would have been right. If I were there now, I'd wrap my arms around you tight and whisper sweet nothings in your ear."

"Would you?"

"You bet, more than that, if you were in the mood."

It made me smile in spite of myself. "I'll remember that."

I could almost see his lopsided grin. "Good," he said. "It's a promise."

I tucked the receiver under my chin.

"Got to go," Charlie said. "Try to get some sleep this afternoon. You'll feel better; you'll see."

For some reason, I felt better already. I pulled the covers up around me.

I was just beginning to doze off when a thought danced into my head. *If the diary had been intact when Aunt Sarah had read it, where were the missing pages now?*

FIFTY-ONE

Lulu started school on Wednesday, two days after the coldest, wettest Labor Day in Deadwood memory canceled an annual community picnic. It was just as well, as Lulu had returned to fretting mode, certain she'd be the outcast of her class.

As it turned out, she came home glowing. Her homeroom teacher was cool, she and Morgan had signed up for Glee Club, and she was pretty sure they would both make the girls' basketball team.

I was glad to hear it because there was a foundation board meeting scheduled that evening, which I hadn't been sure I would attend. But Penny was fine with coming home for the evening, and Lulu's good mood tilted the decision in its favor. We rustled up a quick spaghetti dinner, and I took off for the library.

When I got there, all the board members had arrived, but there was an empty place at the head of the table.

"Anyone know where Rennie is?" I asked.

The question drew only questioning looks and a series of mystified head shakes.

"Maybe he's ill," Mrs. Kovich suggested.

"Or just detained," Father Ruggio said.

We waited, chatting and reading the minutes of the last meeting, until fifteen minutes after the hour. Then we moved on, board Vice President Frank Anderson presiding, through a fairly routine agenda. No income was reported in the previous month, but we approved a grant to help a family in Lead who had lost a son in a motorcycle accident and had no funds to pay for a funeral.

Mrs. Kovich offered to drop by Rennie's on her way home, but the others agreed it was Rennie's responsibility to check in and offer an explanation. So, I drove home, my mind on my B and B to-do list, and I pulled into the driveway in a light mist at a little after nine o'clock.

I squinted at the sight of what appeared to be somebody sitting at the top of the porch steps. I drove in cautiously, stayed where I was, and honked the horn to let Penny know that I was home.

She opened the door, turning on the porch light and peering into the darkness, providing just enough light for me to recognize who had parked himself at the top of the steps.

"Rennie?" I got out of the car and locked it. "We missed you at the meeting tonight. What are you doing here?"

"I have something for you." He rose stiffly. "I thought it expedient to give it to you in person."

I backed up instinctively as he trundled down the steps and began to walk toward me.

"Julie, are you okay?" Penny asked.

I debated briefly. "Yes, I think so. I'll be in in a minute. Thanks."

I met Rennie halfway across the driveway and took the long white envelope he held out.

He stood in front of me at his full height, dressed impeccably as he generally was, in a three-piece suit and tie. He glared directly into my face. "I will no longer give you the opportunity to poison my reputation," he informed me. "Nor will I allow you to undermine my standing with the board. I hereby resign from my post as director of the foundation. Congratulations, Ms. Goldman. You are now free to pursue your own agenda."

"My own—poison your reputation? Rennie, what are you talking about?"

"It was clear from the outset you distrusted my judgment and questioned my value to the foundation, and it appears the majority of the board has now lined up behind you, making it impossible for me to do the job I was paid to do."

I wondered if that included an occasional raid of the bank account, and I was tempted to remind him that anyone who was suspected of embezzlement already had a sullied reputation. But then I remembered that the home of his last accuser had mysteriously gone up in flames.

"I'm sorry you feel your service to the foundation is unappreciated," I said with as much confidence as I could muster. "I can assure you, I had no agenda when I came back to town, and I have no agenda now, except, I suppose, to replace you as soon as possible with thanks for all that you've accomplished."

I hoped my aunt might approve of my response, but Rennie did not seem mollified.

"You have not heard the last of me," he warned. "Be assured I will examine all my options."

With that, he strode down the driveway and up the road, toward the SUV I hadn't noticed when I drove in. I watched him go and reminded myself that I needed to be more observant, especially about what was going on around my own property, for at least for as long, I thought wryly, as it somehow remained my property.

Penny was waiting for me in the living room. "Is everything all right? I had no idea anyone was out there on the porch. He never rang the bell."

I closed and locked the door behind me. "Everything's fine for the moment. That was Rennie Malcolm, the director of my aunt's family foundation. You've seen him once or twice when we were in town. He skipped tonight's board meeting, he's hot under the collar, and he just handed me his resignation."

Penny looked at me. "Is that a good thing?"

"Yes, I think so." I plopped down next to her on the sofa. "Except that Charlie told me he's got something of a rep for being vindictive. Where's Lu, by the way?"

"She's upstairs, out for the night."

"Okay. Well, let's just keep our eyes open, Pen. Now more than ever, we need to be alert for anything out of the ordinary around here."

Penny nodded. "By the way, you had two calls tonight. One was from someone who wanted the rates for a three-day stay over Thanksgiving. You can call her back. Her name and phone number are in the kitchen."

"Great. That makes four inquiries already and three definite reservations and now the website's live. But I should probably post a rate card by the phone so that you, or even Lulu, can provide information if someone calls while I'm out."

"Maybe I should put off my trip back home. It sounds as if you may need me here now more than ever, at least until the business is up and running."

I patted her hand. "Thanks, Pen, we'll manage just fine. You've got your own schedule to meet if you're going to take the bar exam here and then make plans for a wedding."

She considered, "If you're sure . . ."

"I'm sure," I said with the confidence of someone who'd been managing on her own for most of her adult life. "Who was the second call from?"

"Nate Miller," Penny said. "He said to tell you he'll call back tomorrow. He wants to set up a date to meet with you and Harrison to work out some kind of revenue sharing system."

"Revenue sharing. Is that what he called it? How much is half of nothing?"

Penny smiled ruefully. "It won't be nothing for long, Julie. The first guests are already booked."

Yes, and if Nate had title to the property free and clear, as he'd expected he might, he would be reaping a profit from the get-go.

Why did it seem that for every step I took forward, something happened to push me two steps back?

FIFTY-TWO

Petey seemed to have grown four inches over the summer. He stood on the platform, a head taller than either of the other two newly minted Eagle Scouts, grinning and fidgeting in the uncool way only a gangly fourteen-year-old boy can fidget.

I sat with Hannah in the stuffy church sanctuary, a row behind Lulu, Morgan, and Faye, as the Scoutmaster convened the Eagle Court of Honor.

I leaned over and tapped Lulu on her shoulder. "Petey's pretty cute," I stage-whispered in her ear.

Lulu rolled her eyes and looked away. I turned to Hannah, and the two of us exchanged a smile.

Lu and I had lighted the candles and said our Shabbos prayer before a quick meal of soup and sandwiches, and we'd met up with Hannah and her family as we drove into the church parking lot.

It was cold outside, making the sanctuary seem overheated and close. I shrugged out of my jacket and held it on my lap as the Scoutmaster introduced each of the Eagle designees and described the dedication and hard work it had taken for the three designees to reach this highest level of Scouting.

In turn, each of the boys recognized the help of their parents and solemnly reaffirmed their allegiance to live a life of honor and good citizenship. Hannah was beaming, and even I wiped a tear from the corner of my eye as the Eagle badges were pinned on their shirts. Then a round of applause and we were all invited to gather in the social hall for refreshments.

"I made three dozen brownies this morning before I left for the shop," Hannah said, holding the door open for me.

I quickly lost sight of Lulu and Morgan as they made their way through the crowd, briefly spotting them as they heaped their plates and found seats at the back of the social hall with some kids I did not recognize.

"The beginning of the end," I said to Hannah. "I couldn't be happier that she loves her new school, but why is it so hard to cut the apron strings?"

Hannah laughed, surveying the buffet table. "It's a bittersweet rite of passage every mother goes through . . . kind of like shedding a few sentimental tears when you wash out the diaper pail for what you know will be the very last time. They're only toddlers, and you know they still need you, but it's sad to realize they can't run far enough or fast enough!"

I nodded, remembering the scary afternoon Lu was run off the road. But I filled a plate with homemade goodies and tried to put it out of my mind.

We had just found a couple of empty seats when Petey came up beside us. He bent down to give his grandmother a hug. Then he straightened up and shook my hand. "Thanks a lot for coming."

"We wouldn't have missed it, Petey. Congratulations! I know how hard you worked to come this far."

"Let's see that handsome neckerchief slide!" Hannah reached up and fingered the ornament that held his scarf in place. "I hope you like it. It's an old one, Petey. It once belonged to your grandfather."

I peered at the bulky silver slide with a vague sense of recognition, though I certainly had no conscious recollection of having seen it before.

"It's beautiful," I said.

"It is, Grandma." He hugged her again. "Thanks a lot." He took off again, into the crowd, presumably to look for his buddies.

We sampled cookies and sipped coffee until the crowd thinned enough to see where the kids were sitting. It was nearly nine before we slipped into our jackets and exchanged hugs at the door.

"So," I teased as we settled into the car. "You don't think Petey's cute, huh?"

Lulu rolled her eyes again. "Motherrrr . . ."

"Well, I do." I drove out of the lot. "Tall and handsome, if you ask me."

"Well, nobody's asking . . ."

There was a moment of silence as Lu twirled a finger through her ponytail. "And besides," she said, "Morgan says he has a girlfriend."

"Ah hah!" I said. "And just as well. You can be my little girl for a while longer."

"Yeah, right," she said with a distinctly cynical edge.

I smiled, wondering which of two thoughts was making me more anxious—that Lulu was growing into independence or that I felt powerless to protect her forever and always.

It was after ten when I tucked her into bed and headed for my own room. I opened my laptop to check our website for inquiries and was disappointed to find there were none. I turned off the laptop, brushed my teeth, and settled into bed, vaguely aware from the tap-tap-tapping on my window that it had started to rain again.

I burrowed deep into the down-filled comforter, waiting for sleep to come, and it hit me in another flash that made me sit bolt upright. I *had* seen that Eagle Scout emblem before, and now I remembered where. It was on that odd little ring-thing that had languished under my bed for years, the one I'd retrieved from Katy's bedside table on the night she disappeared.

So, it wasn't a ring. The more I thought about, the more convinced I became. It was a neckerchief slide not unlike the one Petey had been wearing tonight. That was why it had seemed so bulky. It wasn't a ring at all.

I sat there, listening to the rain in the trees. *Why was there an Eagle slide in Katy's drawer? Where did it come from, and more importantly, what on earth had become of it?*

What if someone had given it to her—maybe someone she was seeing? Maybe the same someone she'd left home to meet the night she died?

I shook my head. I was getting ahead of myself. Katy could have found the thing anywhere; she could have found it in the street. I turned on the light and rummaged around in the drawer of my bedside table.

I got out of bed and checked the top of my dresser, as though I actually expected to find it there. Finally, I sifted through the drawers of my jewelry box, though I knew in my heart it wasn't there.

Where in the world would I have put the thing?

I stood there thinking for a long moment. *Could I have left it in my old room?* Lulu, of course, was asleep in there, and somehow, although I told myself it could wait till morning, I was unable to put it off.

I crept down the hallway in the dark and quietly opened her door. Lu was sound asleep, but I forgot about Rufus, who'd commandeered the foot of her bed. He raised his head, ID tags clinking, and looked at me hopefully, as though perhaps I'd decided this would be a good time to play.

I shushed him quietly and proceeded into the bedroom, watching the face of my sleeping daughter as I pulled open the drawer of the bedside table.

Rufus hopped off the bed, wagging his tail as though this was some fun new game, but I shushed him again and gave him a warning look as my hands rummaged through the drawer.

"Mom?" Lulu raised her head. "Is that you? What are you doing?"

"It's me," I whispered. "Nothing, Lu, just checking to see you're all right."

She sat up and squinted quizzically. "Why wouldn't I be all right?"

I sighed. "No reason. I was just checking. Everything's fine. Go back to sleep."

Her eyes closed, and she burrowed in a heap back into the warmth of her covers.

Rufus stared at me for a long moment, tail wagging, waiting to play, but I headed for the door, and he whined once before he hopped back onto the bed.

In my own bed, I spent a restless few minutes listening to the sound of the rain. Eventually, I fell into an agitated sleep that left me groggy in the morning.

FIFTY-THREE

Bubbe Lou used to say some things are *bashert*—meant to happen. Something to do with fate, I guessed. I knew it for certain the next day.

Penny let herself in early, carrying a sack of fresh bagels.

"Yum," I said, setting the table. "How's the bride-to-be?"

"Great," she told us, hauling a carton of cream cheese out of the sack. "Harrison left this morning for Pierre. He'll be there on business through Wednesday. I thought this might be a really good time for me to make a quick trip back to California."

She watched as I put the kettle on. "I made a reservation for tomorrow night," she said. "Will you be able to drive me to the airport?"

"Of course." I poured my coffee and set out tins of tea and cocoa.

We ate breakfast in the kitchen. The morning was sunny and the skies clear, and we could see through the window that the rain had left the Black Hills with a glistening crown of snow. It was a glorious sight, and one of the perks of living in South Dakota. It also gave me an idea.

"Penny," I said. "Will you be here tonight? Charlie's been asking for a night out, just the two of us."

"Go for it," she said. "I'll be here."

She slathered cream cheese on a bagel. "You know, I'm thinking of sending some empty suitcases home. It'll be cheaper to ship them ahead as freight than to pay for them at the airport. Lulu can help me get everything ready, maybe come with me to the freight office. Then, unless she's afraid I'll beat her, I'll take her on tonight in a marathon game of Yahtzee."

"Ha!" Lulu scoffed. "And a movie?"

"Sure, why not? We'll make some popcorn and curl up under a blanket on the sofa."

The two of them went out to haul suitcases in from the garage while I washed our few dishes. Then I called Charlie.

"Guess what?" I said. "I think I can manage a free night tonight if you're up for it."

"Great. Tell you what. I'll cook dinner for you. We can eat in front of the fireplace. About six?"

"Sounds perfect. What can I bring?"

"Your smile and a healthy appetite."

I smiled.

"Ever have Shrimp Diablo?"

"I don't think so."

"Good. It's one of my specialties."

I checked our website and found two rate inquiries and a reservation request for the first weekend in January. I checked the credit card, confirmed the reservation, and responded to the other two inquiries.

I was beginning to feel like we were really in business, finally on the road to independence—if the house didn't burn down first, if Nate left me with enough working capital, and if my December court date with Hanford Welty didn't eat too deeply into my claim on the property.

I heard Lu and Penny giggling upstairs. "What on earth?" I heard Penny say.

She came bounding downstairs. "This must be yours. I found it in the side pocket of your suitcase."

She dropped something into the palm of my hand. I stared at it in disbelief. It was an Eagle neckerchief slide, which was similar to the slide Petey had worn the other night, and very likely the same little ring-thing I'd found in Katy's bedside drawer.

Then I remembered. It was my first trip back here. I had dropped it into a pocket of my suitcase.

I looked at the slide with new interest. *Prophetic,* Aunt Sarah would have said.

I turned the slide around in the palm of my hand. I wracked my brain for some buried clue as to where Katy had gotten it. If someone gave it to her, it could have been anyone, and too many years had gone under the bridge for me to remember all of her friends, and even if I did remember, how could I know if any of her boyfriends had ever been Eagle Scouts?

But the Scoutmaster might know, I told myself. There had to be records somewhere, records of boys who had received the award around the time Katy was in her teens.

I called Faye. She gave me the number of the Scoutmaster. He answered his cell phone on the second ring.

"We're friends of Petey Helmond," I told him. "We were at his Eagle Court ceremony the other evening. It was lovely, a really touching tribute, and I wondered if perhaps you might have a record of other local boys who've earned the Eagle rank here in town over the years."

He hesitated. "Maybe . . . . I know there was a fire some time back, but I think I may have some files in my basement. They were given to me by the last Scoutmaster when I took this post a few years ago."

"Oh. Do you think—"

He hesitated again. "I'll have a look when I get home this afternoon."

He took my number, and I thanked him profusely. "I would really appreciate anything you can find, especially from sometime around the mid-eighties."

He promised to call if he found what I wanted, though in truth, he sounded dubious.

It was the best I could do. I sat down in the kitchen with my new reservations book to bring it up to date.

Lu and Penny left to ship off the suitcases. They hadn't been gone a full ten minutes when Nate turned up at the door.

"I haven't heard from you," he said pointedly, looming over me in the doorway. "If we're partners in this business, you really need to keep me informed about how it's going."

He was right. Even I could concede that much. "You're right, Nate, and I apologize. It's going well—for a new venture. At least I think so. Come on in."

I seated him at the dining room table. "Have you seen our website?"

"What website?"

I flushed pink, embarrassed to realize I had never informed him of its existence. I brought over the laptop and brought it up on the screen. "It went live a week ago. I paid a graphics designer to create it."

I gave him a minute to play around with the site.

"Not too bad," he grunted.

"I'm glad to say that it's paying off." I brought over the reservations book. "We'll have our first guests here in a couple of weeks, and there are six more bookings so far through the middle of January."

He nodded. "Not great, in my opinion. We should have had more during the holidays."

He looked at me as though it were my fault.

"I also paid out of my personal funds to furnish the new guest bedrooms."

He nodded, clearly unimpressed. "We need to set up an active ledger. Expenses, revenue, etcetera. We also need to sit down with Harrison, as I told you. I need to start seeing some income."

"So do I," I said frostily. "I don't have bottomless resources."

He glared at me. "All the more reason to work out something equitable, eh?"

I took a beat, my earlier optimism deflating like air out of a tire. "Harrison's out of town until Wednesday," I said. "When he's back, we'll set up a meeting."

"Good," Nate muttered, letting himself out before I could say another word.

I was dressing for my date with Charlie—curve-hugging jeans and a red sweater—when the phone rang. I recognized the voice.

"Seems like you're in luck," the Scoutmaster told me. "The stuff you wanted was in my files, all the Eagle designees in the region, all the way back to 1981. Anything before that, I'm pretty sure was lost in a fire."

"Well, that's just what I want. I appreciate your help. Is there a long list of names?"

"Maybe eighteen or twenty. There aren't too many boys who are committed to all that work. I can scan the list and send it to you, if you like. You can have it in twenty minutes."

I gave him my email address. "I can't thank you enough. I really appreciate your follow-through."

"It's one of the things I tell my boys. Your word is your bond. Live by it."

I brought my laptop up to my room and set it on the bed. Then I twisted my hair into a loose chignon, hoping it would choose to stay in place. By the time I put on lip gloss and blush, I heard the ding that announced a new message.

I opened the list to scan it quickly. What I saw knocked me for a loop.

FIFTY-FOUR

Lu and Penny were playing a heated game of Yahtzee when I was ready to leave for Charlie's place.

"Who's winning?" I asked.

"Me," Lu said. "Call me the shark."

"Well, have a little mercy on Penny, okay? And don't stay up too late."

"Oh, Mom, you are soooo bossy."

I turned on my heel, about to respond, when I caught the impish smile in her eyes.

Oh, boy, if she's old enough to poke fun at herself, she really is growing up.

Her smile widened. "Love you, Mom."

"Love you more." I planted a kiss on the top of her head and scooted out to the car.

I was getting pretty good at having discussions with myself, and this time was no exception. So, as I drove, I thought about what I knew and what it might mean in the scheme of things.

Two names had jumped out at me from the list the Scoutmaster had sent. The first was Nathaniel H., none other than Nate Miller. He had been fifteen in 1990 when he achieved the Eagle rank, which, I realized, would make him just a couple of years older than Katy.

The second name on the list, which floored me completely, was Hanford Eugene Welty. Apparently, the cousin I never knew had lived in the area with his mother, my Aunt Sarah's mysterious sister, until 1989, when he was somewhere in his early teens.

He had, according to the Scouts' records, completed the Eagle requirements. But he had not been inducted in a Court of Honor because he'd been taken into custody as a juvenile offender at some point before that could happen, never to resurface until he'd turned up recently to challenge Aunt Sarah's will.

Surely Aunt Sarah had known of his existence. But she must have had a reason for excluding him entirely from her will.

I was eager to share the news with Charlie, to see what he would make of it, and to be truthful, I was pretty proud of myself for following through on what had seemed like a worthwhile clue.

Woody and Peaches came barreling out to greet me as I turned into Charlie's long driveway, and I heard Charlie shouting as I got out of the car to, "Be nice to my girl or no leftovers."

I smiled, ruffling the dogs' ears and chins and breathing in the scent of butter and garlic.

"I'm starving," I yelled as the screen door slammed behind me. "This better taste as good as it smells!"

Charlie came out to greet me, wiping his hands—I kid you not—on the skirt of a frilly white apron.

"You'd better be hungry. There's enough shrimp here for the czar's army." He circled my waist and drew me in for a kiss.

"Nobody wants to kiss when they're hungry," I said. "Somebody once said that. I can't remember who, but they ought to get a medal for nailing it."

Charlie laughed. "Okay, I hear you. Your table is ready, Madame."

True to his word, he had placed the coffee table in front of a crackling fire. It was handsomely set with white linen and lots of crystal and silver.

"My wife liked nice things," he told me by way of explanation. He fluffed up a couple of big green pillows. "Make yourself comfy," he murmured in my ear. "I'll just go get the wine."

It was a blush-colored Zinfandel, fruity and smooth. "The guy at the wine store recommended it," he said, folding himself down to sit beside me. "And this is a cheese dip my mother used to make." He set it down with a basket of crackers. "Warning: you'd better have a taste for horseradish."

The wine and the horseradish and the fire combined to make me feel mellow and relaxed. I leaned against his shoulder, and we talked about the fireplaces of our childhoods—the big, open hearths, the smell of pine, finding our stockings on Christmas morning. For the first time since Marty died, I talked about the years before my parents died without a crushing sense of loss and grief.

In due time, he brought out the main course—Shrimp Diablo, he called it—angel hair pasta with red-peppered shrimp that put out a heat of its own, and we dipped bread into the garlicky sauce and ate until I thought I would burst.

At that point, he disappeared into the kitchen and brought out dishes of orange sherbet. I watched the sherbet melt into the crevices of my dish, and then I told him about Petey's Eagle Court and the path it set me on.

"Okay." He listened as he picked up a spoon. "So, what are you trying to tell me?"

"Mmm." The sherbet cooled my tongue. "Well, here's the interesting part. The night Katy died, the night I heard her leave the house, I went into her room to snoop around. I found what I thought was a funny little ring in her drawer. Turns out it was a neckerchief slide, an Eagle Scout neckerchief slide."

Charlie looked at me and waited.

"It was a longshot, I know, but I thought maybe it could provide some clue as to who Katy was meeting in secret. So, I called the local Scoutmaster, who sent me a list of all the boys who made Eagle Scout here since 1981."

I turned to face him. "Included on the list is Nate Miller . . ." I paused to let it sink in. "And also, my cousin, Hanford Welty, who apparently lived around here for a while sometime before I got here."

I watched as he processed that.

"For heaven's sake, Charlie. Both of them made Eagle Scouts. Either one of them could have had a neckerchief slide like the one I found in Katy's room. Either one of them could have given it to her as a keepsake and later, for whatever reason, ended up killing her and leaving her in Spearfish Creek."

"They would have been in the right age range for Katy." Charlie nodded slowly. "Although Rennie was, too. Mrs. Kovich was right. He lived in Lead until early 1995."

"Put that in your criminal profiles," I said. "I think it's pretty significant. What if Katy wrote about those boys, or one of them, in her diary? What if Aunt Sarah, reading it years later, realized who Katy had run out in the night to see? Maybe that was why she called you the night she died . . ."

I felt like I was babbling, but the words spilled out, and Charlie was listening closely. "But who? Sarah died of natural causes," he said. "There was no reason to think otherwise. Even if she thought she knew who had murdered Katy, it's a stretch to think she was murdered."

"I still think it's possible. What if she was killed with an untraceable drug, like the drug Doreen Hastings was accused of stealing? The murder might not have been evident."

"Wait a minute." Charlie took a beat. "Are you saying you think Doreen—"

"No, of course not!" *But then, there was Doreen's relationship with*

Rennie Malcolm. "But maybe Doreen took it to help out a friend. Maybe that's why she had to die, to cover it up."

"Julie, that was an accident."

"Not everyone believed that, including Nancy, her best friend, who also wound up dead."

Charlie rubbed a hand over his mouth. "Nancy fell from her own roof, Julie, and you're floating a lot of balloons. Nate Miller. Rennie Malcolm. Hanford Welty. You've come up with motives for every one of them, and any of them could be the one who's been harassing you."

I sighed, exasperated. "I don't know what to think. Any one of the scenarios works. I'm thinking out loud, and I guess I'm depending on you to help me sort it all out."

Charlie took a deep breath and slowly blew it out. "Weirdest thing I ever heard. Three equally viable suspects for a possible twenty-year string of murders. I'm a cop. I thought I'd seen it all. But I don't know. I just don't know."

I sat back in my seat.

"I can tell you this, Julie. I will give it yet another look. Run it all by my profiler friend."

The sherbet had dissolved into orange pools. The tension in the room was palpable. Charlie offered a wry grin. "So much for a romantic dinner."

"Sorry," I said, regretting my outburst. "It's been building for a while, I guess. And then, when I found out about the Eagle thing, it just, it seemed to make sense."

He nodded. "Where's the diary now?"

"I have it, except for the missing pages. Whoever was with Aunt Sarah the night she died must have torn them out to protect himself."

"Strange," he said, getting to his feet. "Why wouldn't he take the whole diary? I don't recall that I saw it around when I found Sarah's body that night."

I shrugged. "I don't know."

He nodded again and started to gather dishes.

"Here, let me help." I started to get up.

Charlie put a hand on my shoulder. "Nope, don't even think about it. Try to relax while I clear this stuff away. Tomorrow will be time enough to try to work this out. Tonight, well, if we try real hard, maybe we can focus on us."

He cleared the dishes onto a big tray and took it all into the kitchen. In a moment, I heard the water running. I stared into the fire. But I was too wrought up to sit still. I got up and began to pace.

I scanned the titles in a big bookcase, filled floor to ceiling with books. I examined a case full of bowling trophies. I wandered over to the desk. The desktop was totally clear. For some reason—I had no idea why—I opened the top right drawer. That was the moment Charlie chose to come back into the room.

I was totally mortified. "Sorry," I murmured. "I wasn't snooping. I don't know what got into me."

He shrugged. "No problem. Nothing in there but a few old bills and receipts. Let me clear away this table and spread out a blanket. We can snuggle in front of the fireplace."

I'd expected nothing less. I'd gone so far as to throw a toothbrush into my purse in case I decided to spend the night. And I tried, I really did try to respond when Charlie took me in his arms. But the questions running around in my head left me distracted and self-conscious.

When I pulled away, Charlie smiled sadly and cupped my cheek in his hand. "I get it," he said. "I understand . . . another time . . . maybe next time."

FIFTY-FIVE

Penny looked at me curiously when I came downstairs the next morning. But I was in no mood even to think about my love life, never mind to discuss it or the lack of it. The truth was, I felt a little foolish that I'd been so busy being Nancy Drew, girl detective, that I ruined what might have been a great evening.

Lulu was making French toast, her most recent claim to fame in the kitchen. I was sitting there, watching the slices pile up on the platter, when the phone rang. I scooted my chair over to answer it.

"Julie?"

"Yes."

". . . This is your cousin, Hanford Welty."

I leaned back in my chair. "Hanford!? Where are you? Why on earth are you calling me?"

There was a short pause. "I'm in Rapid City, and I'm calling to get us both off the hook."

"You should go through my attorney."

"I know, I know. But I'm past that. I need money now."

I was tempted to hang up, and he must have sensed that.

"Wait," he said. "Don't hang up. Look, the truth is, I need bail money here, and I need to pay off some debts. Twenty-five thousand . . . that's exactly what you offered a while back. Well, I need it now, and if you come through for me, I'll drop my claim against the estate."

It was tempting, but I shook my head. "Hanford, I don't know. I won't do anything without talking to my attorney, and he's out of town until Wednesday."

"That's too late. Can you reach him now?"

I glanced at Penny, who was watching me closely. "I don't know. I'm not sure."

"Listen, if you can help me out, there'll be no more hassle, I swear. I'll just get out of your life. Twenty-five grand. But I need it tomorrow. And that will be the last time you hear from me."

Until the next time you need money. I knew in my heart this was wrong.

"Hanford . . . was it you who smashed my front window? And let the air out of my tire?"

A pause. "What? Are you kidding? Who do you think I am?"

I could have answered that, but I chose not to. Still, if he was telling the truth, it could eliminate one of my suspects.

"Look," I said. "I can't give you an answer now. But I will see if I can reach my attorney. Is there a number where I can reach you?"

I heard him blow out air. "No," he muttered. "I'll find a way to call you back."

He hung up, and I listened to dead air for a while before I put the receiver back on the hook. Then I turned to Penny. "Do you know where to reach Harrison?"

"Of course. On his cell, most likely and I have his hotel information. Why?"

"Hey, you guys," Lu said. "Breakfast is on the table."

Rufus came running at the mention of food. I scratched him behind the ears. "My cousin Hanford says he'll drop his lawsuit if I pay him twenty-five thousand dollars."

"That's blackmail."

"Maybe. But we offered him that much when he first threatened to challenge us in court."

"Hmmm . . ." Penny made a wry face. "Don't do anything without consulting Harrison."

"If you don't get to this breakfast now, it's going to be ice cold."

"I won't," I promised, scooting my chair in. "Let me think about it while we eat."

In the end, I left messages on Harrison's cell phone and in his room at the hotel. Then I helped Penny clean up the kitchen.

"Are you ready for your flight tonight?" I asked.

"Absolutely. It's at ten-twenty. We should leave for the airport by eight."

"Or sooner," I said. "No problem. You are the only thing on my agenda."

We found an old movie on TV, Gene Tierney in *The Ghost and Mrs. Muir.* We settled down to watch, but I jumped up to answer when Harrison called an hour later.

"There is no way he'll have funds tomorrow," he said when I'd brought him up to date. "Even if you decide to pay him off, we'd have to draw up papers for him to sign, relinquishing any claim on you or the estate, and agreeing not to initiate any future contact if that's what you want."

I thought about it. Hanford Welty was, to my knowledge, my only living relative. But he was also a jerk and a life-long loser, and I was relieved that legalities could prevent me from helping him out of whatever his latest jam might be.

"And remember what I told you, Julie," Harrison went on. "Based on what we know, the odds will almost certainly be stacked against him in court.

There's no guarantee, but my educated guess is his claim will be thrown out and you can save yourself twenty-five thousand bucks."

I nodded. "Thanks, Harrison. I appreciate your help. Do you want to say hello to your future bride?"

He did, and Lu and I stared at the screen while Penny took the call in the kitchen.

The chilly, gray day sort of ran through our fingers. We built a fire in the fireplace. We watched a special on wedding planning—I could have written it myself—and we talked about the kind of wedding Penny wanted and how we could pull it off on a budget.

We snacked on munchies, made a stab at lunch, and watched the clouds roll in. Twice I got up to check our website and was rewarded with another reservation. I had to admit it was exciting, and a little scary, to think that our first two bed and breakfast guests would be here in a matter of days.

But in truth, I was bored and out of sorts, and when the phone rang at just before six, I leaped out of my chair to answer it.

It was Charlie. "You won't believe what I found out."

"What?"

"It has to do with Nate. But I don't have time to go over it on the phone. I'm down here at the mine, and I'm freezing. Bring me some coffee in an hour or so. I should be through here by then, and we can talk."

It sounded fine to me and maybe a way for me to make it up to Charlie for running out on him last night. I ran upstairs to change, putting a little extra effort into my makeup and taming my wayward locks.

"I'm going to meet Charlie over at the mine," I said, pulling on a fleece-lined jacket. "There's leftover chicken in the fridge for dinner, and Pen, I'll be back in plenty of time to get you to the airport. I promise."

FIFTY-SIX

I stopped at Starbucks for a couple of lattes and headed out to the mine. The fog had rolled in, and it was starting to mist. The parking lot was empty, as I had expected, except for Charlie's police car, but the lights were on in the Visitor Center office. I grabbed the coffees, slammed the car door shut with my hip, and stopped at the office door.

I didn't see Charlie through the glass window, so I set down the coffee and tried the door. It was open. I let myself in and put the coffees on the desk.

"Charlie? It's me. Where are you?"

There was no answer. I figured he was busy somewhere, so I took a seat at one of the desks, glancing around at the old maps and photos that traced the history of the mine. When Charlie didn't appear after a few minutes, I decided to get up and investigate.

Even though I'd been to the mine several times before, including the private tour with Charlie and Lulu, I had never spent much time in the office. So, I peered now around a couple of corners. I called his name, but he didn't answer.

I saw a door marked, "Mine Entrance: Authorized Personnel Only." I pulled it open. "Charlie? Are you in there?"

"Yep. Right here," he called. "Come on in."

It was fairly dark inside the employee entrance, the only light coming from bare bulb fixtures descending into the depths of the shaft. I could make out a railing and a series of concrete steps. I tested my weight against the railing and peered cautiously over it.

Charlie was kneeling about three feet down, hunched over a clipboard.

"Employee safety check," he called. "Every now and then, we do an unannounced inspection to be sure the handrails and catwalks are secure."

I looked around at a patchwork of wooden beams, the catwalks, I assumed. I watched him descend another couple of feet, treading carefully down the stairs.

"Come on down here and have a look. It's pretty interesting. This is the part the public doesn't see."

"Thanks," I said. "But no thanks. It's scary. You come back up here."

"Okay, Chicken Little. Have a seat on one of the steps. I'll be back up in a minute."

I settled myself on the second step down, peering into the vast, dusky space. I peered at the walls of damp concrete and rutted tracks worn smooth over a century of transporting gold out of the mine.

"Hey," Charlie startled me, climbing up to sit beside me.

"Hey, yourself. Okay. Tell me what you found out about Nate."

He paused. His voice, when he spoke, was deadly quiet. "It isn't about Nate, Julie. That was the only way I could think to get you here."

He held out a file folder that had been clipped to the clipboard. "Is this what you were looking for last night?"

I looked at him, confused. "I wasn't . . . I told you . . . I wasn't looking for anything . . ."

"Really?" he said. "Open it."

I stared at the folder.

"Open it."

Inside were a handful of handwritten pages, the edges torn and tattered. I recognized the loopy script, and I knew instantly that these were the pages that had been ripped from Katy's diary.

Raising my head, disbelieving, I tried to read the expression in Charlie's eyes.

"You're a smart girl, Julie. I give you an A. You had it all figured out— the boyfriend, even the Eagle thing." His smile was wry. "You see, I made Eagle Scout, too, the year before the files were destroyed."

My mouth dropped open. A chill snaked down my spine. I tried to speak, but nothing came out.

Charlie didn't stop. "Katy was young, but she was pretty mature . . . and a flirt, I can tell you that. She found the neckerchief slide in my bookcase the first time we were together. She liked the silly thing, so I told her she could have it."

There was something like admiration in his face. "You even managed to figure out it was the drug Doreen pilfered that killed your aunt. I couldn't even pronounce it, but Doreen was a pushover when I told her I needed a single dose of something to put one of my horses out of pain."

I could feel my gaze burning into his face. "But Katy . . ."

He nodded. "You have to understand. Katy told me she was pregnant— with my child. But I was a married man, Julie. I couldn't, I just couldn't . . ."

Charlie looked at me as if he thought I would understand.

"I've regretted it every day of my life, Julie," he said, a quiet pleading in his voice. "But I couldn't let Katy live . . . not when my wife was trying so hard to have a child of her own."

I was beyond shock. The bottom had fallen out of the world, and I was sinking with it. *How could I have been so unaware?*

"But the diary—"

"I never knew about it, I swear, Julie. Not until all these years later. Sarah called me that night, just as I told you. She'd found the diary. She wanted to see me. And somehow, the minute she told me about the diary, I knew what she must have found out."

The clipboard fell out of Charlie's grasp. A long moment passed before I heard a far-away clatter as it hit the bottom of the mine shaft.

But Charlie never lost a beat. He was too caught up in his story.

"I let myself into Sarah's house that night. I had the syringe Doreen had given me." The look on his face was almost tender. "Sarah didn't suffer. I assure you that, Julie. She just—she just quietly slipped away."

As he spoke, he rose, lifting me to my feet, facing me squarely and moving me backward, down the steps, deeper into the mine shaft.

I gripped the railing. *Who was this man . . . ? This madman?*

"I didn't want it to end this way, Julie. I think . . . I think I could really have loved you."

My heart pounded. It was hard to breathe. This was a man with too many secrets to let me get out of this alive.

I needed to buy time, to formulate a plan.

I managed to find my voice. "Is that what Doreen wanted to tell me on my first night back in Deadwood? That she suspected you used the drug she gave you to murder my Aunt Sarah?"

He was backing us further down into the shaft, step by tedious step.

"I have no idea. But I couldn't take the chance. It was easy to fix her brakes . . . and I was the police chief, after all. Nobody questioned my findings."

I looked around for a means of escape. I didn't think I could reach the catwalk, not even if I jumped. But I was damned if I'd be his miner's canary . . . the life crushed out of me at the bottom of the pit while he lived to tell some cock and bull story about how I'd lost my footing in the mine.

"And Nancy?" I asked, to keep him talking.

"Ah, Nancy." His smile was regretful. We descended further into the shaft. "If Nancy had been willing to let Doreen's accident be, she wouldn't have had to die."

I could feel my heart beating in my chest. *How could I have been so blind? This man, this man I might have fallen in love with, had murdered four innocent women.*

"And Lulu." Now I was truly incensed. "You ran her off the side of the road."

"To scare you, Julie. I would never have hurt her. I meant what I said about how much I regret never having children in my life. I can promise you this. I'll take care of Lulu always. You don't need to worry about her, ever. I'll care for her as if she were my own."

It was the last push I needed to clear away the panic—the horrific notion of his raising my daughter as his own.

We stepped in unison to the bottom of the stairwell, where another crosshatch of rugged beams extended to access the tracks. Holding my breath, I vaulted backward and crouched low, scrabbling to press my back and my palms against the slippery concrete wall.

Charlie reached for me, and every question, every doubt, every fear I had felt since the day we arrived in Deadwood rose up as one in my head. I could smell the dank air, feel the hollow quiet, see the cold determination in his eyes. This, from the man I thought I could love, who had all but convinced me he cared.

He came closer. My heartbeat pounded in my ears, but somehow, I managed to rear up with all my strength and butt the top of my head against his chin. I raised one leg and thrust it out as far as I could, and he stumbled as he lost his footing and tumbled into the abyss.

My head throbbed, and my heartbeat was still so loud in my ears that I barely heard his scream. Time stopped. But then I heard the silence, a thunderous silence that told me all I needed to know.

I was shaking, trembling, as much from fear and horror as from the cold this far down in the pit. I felt my fingers clawing the concrete, desperate to maintain my balance.

"Charlie," I called after a long moment, my voice echoing in the shaft. But I didn't hear any answer.

I closed my eyes, heard my breathing slow. Then I looked up, past the crosshatch of catwalks and the steep stairwell, up to the top of the shaft, and I prayed I could find the strength and the footing to make my way back up.

EPILOGUE

I must have passed out from sheer relief when I finally reached the top of the stairs, because the next thing I remembered was Nate Miller's face staring down into mine.

I looked at him, confused. *Was I delusional?*

"Hey, are you all right?" He narrowed his eyes. "I've called an ambulance."

My head hurt. I rose up to inspect myself. "I don't need an ambulance. I'm fine." Then I remembered. "But Charlie Banks is somewhere at the bottom of the pit."

"What?"

I looked into his craggy face. "Nate, what are you doing here?"

He blinked, looking down toward the railing. ". . . Penny sent me."

In typical fashion, his words were clipped as he helped me to a sitting position.

"Apparently, you didn't get home in time to drive her to the airport, and you weren't answering your cell phone. She was worried, and when she couldn't find anyone else around, she called me and asked me to come after you."

I nodded. I heard sirens wailing in the distance. I struggled to get to my feet. Then, to my everlasting chagrin, I must have passed out again.

*　*　*

It turned out, miraculously, that Charlie survived the fall. He had four broken ribs, a fractured knee, a concussion, and a dislocated shoulder. He was recovering in a hospital bed under the guard of state correctional officers until he could be transferred to jail to await his trial.

Penny told me all that as I lay in my hospital bed, convinced I didn't need to be there. I railed and cajoled until the doctor told me I could go home the next day on one condition—if I agreed to overnight observation.

I agreed to stay only if Lulu was allowed to stay there with me.

My daughter leaned over to give me a hug. "See? I told you she was bossy!"

Thank you so much for reading *The Miner's Canary*. If you've enjoyed the book, we would be grateful if you would post a review on the bookseller's website. Just a few words is all it takes!

OTHER BOOKS BY BARBARA PRONIN

Fiction

Syndrome

Thicker Than Water

Sing Sweetly To Me

Finders Keepers (as Barbara Nickolae)

Ties That Bind (as Barbara Nickolae)

Kiss Mommy Goodnight (as Barbara Nickolae)

Non-Fiction

Subbing: A Handbook for Substitute Teachers

West Covina: Fulfilling The Promise

TIDBITS

Finder's Keepers carried enthusiastic cover blurbs by Mary Higgins Clark and Tony Hillerman and was published as a *Reader's Digest* condensed book in nine languages. *Finder's Keepers*, along with *Sing Sweetly To Me* were also optioned for film.

PRAISE FOR BARBARA PRONIN'S WORKS

"Gripping. I loved it from the first page."
MARY HIGGINS CLARK

"Neat, suspenseful plots about the kind of people you worry about, written with skill."
TONY HILLERMAN

"Hooked me from the start and never let me go. A tantalizing puzzle with unexpected twists, engaging characters and high suspense."
PHYLLIS A. WHITNEY